U0006547

# 英美抒情詩新譯

傅正明 ◎譯註

臺灣商務印書館

# Contents

# 目　錄

*Gwendolyn Brooks*

## 再論詩歌翻譯詞曲風味體
### ——序傅正明先生《英美抒情詩新譯》

詩主情。詩言志。誠然。

但詩歌首先應該是一種精妙的語言藝術。

同理，詩歌的翻譯也就不得不首先表現為同類精妙的語言藝術。

若譯者的語言平庸而無光彩，與原作的語言藝術程度差距太遠，那就最多只是原詩含義的注釋性文字，算不得真正的詩歌翻譯。

那麼何謂詩歌的語言藝術？

無他，修辭造句、音韻格律一整套規矩而已。

無規矩不成方圓。無限制難成大師。奧運會上所有的技能比賽，無不按照特定的規矩來顯示參賽者高妙的技能。德國詩人歌德〈自然和藝術〉（*Natur und Kunst*）一詩最末兩行亦彰揚此理：

非限制難見作手，

惟規矩予人自由。

In der Beschränkung zeigt sich erst der Meister,

Und das Gesetz nur kann uns Freiheit geben.

藝術家的「自由」，得心應手之謂也。

詩歌既為語言藝術，自然就有一整套相應的語言藝術規則。詩人一旦達到隨心所欲而不逾矩的程度，那就是達到了真正成熟的境界。當然，規矩並非一點都不可打破，但只有能夠將規矩使用到得心應手程度的人才真正有資格去創立新規矩、豐富舊規矩。創新是在承傳舊規則長處的基礎上來進行的，而不是完全推翻舊規則，肆意妄為。事實證明，

在語言藝術上凡無視積澱千年的詩歌語言規則，隨心所欲地巧立名目，亂來胡來者，永不可在詩歌語言藝術上取得大的成就，所以歌德在上引同詩中認為：

若徒有不羈之心，
則難極頂遨游。
Vergebens werden ungebundne Geister
Nach der Vollendung reiner Höhe streben.

詩歌語言藝術如此需要規則，如此不可放任不羈，詩歌的翻譯自然也同樣需要相類似的要求。這個要求就是文章一開頭就提出的主張：若原詩是精妙的語言藝術，則理論上說來，譯詩也應是同類精妙的語言藝術。

但是「同類」絕非「同樣」。因為，由於原作和譯作使用的語言載體不一樣，其各自產生的語言藝術規則和效果也就各有各的特點，大多不可同樣複製、照搬。所以譯作的最高目標，也就是盡可能在譯入語的語言藝術領域達到程度大致相近的語言藝術效果。這種大致相近的藝術效果程度可叫做「最佳近似度」。它實際上也就是一種翻譯標準。只不過針對不同的文類，最佳近似度究竟在哪些因素方面可最佳程度地（並不一定是最大程度地）取得近似效果，我在拙著《中西詩比較鑒賞與翻譯理論》（清華大學出版社，2010 年版）的相關章節中有詳細的厘定，此不贅。

若原詩是精妙的語言藝術，譯詩也應是同類精妙的語言藝術。這個道理需要舉例加以說明。眾所周知，莎士比亞的詩歌是精妙的格律詩。莎士比亞的全部戲劇作品也基本上是格律性的詩歌語言。按照這個要求，則我們翻譯莎士比亞的作品時，也應該基本上將它們譯成具有一定格律性的詩歌語言。莎士比亞的作品本來是四百多年前的語言藝術品，絕非當代的白話作品。可是翻譯成漢語時，它們幾乎都成了白話作品

（少量譯成了白話詩體，絕大多數實際上都是白話散文，或者是分行的白話散文）。我們想一想，四百多年前只知道寫格律詩的莎士比亞怎麼可能寫出二十世紀才在中國出現的白話詩？這就有點像把莎士比亞幾乎同時代人戲劇家湯顯祖的《牡丹亭》完全改寫成完全的白話劇本一樣！

　　顯然，全白話譯作的語言藝術效果與古典的或近代早期的原作的語言藝術效果差別太大。有沒有補救辦法？有。於是我在 1986 年發表了《西詩漢譯詞曲體略論》。我在文中主張將西詩中格律謹嚴、措詞典雅、短小而又多抒情意味的早期詩作以古體漢詩、詞或曲的風味摹擬譯出，有選擇地借鑒漢詩詞曲體極豐富的藝術規則，以便取得盡可能美的語言藝術效果。因為「古體漢詩詞曲在音美、形美方面已臻絕頂，比之於世界上任何一種語言都不遜色，甚至更佳。而白話體在格律方面尚在草創之期，至多也只在節奏處理方面有些進展而已。……詞曲體句式多變，更宜傳達多樣化的情緒，至少在形式上與英詩長短句可以契合相投。當然，這裏得補充說明一下，我所謂的詞曲體，並不是指嚴格意義上字字講究平仄音韻的詞曲體，而主要是指詞曲體那種長短句式，辭彙風味等，使人一讀，覺得像詞曲，仔細辨別，卻又不是，恰在似與不似之間，凡所措詞，總以達志傳情摹形追韻為宗旨。」（見《四川師範大學學報》，1986 年第 5 期）依據自己提出的翻譯對策，我也在八〇年代以這種詞曲風味體翻譯了若干西詩。例如：

|  |  |
|---|---|
| The Wild Honeysuckle | 野忍冬花 |
| By Philip Freneau (1752-1832) | 菲力浦・佛瑞諾 作 (1752 – 1832) |

| | |
|---|---|
| FAIR flower, that dost so comely grow, | 豔花，似這般嬌滴滴任招展， |
| Hid in this silent, dull retreat, | 無言，廝守著冷落荒原。 |
| Untouched thy honied blossoms blow, | 少攀折，你隨意綻出甜花蕊； |
| Unseen thy little branches greet: | 無人顧，你柔枝仍作寒暄顏。 |
| 　No roving foot shall crush thee here, | 　喜無有遊蕩腳踏碎你玉容花面， |
| 　No busy hand provoke a tear. | 　更無有忙碌手令你把熱淚輕彈。 |

By Nature's self in white arrayed, 　是造化安排你身著素衫，

She bade thee shun the vulgar eye, 　好令你躲開那俗眼塵凡；

And planted here the guardian shade, 　又為你栽植出輕蔭一片，

And sent soft waters murmuring by; 　還送來做伴流水聲潺湲。

　　Thus quietly thy summer goes, 　　悄聲兒去也，你夏日芳枝，

　　Thy days declining to repose. 　　到頭來妙齡須老花自殘。


Smit with those charms, that must decay, 　歎只歎萬般媚態終須朽，

I grieve to see your future doom; 　忍見你眼睜睜來日遭劫難！

They died — nor were those flowers more gay, 　終須朽也——縱然是別樣群芳，

The flowers that did in Eden bloom; 　別樣嬌容，盛開在伊甸。

　　Unpitying frosts and Autumn's power 　　恨無情霜欺，金秋肅殺，

　　Shall leave no vestige of this flower. 　　此花當零落，便留下殘骸也難！


From morning suns and evening dews 　想當初，朝暉夕露，

At first thy little being came; 　托出你體態玲瓏面，

If nothing once, you nothing lose, 　來也空空，去也空空，

For when you die you are the same; 　但芳消香殘，惟留花魂不變。

　　The space between is but an hour, 　　悵妍紅易褪浮生短，

　　The frail duration of flower. 　　呀，只在一瞬間！

（辜正坤譯）


　　以同樣的風格，我還翻譯了一些莎士比亞的十四行詩。有人或許問，這是莎士比亞的十四行詩嗎？言外之意是：莎士比亞怎麼會寫出元明散曲味的詩來？我會回答：你問得很好。既然莎士比亞身處時代與

中國明朝年代相當，卻寫不出明散曲來，他又怎麼可能寫出他死後三百多年才出現的當代白話漢詩來？！邏輯上說來，莎士比亞若偶然寫出與他的同時代人湯顯祖相類似的散曲味詩歌來，這是無須驚詫的；若他居然寫出要在他死後三百多年才出現的白話體詩歌，這才真正令人感到滑稽！

　　當然，要補充的是，我並不反對用白話詩形式翻譯西方的詩歌，我主張的是詩歌翻譯標準多元互補論。由於存在著各式各樣的審美趣味，各式各樣的讀者群、各式各樣的語言藝術風格，也就自然會有相應的各式各樣的詩歌翻譯標準。詩歌翻譯詞曲風味體的產生就是這種理論的產物。

　　事隔二十多年，突然收到老校友傅正明先生從海外寄來的《英美抒情詩新譯》，走的竟然正是這條詩歌翻譯詞曲風味體的路子，我的欣喜、我的感動、我的欽敬自然不言而喻。所以當傅先生命我為其大作寫一篇序言時，我儘管極為忙迫，也於百忙中抽空倉促成篇，為我詩歌譯林詩友寫一篇力盡其能的短序，舊論重申，號角復鳴，聊以為詩苑譯林助興。傅先生苦心經營多年，嘔心瀝血，精益求精，今碩果在茲，譯林何幸，詩苑何幸！惟願此詩歌翻譯詞曲風味體嘗試之花越開越繁，遠播四海五洲。

　　是為序。

辜正坤（北京大學外語學院世界文學研究所教授）

2012 年 5 月 4 日於北京大學世界文學研究所

## 兩頭鸚鵡 一心創造
### ── 英詩漢譯漫談

# A Two-Headed Parrot's Creation with One Heart
# On Translating English Poetry

　　譯詩，是翻譯的跑馬場上最難駕馭的一匹野馬。考察前人馭術，總結自身心得，興許可以給這個跑馬場增添一道景觀。但願它既是歷史和思想的景觀，也是美學和藝術的景觀。

── I ──

　　從比較翻譯學的角度來看，中西翻譯理論頗多可以互相闡發或作平行研究、影響研究的要義。不同時代的各國學者，好像時而遙相呼應，時而隔代辯難。與耶穌同時代的猶太哲學家斐洛（Philo），為了融合希臘文化與希伯來文化倡導寓意解經時，翻譯就有了意譯（paraphrase）之說（Baker, 1998:166）。十七世紀法國學者梅納日（Gilles Ménage）以「不忠的美人」（les belles infidèles）比喻一位翻譯家的譯筆（Baker, 1998: 94），道出了翻譯的兩難。稍後的英國詩人和翻譯家德萊頓（John Dryden）在〈序《奧維德信箚》〉中，一方面讚揚該書幾位譯者把翻譯從株守原文的窠臼中解放出來，另一方面，又告誡自己防範他們那種過度偏離原作的傾向。在此基礎上，德萊登提出了直譯（metaphrase）、意譯（paraphrase）和擬作（imitation）三分法（Dryden, 1861）。後來，針對紐曼（John Henry Newman）強調「忠實」（to be faithful）乃譯者首要歷史責任的觀點，阿諾德（Matthew Arnold）進一步提出了何為

「忠實」的問題（Arnold, 1861: 2-3）。

在中國，類似的考量始於符秦時代的佛經翻譯，意譯日漸占了上風。嚴復「信、達、雅」的翻譯標準，首推「信」，即忠實。林語堂〈論翻譯〉一文，提出忠實、通順和美的三條翻譯標準以及相應之譯者的責任。他肯定了作為一種藝術的翻譯既信又美的可能性（林語堂，1932）。

與「忠實」或「信」大相徑庭的，是西諺「翻譯者叛逆也」（traductore-tradittore）的極端主張。但是，正如許淵沖先生在〈譯詩六論〉中認為的那樣，「譯者易也」與「譯者一也」這樣對立的命題都是可以言之成理的（許淵沖，1991）。這就觸及了西方翻譯理論中重要的源語（source language）、譯語或目標語（target language）之間的「對等」（equivalence）概念。

實際上，翻譯中最早採用「對等」一詞，原本指文化上的轉換，例如，法國軍隊喝「湯」（la soupe），英國士兵喝「茶」（tea），詞不同功能為一，就是對等。可見這個概念一開始就不是數學意義上的等值（Vinay, 1958: 55）。如果譯員把法軍的「湯」譯為英軍的「茶」，就冒出了翻譯中的歸化（Domestication）問題，如果他尊重法軍風俗，把 la soupe 譯為 soup，就是一種異化（Foreignization）。

在西方翻譯家對翻譯中的「對等」日益質疑之時，奈達（E. A. Nida）在《靠近一種翻譯科學》中區分了兩種對等：形態對等（formal equivalence）與動態對等（dynamic equivalence）。後來，他進一步把形態對等稱為「形似」（formal correspondence），把強調對等效果原則的動態對等重新命名為功能對等（functional equivalence），要求譯文「貼近」（closest）原文，謀求最大「近似值」（approximation）（Nida, 1964: 159-66; Nida and Taber, 1982 [1969]: 200）。

奈達之後，翻譯理論家貝雅（Monia Bayar）在她的《表意還是不表意》（*To Mean or Not to Mean*）一書中進一步列出多種級別的翻譯，首推最佳翻譯（optimum translation），即達到與原作的最大近似值或最高層次的功能對等的翻譯。用中國繪畫美學中的形神俱似的主張，馬建中早就提出「善譯」的翻譯觀，或錢鍾書「化」的標準，可以與之相互闡釋：最佳翻譯的譯者，像馬建中所說的那樣，對於原作必須「確知其意旨之所在，而又摹寫其神情，彷彿其語氣，然後心悟神解，振筆而書」（馬建中，1894）。或如錢鍾書所言，最佳翻譯，「既能不因語文習慣的差異而露出生硬牽強的痕跡，又能完全保存原有的風味」（錢鍾書，1997：269）。而所謂「善譯」或「化境」，就必須達到貝雅所說的「風格對等」（stylistic equivalence）或「風味對等」（connotative equivalence），傳達原作「字面的和言外的巧妙」（linguistic and extralinguistic resources）（Bayar, 2007: 214）。

明末清初以降，西學東漸，譯詩中的歸化策略和異化策略並出兼用。梁啟超批評的「徇華文而失西義」和「徇西文而梗華讀」的兩種翻譯弊病（梁啟超，1897），百多年後，仍然在所難免。用著名語言學家王力的比喻來說，這是或左或右的兩種「偏枯」癥（王力，1980）。❶因此，有必要復譯。正如法國翻譯學者伯曼（Antoine Berman）所說的那樣，作為經典的原作始終「年輕」，譯文卻可能衰老，或遲或早會被復譯（Antoine, 1985: 281）。多次復譯之後，也不排除後來的譯者可能會發出感嘆：眼前有詩譯不得，前人佳譯在上頭！魯迅先生在〈非有復譯不可〉一文中更為詳盡地表達了類似看法，指出復譯的必要性：「復譯還不止是擊退亂譯而已，即使已有好譯本，復譯也還是必要的。曾有文言譯本的，現在當改譯白話，不必說了。即使先出的白話譯本已很可觀，但倘使後來的譯者自己覺得可以譯得更好，就不妨再來譯一遍，無須客氣，更不必管那些無聊的嘮叨。取舊譯的長處，再加上自己的新心得，這才會成功一種近於完全的定本。但因言語跟著時代的變化，將來還可以有新的復譯本的。」（魯迅，1935）

我的復譯，就是基於這樣的考量，嘗試如何譯得更好一些。已有一家或多家古體譯本的，我以較為通俗的古體或自由體重譯，與此同時，對一些自由體譯詩感到韻味不足時，則以古體復譯。這不僅僅需要閒情逸致，而且需要求真向善的審美情趣。復譯需要借鑒舊譯長處，但對前人創造性的意譯不敢掠美，在不得已的情況下，包括「一名之立」的襲用，我均以注釋說明。此外，我也新譯了不少就我所知前人沒有譯過的英詩。

── I I ──

　　悠久的歐洲人文主義傳統，是西義的核心。這是滲透在希臘文化和希伯來文化中的愛的渴望，死的沉思。是葉慈（W. B. Yeats）在〈長久緘默過後〉（*After long silence*）中所說的「藝術和詩歌的至上主題」。中國詩人和語言學家陸志韋在 1913 年《東吳》雜誌創刊號發表的龍費羅（朗費羅）〈野橋月夜・調寄浪淘沙〉（*The Bridge*），可以視為「失西義」的一個例證，陸譯如下：

　　夜靜小橋橫，遠樹鐘聲。／浮圖月色正三更。／橋下月輪橋上客，沉醉金觥。
　　潮水打空城，舉目滄瀛。／浮萍逐浪野花迎。／兩岸蘆花斜月影，似溯空明。

　　原詩四行一節，共十五節，陸譯是原詩前六節摘譯。我的譯詩（以下簡稱傅譯）以七首「巫山一斷雲」加一個單片譯出全詩，見本書第187頁。

　　陸譯以精練的詞句把原詩第一、二節，第五、六節的內容大致意譯出來了，第三、四節基本上省略了，卻仍然再造了原詩意境。其中一個歸化策略是把西方教堂塔樓轉換成佛家「浮圖」，即佛塔。儘管原詩意

境與佛教禪宗有相通之處，但詩人最後直接提到「上帝之愛」。真正能表達詩人的人文精神的思想內容，由於陸譯是節譯，自然沒有迻譯出來。這首詩寫於朗費羅喪妻之後的孤獨中，構思於他常去的波士頓查理斯河上的橋頭（The bridge of the Charles）。詩人想到自己一生，也曾像那些匆忙過橋頭的名利之徒一樣，揹著俗世的沉重負擔，並為之煩惱，此刻獨立橋頭，他自己的煩惱彷彿拋諸流水，可是，就在這一刻，詩人想起了他人的煩惱並寄予同情：「他人尚有斷腸愁／擲影我心舟」（And only the sorrow of others / Throws its shadow over me）。正是這種人類關懷，使得朗費羅的這首詩成為一首偉大的詩，使得詩人曾經流連忘返的這座橋，被後人改名為「朗費羅橋」。後來，這首詩有了不失西義的全譯。

—— I I I ——

從譯詩的體裁來看，百多年前，英詩古譯幾乎是一種別無選擇的選擇，直到白話文運動興起，才打破了這種形態上的歸化現象。無可否認，中國古典詩詞具有永恆的藝術魅力。最早的英詩古譯留下了仍然具有可讀性或琅琅上口的譯作，例如「清末怪傑」辜鴻銘譯考伯（William Cowper）〈癡漢騎馬歌〉（*John Gilpin's Ride*），馬君武譯虎特（胡德，Thomas Hood）〈縫衣曲〉（*The Song of the Shirt*）以及此後胡適和劉半農的重譯，詩僧蘇曼殊譯師梨（雪萊 Shelley）〈冬日〉（*A Song*），胡適譯堪白爾（Thomas Campbell）〈軍人夢〉（*A Soldier's Dream*），郭沫若譯雪萊〈轉徙〉（*Mutability*）和洛威爾（J. R. Lowell）〈噴泉〉（*The Fountain*），吳宓譯羅塞蒂（C. G. Rossetti）〈願君常憶我〉（*Remember*），等等。但是，過去的不少譯詩也許只有翻譯史的意義了，因為它們給當時的讀者帶來了閱讀障礙，今天更難於為一般讀者接受。

導致閱讀障礙的原因，除了「徇西義」之外，大致有三個方面，第

一，是因為英詩古譯，採用五言和七言，有時難免削足適履或省略失當；第二，有些譯者好用冷僻的字詞；第三，由於難以避免的誤譯。

依照原詩適當選體，有時五言和七言，仍然是最佳選擇，例如雪萊（Shelley）〈轉徙〉（*Mutability*），的確適合五言，朗費羅（Longfellow）的〈人生禮贊〉（*A Psalm of Life*），華茲華斯（William Wordsworth）的〈詠水仙〉（*The Daffodils*），斯溫伯恩（A. C. Swinburne）的〈伉儷〉（*A Match*）等詩作，很適合七言。〈人生禮贊〉原詩採用揚抑格四音步句（trochaic tetrameter），其整齊的詩行、鏗鏘的節奏，以七言古體迻譯能順應原詩音步。晚清董恂把英使威妥瑪（Thomas Francis Wade）「有章無韻」的漢譯改為七言，就是一種非常得體的剪裁，只是在貼近原文的形似方面有所欠缺，或有失當的歸化譯筆。

應當留意的是，許多英詩詩句是參差不齊的，例如阿諾德的名詩〈多佛海灘〉（*Dover Beach*），詩句最長的十一個音節（syllable），最短的四個音節。郭沫若和聞一多都曾採用五言古體迻譯，給譯筆戴上沉重鐐銬。郭譯中的「英倫森峭壁，閃爍而屹嵲」（郭沫若，1981），原文是下述一行半：the cliffs of England stand,／Glimmering and vast, out in the tranquil bay。郭譯把寧靜的港灣這一意象不恰當地省略了，還出現了冷僻詞「屹嵲」。以該詞狀山高聳、顛簸貌，雖然貼切，卻可能令讀者望而生畏。因此，傅譯的詞曲體把這一句譯為：「英格蘭危崖壁立，／光閃閃，影森森，港灣無語相對。」

著名詩人和學者吳宓譯詩，有時也有類似弊病。他以五言古體譯安諾德（阿諾德）〈輓歌〉（*Requiescat*，參看傅譯〈安魂曲〉），前三節瑯瑯上口，第四節卻用詞冷僻：「小鳥困樊籠，嬌喘怨偪窄。今宵從所適，廣漠此窀穸」（吳宓，1923）。「偪」，同「逼」，但許多讀者認得「逼」卻不認得「偪」。窀穸，即墓穴，也不是常用詞。試比較原詩和徐志摩以自由體譯為〈誄詞〉的同一詩節：

Her cabin'd, ample spirit, / It flutter'd and fail'd for breath. / To-night it doth inherit / The vasty hall of death.

局促在人間，她博大的神魂，／何曾享受呼吸的自由；／今夜，在這靜夜，她獨自的攀登／那死的插天的高樓（徐志摩，1915）。

誤譯帶來的閱讀障礙更大。任何學識淵博的翻譯家都難以完全避免誤譯。但譯者必須盡可能減少誤譯。指出誤譯，同樣體現了翻譯的責任。百年來屬於誤譯或多少有所誤解的譯筆，例如：馬君武譯詩之「訛」，蘇曼殊譯詩之「晦」，已有不少學者作了分析。

蘇曼殊比較看重五言、七言古體或律絕。已有學者指出，對於英詩中六行的處理，蘇譯減縮為四行，或是拉長為八行。帶來的弊病，一是省略過多，二是增添過多。這也是導致他誤譯的原因之一。例如他從擺倫（拜倫，Byron）長詩〈島嶼〉（*The Island*）節譯的〈星耶峰耶俱無生〉，原文和蘇譯如下：

Live not the Stars and Mountains? Are the Waves / Without a spirit? Are the dropping caves / Without a feeling in their silent tears?
No, no; they woo and clasp us to their spheres, / Dissolve this clog and clod of clay before / Its hour, and merge our soul in the great shore.

星耶峰耶俱無生，浪撼沙灘巖滴淚。
圍範茫茫寧有情，我將化泥溟海出。（蘇曼殊，1927）

在二十世紀初已經引進西式標點的情況下，蘇譯把原詩問句一概譯為敘述句。第三句的「寧」字應當不是語助詞而是副詞，即「豈」或「難道」的意思，一般見於反問句，如「王侯將相寧有種乎？」。拜倫要提出的反問是：圍範茫茫寧無情？像英國的浪漫詩人一樣，拜倫深受

泛神論（pantheism）影響。在中國詩學中或詩人眼裏，「煙雲泉石，花鳥苔林，金舖錦帳，寓意則靈。」「落紅不是無情物，化作春泥更護花」。泛神論者認為，無須寓意或移情，造化萬物，原本就是有靈有情的。無論有沒有泛神論信仰，詩人一般都不會把造化萬物寫成無情之物。拜倫首先提出問題，接著肯定了它們（They，即首字母大寫，帶有擬人特徵的星辰、山嶽、波浪等）都是活生生、有靈有情的。這一詩節的最後一行是：「整個大自然是他的王國，愛是他的寶座」（All Nature is his realm; and Love his throne），由此可見詩人對萬物傾注的深情。試比較詞體重譯的傅譯〈星辰山嶽（少年游）〉：

　　星辰山嶽，悄然寂滅？／波浪少精神？野洞幽深，／水珠滴落，無語淚無情？
　　何須問：有靈之物，求愛解人心。／蘽土銷形，此身歸去，／魂魄入洪溟。

　　此外，蘇譯用七言四行，過多省略原詩意象。如果採用七言，像原詩一樣，大致需要六行才能達意。其實，孟郊的〈遊子吟〉就只有六行，卻是唐詩佳作。《浣溪沙》詞調也是七言六行。譯詩為什麼不可以採用五、七言六行詩體呢？

## ─ I V ─

　　李思純先生對上世紀初的譯壇作了這樣的歸納：「近人譯詩有三式。一曰馬君武式。以格律謹嚴之近體譯之。如馬氏譯囂俄（雨果）詩曰『此是青年紅葉書，而今重展淚盈裾』是也。二曰蘇玄瑛（曼殊）式。以格律較疏之古體譯之。如蘇氏所為《文學因緣》、《漢英三昧集》是也。三曰胡適式。則以白話直譯，盡馳格律是也。」（李思純，1925）。李思純對於各家評論是否妥當，當作別論，但從中可以看出，以詞曲體譯詩，鮮有嘗試，未能形成一派。

就我所知，前輩翻譯家謹守格律以詞體譯詩並標明詞牌的，除了上文論及的陸譯朗費羅之外，還有下述兩例：一是陸志韋在 1914 年 3 月《東吳》雜志（1 卷 2 號）發表的〈譯彭斯詩調寄虞美人〉，二是吳宓把朗法羅（郎費羅）的長詩〈伊芳吉琳〉（Evangeline）「意譯」為〈滄桑豔傳奇〉時，首齣有一曲〈蝶戀花〉，載於達德學會《益智雜誌》1913 年 1 卷 3 期，吳宓自稱是從〈伊芳吉琳〉序曲「直譯原文」。

　　在中國翻譯史上，這幾個例子值得研究。但據我所知，對陸譯和吳譯，論者大都泛泛提及而已。陸譯彭斯，沒有注明原作，後來也沒有人論及原作。因此，下文著重討論陸譯、吳譯及其重譯。陸譯〈譯彭斯詩調寄虞美人〉如次：

　　匿斯河上延空翠，頗領心頭事，思量到此強開眉，忽憶桃花流水賞心時。
　　淡山窈宛連江繡，忍感春懷舊。幾尋蹤跡曲江濱，爭奈素心難遇素人心。

　　據我的查考，原詩當為彭斯寫於 1793 年的〈美后菲莉絲之歌〉（Phillis the Queen o' the fair）。菲莉絲是彭斯一位朋友的女兒，她的麗質啟迪了詩人的靈感。陸譯從該詩的前四節摘譯。王佐良譯《彭斯詩選》沒有譯這首詩。傅譯全詩譯出，參見本書第 95 頁。不難發現，陸譯的摘譯，半是擬作半是意譯。除了詞體形態歸化之外，陸譯的歸化策略，就是把原文的「玫瑰花蕾」（The rose-bud）改為桃花，像詩人朱湘譯勃朗寧（Robert Browning）〈異域鄉思〉（Home-Thoghts, from Abroad）時把「梨樹」（elm-tree bole）譯成「夭桃」（朱湘，1986）一樣。

　　除了詩題之外，傅譯把專有名字菲莉絲意譯為「芳心」。因為這個名字來自希臘文，相當於拉丁文的「芙羅拉」（Flora），意為草木花卉，源於羅馬神話的花神和春神的名字。彭斯把菲莉絲視為「純美皇

后」的化身，所以譯為「芳心」，以便襲用陸譯「素心」一詞，寄寓素樸乃芳美之母的詩意。因為用韻和對仗的緣故，譯詩中有一種「詩的破格」（poetical licence），即詞序變化或倒裝句：「玫紅羞我臉頰／甘甜銜她皓齒」。在中西詩詞中，這都是有前例的，杜甫就有「香稻啄餘鸚鵡粒，碧梧棲老鳳凰枝」的名句。

像陸譯一樣，吳譯〈蝶戀花〉，也很難稱之為「直譯」：

蒼莽松林千年老，敗葉殘蛋，瀟地鳴愁惱。陵穀劫殘人不到，高山流水哭昏曉。
商婦弦絕伶工杳，片羽只鱗，舊時傳來少。今我重臨蓬萊島，原野淒迷空秋草。

吳譯依據的原文見本書第 94 頁，朗費羅〈伊芳吉琳‧序曲〉前半部分。整個〈序曲〉傅譯用兩首〈玉蝴蝶慢〉迻譯，請參照比較。朗費羅這部長詩以十八世紀法印戰爭（the French and Indian War）為背景，描述北美阿卡狄亞一個和平村莊遭英國殖民者焚毀，少女伊芳吉琳與其未婚夫悲歡離合的故事。原文寫到的德魯伊高僧（Druids of eld），是古老的凱爾特 （Celt）神職人員；他們不僅掌管祭祀，同時也是巫醫、魔法師、占卜者、詩人、樂師和部族歷史的記錄者。Druid 一詞原義為「橡樹的賢者」或「深諳樹理之人」，因此，在後世詩文中，凱爾特高僧常以橡樹精的形象出現。朗費羅想像自己身處橡樹林中，彷彿看到德魯伊高僧成為鬚髮蒼白的豎琴師，仍然在彈唱阿卡狄亞的歷史故事。對於中國人陌生的這一藝術形象，吳譯的歸化策略，是用琴師伯牙和「老大嫁作商人婦」的琵琶女子來代替。

在理論上，吳宓對德萊頓的三分法，獨尊意譯，認為「直譯窒礙難行，擬作並非翻譯，過與不及，實兩失之，唯意譯最合中道，而可以為法」（吳宓，1923）。既然如此，他何必標榜帶有意譯因素的〈蝶戀

花〉係直譯？如某些學者已指出的那樣，吳譯中頗多中國典故和成語。譯筆雖然典雅流暢，但難以完整地保留原作內容。

除了上述三首標明詞牌的譯作之外，早在 1902 年，梁啟超就嘗試採用詞體譯詩了。他出版的從日文轉譯的小說《十五小豪傑》，原作是焦士威爾奴（儒勒・凡爾納，Jules Veme）的《兩年假期》（*Deux ans de vacances*）。梁譯以一曲「調寄摸魚兒」作為開篇。但是，該小說日文本是從英文轉譯的，梁譯又採用時人所謂「豪傑譯」的筆法，任意增刪或改變原作主題、結構和人物，因此，這首詞離法文原文有多遠，有待考察。

十分值得推崇的，是梁啟超在章回小說《新中國未來記》第四回插入他以曲本體翻譯的擺倫（拜倫）關於希臘的詩，即長詩〈渣阿亞〉（*Giaour*，通譯〈異教徒〉）選節；〈端志安〉（*Don Juan*，即〈唐・璜〉）選節，譯詩標明元曲曲牌「沈醉東風」和「如夢憶桃園」，但並不完全受曲牌定字、定句和平仄的限制（梁啟超，1902）。

後來以〈哀希臘〉為題聞名中國的拜倫詩，早期四家譯文，即梁譯曲本體，馬君武七言古體（〈哀希臘歌〉），蘇曼殊譯五言古體和胡適譯騷體，我以為以梁譯採用文白夾雜的長短句，較貼近原作風味，對今人頗有啟發。梁啟超本人也非常看重自己的譯筆。「沉醉東風」眉批曰：「著者常發心欲將中國曲本體翻譯外國文豪詩集。此雖至難之事，然若果有此，真可稱文壇革命巨現。吾意他日必有為之者。此兩折亦其大。」那時，現代白話文運動已呼之欲出。作為「詩界革命」的倡導者之一，梁啟超提倡以曲本體譯詩，實際上是在譯壇提倡與「廟堂文學」相對的歌謠、彈唱等中國民間詩歌形式，希望譯詩像中國詞曲一樣，與「歌」不分家，可以吟唱。他的表率啟迪了白話詩譯詩的發展，但是，在他之後，鮮有以詞曲體譯詩者。吳宓譯羅色蒂（羅塞蒂，C. G. Rossetti）的〈逝矣逝矣〉（*Passing Away*），堪稱帶有詞曲風味的佳

譯（吳宓，1935）。總體來看，梁啟超對詞曲體譯詩的期望沒有蔚為大觀。

八〇年代，現為北京大學英語系教授的辜正坤先生成為梁啟超所期望的「他日有心人」。辜先生提出了多元互補翻譯標準與西詩漢譯詞曲體問題，把詞曲體譯詩視為多元中的一元。他認為西詩許多作品，詩句原本長短不齊，有一種「參差美」，尤其是這類短詩，不妨以詞曲體譯之，但不必字字講究平仄音韻，即不用詞牌，只借長短句式和詞彙風味。他自己就是這樣採用所謂「自度曲」譯詩（辜正坤，1990：32-4）。

辜先生在主編《世界名詩鑒賞詞典》時，邀我擔任編委，負責古羅馬部分的翻譯賞析。該詞典1990年出版後，我更多瞭解到他的翻譯理論和實踐。在此影響下，我開始嘗試以詞曲體譯詩，斷斷續續翻譯的數百首詩，正在整理中，其中標明詞牌謹守格律並且可以與原作逐行對照的，只有十多首，所謂「自度曲」，也只有數十首。這正好說明，詞曲體譯詩可以聊備一格，卻不可能成為譯詩體裁主流。西方詩歌，尤其是鴻篇巨制，仍宜以自由體翻譯。

或曰，英詩古譯，難免削足適履或因韻害意。我的回應是：就有些詩來說，以自由體迻譯，缺乏詩味，古譯亦有其弊；兩弊相權，取其輕。西方的十四行詩等格律詩，中國的格律詩詞，其嚴謹的要求對優秀詩人來說並非一種窠臼。同樣，高明的譯者完全可以把古譯之弊降低到最低程度甚至完全避免，化弊為利。借吳宓譯解尼埃（André Chénier）〈創造〉（*Invention*）中的詩語來說：「今天的詩歌翻譯者，仍然可以「用新來之俊思兮，成古體之佳篇」（吳宓，1935）。

相對於五言七言，詞曲體譯詩在這方面的長處和潛力，可以用英國詩人豪易特（William Howitt）的〈去燕〉（*Departure of the Swallow*）中譯

為例。請先比較原文和蘇曼殊所譯五古：

And is the swallow gone? / Who beheld it? / Which way sail'd it? / Farewell bade it none?

No mortal saw it go: / But who doth hear / Its summer cheer / As it flitteth to and fro?

So the freed spirit flies! / From its surrounding clay / It steals away / Like the swallow from the skies.

Whither? wherefore doth it go? / 'T is all unknown: / We feel alone / That a void is left below.

燕子歸何處，無人與別離。女行藪誰見，誰為感差池。

女行未分明，躞蹀復何為？春聲無與和，呢喃欲語誰？

遊魂亦如是，蛻形共馳騁。將翱復將翔，隨女天之涯。

翻飛何所至，塵寰總未知。女行諒自謫，獨我棄如遺。（蘇曼殊，1927）

蘇譯把原文的許多問句改為敘述句，這種變通並無不可。但原詩詩句很短，從譯詩選體的角度來看，似乎以詞體為妥。相傳黃帝所作〈彈歌〉，是一首短小精悍的兩言詩。宋詞中兩言句不少。我用詞牌「河傳」五十五個字，譯出了蘇譯用一百字迻譯的這首詩，題為〈離燕〉：

離燕？／誰見？／孤帆飄遠？／誰送它行？／有無凡眼？／春夏笑語／誰聞？／去來／瀟灑魂！

塵寰隱逸／如歸燕。／花季晚？／底事尋他岸？／竟無人曉，／高瞰寂寞空枝，／夢魂飛。

傅譯保留了原詩全部問句，內容上少有遺漏。蘇曼殊自言譯拜倫詩：「按文切理，語無增飾」（蘇曼殊，1914），這實際上是做

不到的，有時也是不必要的；因為，詞語的省略（omission）和增添（addition）是翻譯的重要手法，用得適當，前者無傷大雅，甚至可以取粗存精，後者可為譯文增色或營造意境。

— V —

意象、意境或境界，是中國古代文論中的重要範疇。「意象」一詞，與英文的 image 非常貼近。意境的概念大一些，沒有一個完全對等的英文詞，一般譯為 imagery，artistic state 等。我認為，更貼近的英文詞，也許是 imaging，該詞在藝術上的意義是心靈圖畫的成象，或借想像達成的表現。德萊頓對該詞的解說是：「Imaging 就其本身而言是詩的極致和生命，經由一種熱情（enthusiasm）或靈魂特有的情感，這一過程使得我們仿佛看到詩人所描繪的事物。」❷詹森（Samuel Johnson）在著名的《英語詞典》中解釋 enthusiasm 一詞，引德萊頓的用法為例，把它與想像和幻想聯繫在一起，第二義和第三義分別為「想像的熱度；情感的強烈；看法的自信」（Heat of imagination; violence of passion; confidence of opinion）和「幻想的提昇；觀念的得意」（Elevation of fancy; exaltation of ideas）（Johnson, 1755）。可見德萊頓和詹森關於 imaging 和藝術想像的觀點，完全可以借用中國詩學的意象、意境、神思和「詩緣情」之說來相互闡發：「……獨照之匠，窺意象而運斤；此蓋馭文之首術，謀篇之大端。夫神思方運，萬塗競萌，規矩虛位，刻鏤無形。登山則情滿於山，觀海則意溢於海……」（劉勰《文心雕龍‧神思》）。或如歐陽修引梅聖俞語：「必能狀難寫之景如在目前，含不盡之意見於言外，然後為至矣」（《六一詩話》）。

由此可見，詩的意象或意境的傳譯，同樣是譯詩的「極致和生命」或「首術」、「大端」。西方詩歌中的意象派（imagism），原本就是在法國象徵主義和中國古典詩歌豐富意象的影響下形成的。因此，在翻譯意象派的創立者龐德（Ezra Pound）等詩人的某些作品中，如果可能

的話，在詩體上採用歸化策略，順理成章。例如龐德早期詩集《大祓集》（*Lustra*,1916）中的一首短詩和傅譯：

'Ione, Dead The Long Year'
Empty are the way, / Empty are the way of this land/And the flowers / Bend over with heavy heads. / They bend in vain. / Empty are the way of this land / Where Ione / Walked once, and now does not walk / But seems like a person just gone.

〈伊昂妮離世的漫長一年〉：
條條小徑，／空空蕩蕩寂寂。／簇簇野花，／低眉垂首，／徒然掩泣。／但憶當年附素足，／而今足音何處覓？／恰似離人方才去，／無聲息。

試比較申奧譯〈伊昂妮，死去多年〉：
道路是空曠的，／這片土地上的道路是空曠的／花朵／沉重地低下了頭。／它們徒然低頭。／這片土地上的道路是空曠的／伊昂妮曾在這兒／漫步，如今沒有漫步／但好像一個人剛剛離開。（申奧，1985）

龐德此詩悼念的，是詩人的情人，一位自殺身亡的法國芭蕾舞女。詩的寫作年代正是愛因斯坦相對論問世之際。龐德寫到的「漫長一年」，可以視為熱力學時間箭頭的行進，「恰似離人方才去」，則表達了詩人精神軌跡中，心理時間的相對短暫。與此相反的是，在李清照〈聲聲慢〉中，「守著窗兒，獨自怎生得黑」的心理時間是相對緩慢的。兩個詩的主人公，一個對故人記憶猶新，度年如日，一個一起床便難耐寂寞，度日如年。可是，龐德詩與易安詞通過重復和疊詞的手法營造的「尋尋覓覓」、若有所失的意境卻頗為接近。以王國維境界說觀之，前者是借花說事的「無我之境」，後者是借酒說愁的「有我之境」。因此，借鑒詞體和易安詞的疊字手法來轉換龐德的詩行重複，可

以賦予原詩以意境。

中西詩歌意境相通的例子很多。例如，活躍於二十世紀初葉英國文壇的托馬斯（Edward Thomas），作為評論家，是他最早擢昇從美國來到倫敦初露頭角的弗羅斯特（Robert Frost）和龐德的詩名，可能通過龐德接觸到中國文化。作為詩人，他深受華茲華斯的影響，像湖畔派詩人（Lake Poets）一樣，曾經在著名的英國湖區，或獨自徜徉於湖畔，或游泳擊槳於湖中。他的〈七月〉（*July*）一詩，可謂意境深遠，氣韻生動，渾厚質樸。下面是宗白的中譯：

萬物寧謐，惟有流雲，晶瑩的湖泊，／雲影緩移，浮泛著舟影。／扁舟輕蕩，我用槳兒劃破／沉沉的炎熱，和迷離的寂寞，／為了辨認：望見的是鳥和纖塵。／為了探明：湖畔樹林是否蘇醒。

晨曦早已微明──彌漫──飄向晴空／又溶於碧波；我久久凝視冷冷的蘆葦／影入雲天氄氄的水中，涼意更濃；／在這悠悠的時光，物我兩忘／遠處樹叢，斑尾鴿禺禺細語，／我靜臥啼聽，恍惚置身仙境（見孫梁，1987）。

原詩見本書第 306 頁。詩中唯有斑尾鴿或斑鳩，是帶有西方文化色彩的意象，在基督教文明中往往是愛的象徵。托馬斯在1908年的一封書信中寫道：「對我來說，人似乎是大自然的一小部分（Man seems to me to be a very little part of Nature）」（Thomas, 1995: 51）。這句話與「天人合一」的觀念非常吻合。詩的第二節第四行，直譯是「沒什麼值得如次長久地思考」。宗譯從中國文化中信手拈來「物我兩忘」一語，這種歸化，在意境上與原詩是對等的。傅譯在重譯時襲用了這一成語，譯為〈七月（水調歌頭）〉，起筆也許能見出一種意境：

Naught moves but clouds, and in the glassy lake
Their doubles and the shadow of my boat.

萬籟靜無念，但見白雲飄，平湖如鏡，
舟影輕蕩共雲搖。

— Ⅵ —

　　托馬斯的詩風，詩如其人。「風格即人」（Le style est l'homme même），是千古不刊之論。泰特勒（Alexander Tytler）在《論翻譯的原則》一書中提出的翻譯三標準之一，就是譯文的風格（style）和筆調（manner）應與原文性質相同（Tytler, 1791: 109）。如奈達所認為的那樣，翻譯的風格對等具有僅次於意義對等的重要性。（Nida, 1964: 166）。劉半農先生〈關於譯詩的一點意見〉（1921）一文比奈達的書早發表，他認為翻譯必須做到三點：第一，要傳達出原詩的意思；第二，要盡力的把原文中的語言方式保留下來；第三，要傳達出原詩的情感（劉半農，1935）。他提出的第一、二個要求，與奈達的觀點一致，因為語言是體現風格的媒介。

　　在英國詩歌史上，曾有過各種流派，如玄學派（Metaphysical poets）、感傷派（Sentimental poets）、墓園派（Graveyard poets）、湖畔派（Lake poets），以及後來蔚為大觀的浪漫主義運動和五花八門的現代派和後現代派。如果用中國詩歌史上關於流派的美學區分，就不難發現，英美詩歌也有類似於宋詞的婉約派與豪放派的分野。

　　例如，十七世紀的宮廷派詩人考利（Abraham Cowley），不少詩歌採用阿那克里翁詩體（Anacreontics），即源於希臘抒情詩人阿那克里翁（Anacreon）專寫酒色的詩體，就可以目為婉約派。他的〈燕子〉（Swallow）一詩，傅譯為「虞美人」，酷肖婉約詞風。它也許可以令中國讀者想到金昌緒〈春怨〉（打起黃鶯兒），（唐）無名氏〈鵲踏枝〉（叵耐靈鵲多謾語）或南唐馮延巳的〈鵲踏枝〉（雙燕來時）。在中西詩歌中諸如此類人與鳥之間的對話，大凡可以視為一個孤獨寂寞的人

與他或她自己心靈的對話。傅譯胡德〈水娘（西江月三首）〉（*Water Lady*），亦有婉約詞風，同樣可以如此解讀。

在浪漫派中，華茲華斯的詩風既與拜倫、雪萊有別，又與考利不同。華茲華斯兩首〈致蝴蝶〉（*To A butterfly*），可見其纖穠、典雅、飄逸之一斑。例如其二的原文第一節和傅譯〈聲聲慢〉上片：

I've watched you now a full half-hour; / Self-poised upon that yellow flower / And, little Butterfly! Indeed / I know not if you sleep or feed. / How motionless!--not frozen seas / More motionless! and then / What joy awaits you, when the breeze / Hath found you out among the trees, / And calls you forth again!

觀花賞蝶，蝶落黃花，／神思恍恍惚惚。／靜靜悄悄良久，／不知飛蝶，／安然收翼入睡，曉夢迷，／或吸花汁？／汝不動，／若冰河，／醒悟待風吹拂。

英詩古譯，往往可以省略主語和人稱代詞所有格，此處的省略正好可以造成一種「莊生曉夢迷蝴蝶」的境界。所引原詩最後三行，譯詩也有省略，但省略的重要詞，在下片延後出現（綠樹黃花園圃，我亦有……）。這種情況，我視為類似於律詩隔行「拗救」的一種翻譯技巧。

與華茲華斯的詩風不同，拜倫、雪萊等浪漫主義詩人，不遜蘇軾的廣闊社會人生視野及其「大江東去」的氣魄。梁啟超推崇拜倫，著意「取泰西文豪之意境之風格，熔鑄之以入我詩」，作為「詩界革命」的一種創舉（梁啟超，1903）。

拜倫、雪萊，堪稱英國浪漫主義詩歌的豪放派雙璧。以雪萊〈西風

頌〉（Ode to the West Wind）而言，排山倒海之強力，不足以況其磅礴之氣勢，弓道箭術之張弛，不足以比其節律之和諧，正劇悲劇之範疇，不足以總其精神之豐富，海天糾結之奇觀，不足以壓其浪漫主義之崇高。以中國詩學觀之，屬於二十四詩品首品「雄渾」，兼具第八品「勁健」、第十二品「豪放」的特徵。狂野的西風，是詩人雪萊的「真體內充」，「橫絕太空」的「寥寥長風」，有「吞吐大荒」的宏偉氣派。

辜正坤認為，譯〈西風頌〉，不妨摹擬元曲關漢卿雜劇《單刀會》的氣勢，謂之「偷勢」，摹擬其長於表現壯懷激烈感的入聲韻，謂之「偷語」。但辜正坤只譯了〈西風頌〉的第四、五節（辜正坤，1990）。

帶有詞曲體風味的傅譯〈西風頌〉全詩近年發表後，北京國際關係學院英語系教授張世紅先生在該院學報上發表專文評論，題為〈從西風頌的兩個譯本比較看經典名作復譯的必要性〉。通過對中國著名翻譯家王佐良譯文和傅譯進行對比分析，張世紅肯定了傅譯的價值（張世紅，2010）。

傅譯之前，〈西風頌〉英譯多達十多家，這裏只就郭沫若（〈西風歌〉，1928）、楊熙齡（1980）、查良錚（1982）、王佐良（1982）、卞之琳（1983）等幾家的第一節和第二節的幾行詩與傅譯進行比較。首先是〈西風頌〉突兀崢嶸的起筆。能否譯好這個「鳳頭」，傳達原文氣勢，至關重要。試比較原文和多家譯文：

O wild West Wind, thou breath of Autumn's being / Thou from whose unseen presence the leaves dead / Are driven like ghosts from an enchanter fleeing

郭譯：哦，不羈的西風！你秋之呼吸，／你雖不可見，敗葉為你吹

飛，／好象魍魎之群在詛咒之前逃退

　　楊譯：你是秋的呼吸，啊，奔放的西風；／你無形地蒞臨時，殘葉
們逃亡，／它們像回避巫師的成群鬼魂

　　查譯：哦，狂暴的西風，秋之生命的呼吸！／你無形，但枯死的落
葉被你橫掃，／有如鬼魅碰到了巫師，紛紛逃避

　　王譯：呵，狂野的西風，你把秋氣猛吹，／不露臉便將落葉一掃而
空，／猶如法師趕走了群鬼

　　卞譯：狂放的西風啊，你是秋天的浩氣／你並不露面，把死葉橫掃
個滿天空，／象鬼魂在法師面前紛紛逃避

　　傅譯：啊，狂野的西風，你這秋神的浩氣／吞吐呼嘯無形跡，抖落
滿地枯萎／猶如巫師念咒語，群鬼紛紛逃逸。

　　雪萊一開始就採用了人格化（personification）或神格化（deification）
的表現手法。在「神人同形同性論」（anthropomorphism）的希臘神話
中，西風 Zephyrus 是泰坦巨人族的佔星之神（Astroeus）和黎明女神
（Aurora）的兒子；在荷馬史詩中被當作暴風雨之神來描寫。在後世文
學中，西風經常被描繪為春天的和風。在基督教文化中，西風是上帝吹
進亞當鼻孔中的「生命之氣」。雪萊的西風，更像荷馬筆下的西風，同
時帶有基督教文化的意味；傅譯因此譯為秋神。其浩蕩氣勢，在中國文
化中，也許只有孟子所說的「浩然之氣」才能與之匹配。多家把 breath
直譯為呼吸，缺乏力度，卞譯「浩氣」，是恰到好處的歸化，傅譯因此
襲用卞譯的擇詞。王譯採用了詞類轉譯手法，這在翻譯中是常見可行
的，但是，張世紅指出：「〈西風頌〉裏多處使用同位語結構，讓西風
與不同的意象成為一體，使整個詩篇生動有力、節奏明快。」王譯：
「你把秋氣猛吹」，「把同位元結構變為主謂結構，使西風與秋天的氣
息一分為二，儘管第一行的『吹』與第三行的『鬼』押韻，在形式上與
原文保持一致，但內容違背了原文的旨義」（張世紅，2010）。此外，
我認為「猛吹」一詞，擇詞較俗。第二行，郭譯和查譯均採用被動語
態。英語中被動語態比中文要常用得多（當代中國被動語態流行當作別

論）。中譯有時可以保留被動語態，但此處為了加強西風的氣勢，宜像卞譯和王譯那樣用主動語態。傅譯的「抖落」不是被動語態，可以視為使動詞的主動語態。

第二節開頭三行詩的景觀，是詩歌中罕見的浩大形象：

Thou on whose stream, 'mid the steep sky's commotion, / Loose clouds like earth's decaying leaves are shed, / Shook from the tangled boughs of heaven and ocean, / Angels of rain and lightning!

郭譯：太空中動亂嶔崎，／鬆散的流雲被你吹起，／有如地上的落葉辭去天海的交枝；／那是雨和電光的安琪

楊譯：你在動亂的太空中掀起激流，／那上面飄浮著落葉似的雲塊，／掉落自天與海的錯綜的枝頭／它們是傳送雨和閃電的神差

查譯：沒入你的急流，當高空一片混亂，／流雲象大地的枯葉一樣被撕扯／脫離天空和海洋的糾纏的枝幹。／成為雨和電的使者

王譯：你激盪長空，亂雲飛墜/如落葉；你搖撼天和海，/不許它們象老樹纏在一堆;/你把雨和電趕了下來

卞譯：你啊，順你的激流，趁高空騷動，／鬆開了雲朵，象大地上殘葉飛飄，／朵朵搖脫了天海交結的枝叢，／那些雨電的神使

傅譯：海天糾結為樹，亂雲翻飛為葉，／你湧上高天險關，沖落敗葉撼大樹，／豈容這蒼老古木盤根錯節！／你這雨電的天使

原詩主句是一個無須系動詞的驚嘆句（你，雨電的天使！），中間帶了個很長的從句。原詩不著「樹」字，卻以 decaying leaves 和 boughs 的意象渲染了一棵龐然大樹。它是當時歐洲封建反動勢力的象徵。其中 stream 一詞，以卞譯的「激流」或查譯的「急流」為妥，傅譯詞類轉譯為「湧上」。郭譯省略了這個比喻，繼續採用被動語態，可是寫到落葉，卻讓它們主動「辭去」枝頭，這種處理是不大恰當的。王譯第三行同樣有用詞較俗的問題，缺乏詩意。多家譯文都大致依照原文語序。

根據喬姆斯基（Noam Chomsky）的句法理論觀點，句子的深層結構（deep structure）蘊含著唯一能解釋這個句子的全部資訊（Chomsky, 1965: 16）。有時，譯者可以僅僅把源語的表層結構（surface structure）轉換成譯語，以保持原詩的修辭格或含蓄。有時，要求得神似，就不妨捨棄表層結構，謀求深層結構的一致性，以達到風格對等的效果；用中國美學的術語來說，就是「離形得似」。如奈達所言，當源語與譯語的語法結構和語義結構之間差異很大時，就需要經歷分析（analysis）、轉移（transfer）和重組（restructuring）的曲折過程（Nida, 1969: 33）。

　　傅譯與多家譯文不同，「離形」之處首先在於顛倒了原文語序，以「海天糾結為樹」一語渲染此一形象，強化了原詩中立詞義所隱含的褒貶色彩，以便反襯出西風彌滿宇宙的形象。傅譯摹仿了源語的比喻和中國古典詩詞的句法，間或採用英語中所沒有的對仗等手法。

—— VII ——

　　郭沫若雖然深諳譯中之「易」，卻在理論上有失偏頗。他早期談論譯雪萊詩的體驗時說：「譯雪萊的詩，是要使我成為雪萊，是要使雪萊成為我自己。譯詩不是鸚鵡學舌，不是沐猴而冠」（郭沫若，1923）。這種翻譯狀態，像蘇曼殊譯拜倫而以「中國的拜倫」自居一樣，像吳宓以「東方安諾德」自居一樣，屬於審美中的「移情」（Einfühlung）和「內摹仿」（innere Nachahmung）狀態。王力談到譯波德萊爾的體驗時說：「莫作他人情緒讀，最傷心處見今吾。」（王力，1980）。更正確地說，譯詩所表達的，應當既是他人（原作者）的情緒，也是譯者的情緒。譯者與原作者異域隔代，卻有可能靈犀相通。我譯〈西風頌〉，同樣處在這種狀態。我們既需要偏重情感的移情性翻譯，也需要偏重理性保持審美距離的翻譯。但是，郭沫若在強調前者時不恰當地否定了翻譯中的摹仿。

值得注意的是，德萊頓所說的擬作，不同於淵源於古希臘的摹仿（mimesis），前者的另一極是直譯，後者的另一極是創造。有趣的是，在西藏傳統藝術和佛教造像中，經常用幻想中長於摹仿的兩頭鸚鵡來象徵佛教大譯師。納博科夫（Vladimir Nabokov）在〈論翻譯普希金《歐根·奧聶根》〉一詩中，就把翻譯比喻為「一隻鸚鵡的尖叫，一隻猴子的聒噪，／以及對死者（原作者）的失敬」（Nabokov, 1955）。由此可見，盛行於西方的「翻譯即摹仿」、「譯者如畫家」的說法，只有加上強調對原作者失敬的另一極，即創造性的另一極，才能相反相成地闡明翻譯的本質。「創造性的摹仿」（creative mimeses）的矛盾語（oxymoron）是有效的。翻譯英詩，不是像繪畫學生那樣以油畫摹仿油畫，而是以中國彩墨摹仿西方油畫。除了調動自己的人生體驗把握原作的精神風貌之外，也要懂得原作的基本技法，是透明薄塗畫法，還是不透明厚塗畫法或兩者的折衷？在轉換為國畫時，既要採用某些中西共通的技法，也要採用一些國畫獨有的技法，例如用筆、用墨、敷色等多方面的手法，達到一種與原作「似與不似之間」的藝術效果。詩畫相通，真正的詩歌翻譯家既是畫家，也是詩人，最好是他自己也以母語寫詩的詩人。

歸化和異化，像翻譯中的對立概念一樣，是兩個極端。兩者之間有「黃金中道」（the golden mean）。但是，「黃金中道」是個無法測定的模糊點。英國詩人赫里克（Robert Herrick）的〈美的定義〉（*definition of beauty*）是：「美是中道與極端之間的一束閃光。」這一警句也許同樣適合於翻譯之美，有助於譯者尋找理想的「黃金分割」。翻譯有時可以向歸化靠近一點，有時又可以向異化靠近一點，以拓寬創造性空間。

借用英國詩人鄧約翰（John Donne）的〈跳蚤〉（*The Flea*）奇喻（conceit）來說，翻譯家好比一隻跳蚤，對於兩種文化，先叮你後叮他，然後在自己的肚子裡搞名堂，搞出一個鴛鴦床。弄得不好，它蹦跳一下就被人搯死了——被譯語的讀者和批評家搯死。弄得好，就弄出了

一個陰陽和合大殿宇——像鄧約翰的創造性的詩歌〈跳蚤〉一樣，贏得永恆的藝術生命。

再回到鸚鵡這個比喻。翻譯家應當承認這個悖論（paradox）：譯者即是鸚鵡，又不是鸚鵡，既是鸚鵡本身又是玩鸚鵡的主人。從形式上看，摹仿，或戴著源語和譯語的雙重鐐銬跳舞，卻有可能跳得瀟灑徇美，求得與原作形神俱似。從內容上看，對原詩的深層結構或神韻的把握和轉換，必須用心，甚至要嘔心瀝血才能創造性地傳情達意。我可以懸為座右銘的，是我博採眾說所概括的八個字：

兩頭鸚鵡，一心創造。

傅正明
2012 年 3 月於瑞典

注釋：

❶ 王力譯波德萊爾〈《惡之花》譯者序〉：「頻年格物歡偏枯，偶譯佳詩只自娛。」

❷ 德萊頓這句話，多家西方學者誤以為出自他的〈詩畫比較〉（*The Parallel of Poetry and Painting*），我在該文中沒有查到這句話。依照詹森權威的《英語詞典》，當出自德萊頓〈朱文科書序〉（*Juv. Preface*），是德萊頓為四世紀西班牙詩人朱文科（Juvencus）的四福音書詩體改寫本所寫的序言，寫作年代不詳。

# 參考及引用書目

## 西文部分

Arnold, Matthew. *On Translating Homer*. London: Longman, Green, Longman, and
    Roberts, 1861.

Bayar, Monia. *To Mean or Not to Mean*, Kadmous cultural foundation. Khatawat for
    publishing and distribution. Damascus, Syria, 2007, pp. 213-223.

Brown,John Pairman. *Israel and Hellas*, Vol. 3, Berlin: Walter de Gruyter, 2001.

Chomsky, Noam. *Aspects of the theory of syntax*. Cambridge: The MIT Press. 1965.

Dryden, John. 'Preface to Ovid's Epistles'.*Ovid's Epistles, Translated by Several
    Hands*. London: Jacob Tonson, 1681.

Johnson, Samuel. *The Dictionary of the English Language*, 1755.

Nabokov, Vladimir. 'On Translating Eugene Onegin'. *New Yorker*, January 1955.

Nida, E. A. *Toward a Science of Translating*, Leiden: E. J. Brill, 1964. Nida, E. A. and
    Taber, C. R. *The theory and practice of translation*. Leiden: Brill, 1982.

Thomas, Edward. *Selected Letters*, Oxford University Press, 1995.

Tytler, A. F. *Essay on the Principles of Translation,* 1791. Ed.Huntsman, J. F.,
    Amsterdam 1978.

Vinay, J. P. & Darbelnet, J. *Stylistique Comparée du Français et de l'Anglais*, Didier-
    Harrap, 1958.

中文部分

（一）

卞之琳（1983）。英國詩選。湖南：湖南人民出版社。

王力（譯）（1980）。惡之花（原作者：Charles Pierre Baudelaire）。北京：外國文學出版社。

王佐良（1982）。英國詩文選譯集。北京：外語教學與研究出版社。

申奧（1985）。美國現代六詩人選集。湖南：湖南人民出版社。

朱湘（1986）。朱湘譯詩集。湖南：湖南人民出版社。

吳宓（1935）。吳宓詩集。上海：中華書局。

林語堂（1932）。論翻譯。語言學論叢（32-47 頁）。北京：開明出版社。

查良錚（1982）。雪萊抒情詩選。北京：人民文學出版社。

馬建中（1894）。擬設翻譯書院議。

徐志摩（1915）。詠詞。徐志摩譯詩集（52 頁）。湖南：湖南人民出版社，1989。

許淵沖（1991）。文學與翻譯。北京：北京大學出版社。

孫梁（1987）。英美名詩一百首。香港：商務印書館。

郭沫若（1928）。沫若譯詩集。上海。：創造社出版部。

郭沫若（1981）。英詩譯稿。上海：上海譯文出版社。

梁啟超（1897）。飲冰室合集（文集之一，變法通議‧論譯書）。北京：中華書局，1936。

梁啟超（1902）。飲冰室合集（專集之八十九，新中國未來記）。北京：

中華書局，1936。

辜正坤（主編）（1990）。**世界名詩鑒賞詞典**。北京：北京大學出版社。

楊熙齡（1980）。**雪萊抒情詩選**。上海：上海譯文出版社。

魯迅（1981）。非有復譯不可。**魯迅全集**（第六冊，274 頁）。北京：人民文學出版社。

劉半農（1935）。關於譯詩的一點意見。**半農雜文二集**。北京：良友圖書公司。

錢鍾書（1979）。林經的翻譯。**舊文四篇**。上海：上海古籍出版社。

羅新璋（1984）。**翻譯論集**。北京：商務印書館。

蘇曼殊、柳亞子（編訂）（1927）。**蘇曼殊全集**。北京：中國書店據北新書局 1927 本影印（第一冊 75-78，譯詩集），1985。

蘇曼殊、柳亞子（編訂）（1914）。拜倫詩選自序。**拜倫詩選**。日本：東京三秀舍印刷，梁啟莊發行。

（二）

李思純（1925）。仙河集自序。**學衡**，47。

吳宓（1923a）。英詩淺釋。**學衡**，14。

吳宓（1923b）。論今日文學創造之正法。**學衡**，15。

郭沫若（1923）。雪萊的詩小引。**創造季刊**，第 1 卷第 4 期。

張世紅（2010）。從西風頌的兩個譯本比較看經典名作復譯的必要性。**國際關係學院學報**，3。

梁實秋（1933），論翻譯的一封信，**新月**，第 4 卷第 5 期。

春天（*Primavera*）／波提伽利（Sandro Botticelli），ca：1482，蛋彩畫。

一〇八是個神祕的數字

一是真善美的統一

〇是精神證悟的空性和圓滿

八是八方的遼闊和久遠

——譯者題記

# Geoffrey Chaucer (1343-1400)

## Canticus Troili

'If no love is,* O God, what fele I so?                         *there is*

And if love is, what thing and which is he!

If love be good, from whennes* cometh my wo?          *whence*

If it be wikke,* a wonder thinketh me,                              *bad*

When every torment and adversitee                                   5

That cometh of him, may to me savory* thinke;          *pleasant*

For ay* thurst I, the more that I it drinke.                        *ever*


And if that at myn owene lust* I brenne,*        *pleasure/burn*

From whennes cometh my wailing and my pleynte?*   *commplaint*

If harm agree me, wherto pleyne I thenne?                        10

I noot,* ne why unwery that I faynte.                   *do not know*

O quike* deeth, O swete harm so queynte,         *living/curious*

How may of thee in me swich quantitee,

But if that I consente that it be?


And if that I consente, I wrongfully

# 傑弗雷‧喬叟 (1343-1400)*

## 001. 特羅勒斯情歌 ❶

若言人間無愛，心底何物襲來？
若言人間有愛，誰能知其真宰？
若言愛本性善，為何令我憂慮？
若言愛本性惡，令人百思不解：
儘管愛之苦澀，儘管愛之乖戾，
卻似生命之源，湧出無窮愉快；
痛飲愛之瓊漿，反而唇焦舌蔽。

若言我戀女色，欲火燃燒不熄，
悲號哀怨之聲，不知從何而來？
若言堪忍災禍，何以笑口難開？
若言並未疲憊，何以暈厥倒地？
怪哉生中有死，受傷反覺痛快。
若非我之恩准，豈能容你藏匿，
如此重重疊疊，壓在我的心懷。

既然我已容許，為何錯得離譜，

Compleyne, y-wis;* thus possed to and fro,     *certainly* 15
Al sterélees withinne a boot am I
Amid the see,* bytwixen* windés two,     *sea/between*
That in contrarie stonden* evermo.     *opposition stand*
Allas! what is this wonder* maladye?     *strange*
For hete* of cold, for cold of hete, I deye.'     *heat* 20

一再怨天尤人，傾訴心頭悲苦。
我如無舵孤舟，日夜浮游大海，
茫茫不見邊際，風從兩邊吹來，
終身漂泊無依，沉舟今又泛起，
何種疑難雜病，如此古怪離奇，
冷熱相間發作，送我魂歸故里。

＊：譯註請參照頁 P.346～P.407

# Sir Philip Sidney (1554-1586)

## WHEN NATURE MADE HER CHIEF WORK

When Nature made her chief work, Stella's eyes,

In colour black why wrapt she beams so bright?

Would she in beamy black, like painter wise,

Frame daintiest lustre, mixed of shades and light?

Or did she else that sober hue devise,                              *5*

In object best to knit and strength our sight;

Lest, if no veil these brave gleams did disguise,

They, sunlike, should more dazzle than delight?

Or would she her miraculous power show,

That, whereas black seems beauty's contrary,                        *10*

She even in black doth make all beauties flow?

Both so, and thus, — she, minding Love should be

Placed ever there, gave him this mourning weed

To honour all their deaths who for her bleed.

# 菲力普・錫德尼 (1554-1586)*
## 002. 當造化創造她的傑作❶

當造化創造她的傑作：史黛拉的雙眼，

為什麼用黑墨把眸子裹得如此鮮亮？

莫非她像丹青妙手那樣用璀璨的黛螺

以明暗對比給絕妙眼神加上畫框？

抑或她額外構想了適度的冷色，

不尚乖巧的編織，讓天姿經久耐看，

以免撩開黑紗時，那奪目的光彩

亮如不能直視的日照，叫人眼花繚亂？

莫非她要顯示非凡的功力：

儘管黑色似乎是醜的象徵，

她也能用黑色讓羣芳爭相模仿？

原來如此：她忘不了愛應當始終在場，

才送給他這雙著喪服的眼睛——❷

紀念一切為她癡迷氣絕的情郎。

# Edmund Spenser (1552-1599)

## OF THIS WORLDS THEATRE IN WHICH WE STAY

Of this worlds Theatre in which we stay,

My love lyke the Spectator ydly sits

Beholding me that all the pageants play,

Disguysing diversly my troubled wits.

Sometimes I joy when glad occasion fits,                              5

And mask in myrth lyke to a Comedy:

Soone after when my joy to sorrow flits,

I waile and make my woes a Tragedy.

Yet she beholding me with constant eye,

Delights not in my merth* nor rues my smart:                   *mirth* 10

But when I laugh she mocks, and when I cry

She laughes, and hardens evermore her hart.

What then can move her? if not merth nor mone,*          *moan*

She is no woman, but a sencelesse stone.

# 艾德蒙・斯賓塞 (1552 -1599)*

## oo3. 我們在世界大舞臺演戲❶

我們在世界大舞臺演戲，
臺下悠閒坐著我那情侶；
她像觀眾一般看我登臺，
設法為我掩飾紊亂思緒。
歡樂的場面我歡歌笑語，
仿佛戴著一張喜劇面具，
很快我的歡樂化為憂愁，
哭號著把煩惱變成悲劇。
可她以不變的眼光看戲：
我悲她不悲我喜她不喜，
我哭她就笑我笑她揶揄，
何以硬著心腸薄情如斯？
大悲大喜無法使她動情，
那就不是女人而是木石。

# William Shakespeare (1564-1616)

## ONE TOUCH OF NATURE MAKES THE WHOLE WORLD KIN

One touch of nature makes the whole world kin:

That all with one consent praise new-born gauds,

Though they are made and moulded of things past,

And give to dust that is a little gilt

More laud than gilt o'er-dusted.                                                5

The present eye praises the present object.

Then marvel not, thou great and complete man,

That all the Greeks begin to worship Ajax,

Since things in motion sooner catch the eye

Than what not stirs. The cry went once on thee,              10

And still it might, and yet it may again,

If thou wouldst not entomb thyself alive

And case thy reputation in thy tent,

Whose glorious deeds, but in these fields of late,

Made emulous missions 'mongst the gods themselves        15

And drave great Mars to faction.

# 威廉·莎士比亞 (1564-1616)*
## 004. 人性自然的一觸，世人都來套近乎❶

人性自然的一觸，世人都來套近乎：

大家一致贊美新生的小玩意兒，

儘管它們是打造翻新的古玩，

他們喜歡拂拭鍍金的把戲，

贊美有加，卻不理會蒙塵的真金。

現在的眼睛贊美眼下的事物。❷

因此你這偉大的完人不必詫異，

所有的希臘人都開始崇拜阿賈克斯了，❸

因為動態的事物比呆滯的東西，

能更快地鉤住人們的眼睛。

過去你是眾望所歸，現在將來仍可如此，

只要你不想活埋你自己，

不把你的威名封閉於帷幄。

別忘了，你曾威震一時，在疆場上

促使爭勝好強的天神重新選邊對壘，

把顯赫的戰神拉到你的陣營。❹

# Sonnet I

## From Fairest Creatures We Desire Increase

From fairest creatures we desire increase,

That thereby beauty's rose might never die,

But as the riper should by time decease,

His tender heir might bear his memory:

But thou, contracted to thine own bright eyes,     5

Feed'st thy light's flame with self-substantial fuel,

Making a famine where abundance lies,

Thyself thy foe, to thy sweet self too cruel.

Thou that art now the world's fresh ornament,

And only herald to the gaudy spring,     10

Within thine own bud buriest thy content,

And, tender churl, makest waste in niggarding:

  Pity the world, or else this glutton be,

  To eat the world's due, by the grave and thee.

# 十四行詩・一

## 005. 人類有良種，菁英求繁衍❶

人類有良種，菁英求繁衍，

以免芳美玫瑰，一朝枯萎不繼，

在他熟透之後，終將凋殘，

子孫稚嫩，卻能銘刻先賢印跡。❷

君卻獨戀自我，為自身明眸所役❸，

以身燭之蠟熬夜，讓烈焰燃燒不熄，❹

豐饒田園裏耕耘一片荒地，❺

與自我為敵，殘忍撻伐內美。

君乃裝點世界之新鮮花卉，

君乃嫩綠新春之珍稀使者，

何故於蓓蕾中埋葬自身精髓❻，

精明反作粗人，於吝嗇中揮霍？——❼

　　望君可憐人世，勿再饕餮人類後嗣，

　　晚輩葬身君腹內，君將葬身孤墳裏。❽

# Sonnet XVIII

## SHALL I COMPARE THEE TO A SUMMER'S DAY?

Shall I compare thee to a summer's day?

Thou art more lovely and more temperate:

Rough winds do shake the darling buds of May,

And summer's lease hath all too short a date:

Sometime too hot the eye of heaven shines,                    5

And often is his gold complexion dimmed,

And every fair from fair sometime declines,

By chance or nature's changing course untrimmed;

But thy eternal summer shall not fade

Nor lose possession of that fair thou owest,                  10

Nor shall Death brag thou wander'st in his shade,

When in eternal lines to time thou growest:

   So long as men can breathe or eyes can see,

   So long lives this and this gives life to thee.

# 十四行詩・十八

## oo6. 問君何所似，可否比春日？

問君何所似，可否比春日❶？

春輸一段柔情，君多三分麗質：

五月瘦蕾，難堪晚來風急，

春宵苦短，租賃只在片時；

日高起時懸巨眼，灼熱如火炙，

又常見金容蒙陰翳，愁雲密。

便縱有芳菲滿地香馥鬱，

怎奈萬物變易，美更容易遇劫❷。

唯君挽住春光夏時，

神采豐韻，永不凋敝。❸

任它死神陰雲匝地催命急，

自有名家詩行賦佳麗：❹

    只要人類繁衍好書有人讀，

    借我詩筆，賜君生命傳永世。

# Sonnet XX

## A Woman's Face with Nature's Own Hand Painted

A woman's face with Nature's own hand painted

Hast thou, the master-mistress of my passion;

A woman's gentle heart, but not acquainted

With shifting change, as is false women's fashion;

An eye more bright than theirs, less false in rolling,    5

Gilding the object whereupon it gazeth;

A man in hue, all 'hues' in his controlling,

Much steals men's eyes and women's souls amazeth.

And for a woman wert thou first created;

Till Nature, as she wrought thee, fell a-doting,    10

And by addition me of thee defeated,

By adding one thing to my purpose nothing.

    But since she pricked thee out for women's pleasure,

    Mine be thy love and thy love's use their treasure.

## 007. 造化大手筆，為君繪容顏

造化大手筆，為君繪容顏

我之情欲所在，君兼情婦情郎❶；

有芳菲柔嫩之心，無贗品塵垢之染，

更不像時髦女郎變幻異常；

明眸流轉不矯情，勝過彼等亮麗❷，

一旦蒙君顧盼，無不鍍上金黃；

君之男相❸，駕臨萬種雅態妍姿，

竊得男人回眸，令女人心神搖盪。

造化原本想塑造女相，

可她落筆時情迷意亂，

誤添一筆耍我的花樣──❹

那把戲使我無權把君獨佔。

　　可造化為君塑身想取悅於女郎，❺

　　君之情歸我，愛撫技巧由別人珍藏。

# Sonnet LXVI

## TIRED WITH ALL THESE, FOR RESTFUL DEATH I CRY

Tired with all these for restful death I cry,

As to behold Desert a beggar born,

And needy Nothing trimmed in jollity,

And purest Faith unhappily forsworn,

And guilded Honour shamefully misplaced,                    5

And maiden Virtue rudely strumpeted,

And right Perfection wrongfully disgraced,

And Strength by limping Sway disablèd,

And Art made tongue-tied by Authority,

And Folly, Doctor-like, controlling Skill,                  10

And simple Truth miscalled Simplicity,

And captive Good attending captain Ill:

  Tired with all these, from these would I be gone

  Save that, to die, I leave my love alone.

# 十四行詩・六十六

## oo8. 萬事令人煩惱，不如一死了之

萬事令人煩惱，不如一死了之，

眼看天才❶生來命苦去行乞，

穿金戴銀的❷，一肚子敗絮，

發過聖誓的，誓言早拋棄，

行善受懲罰，作惡有獎掖，

童真女子被迫做娼妓，❸

缺德衙門抓了義人亂定罪，

跛足權貴打斷平民英雄腿，

官媒成言霸，堵住書生嘴，

蠢才耍花招，江湖充良醫，❹

純真被人當作頭腦簡單好欺負，

邪惡橫行逼良為盜賊：

　　萬事令人絕望，只剩一條死路，

　　怕只怕，平生所愛❺怎一個獨字了得。

# Sonnet CXXVII

## IN THE OLD AGE BLACK WAS NOT COUNTED FAIR

In the old age black was not counted fair,
Or if it were, it bore not beauty's name;
But now is black beauty's successive heir,
And beauty slander'd with a bastard shame:
For since each hand hath put on nature's power,                5
Fairing the foul with art's false borrow'd face,
Sweet beauty hath no name, no holy bower,
But is profaned, if not lives in disgrace.
Therefore my mistress' brows are raven black,
Her eyes so suited, and they mourners seem                     10
At such who, not born fair, no beauty lack,
Slandering creation with a false esteem:
　　Yet so they mourn, becoming of their woe,
　　That every tongue says beauty should look so.

# 十四行詩 · 一二七

## 009. 往古之時黑色豈能作風流❶

往古之時黑色豈能作風流，

真有黑美，芳名亦難載春秋；

而今黑美成了嫡傳真美人，

白美反被目為庶出蒙其羞。

凡手竟想巧奪造化工，

濃施黛色遮其容貌醜。

真美無美名，何處覓閨秀，

美被逐出神廟甚而蒙污垢。

我那情人因此入時髦，眉宇鴉黑，

雙眼含愁，恰如服喪哀俗女❷：

雖無天姿，卻並不乏美質，

何苦扭曲造化故作假風流。

　　悲傷眼神倒有動人處，惹得世人

　　紛紛說，美中原本帶隱憂。

# John Donne (1572-1631)

## The Good-Morrow

I wonder, by my troth, what thou and I

Did, till we loved? Were we not weaned till then?

But sucked on country pleasures, childishly?

Or snorted we in the Seven Sleepers' den?

'Twas so; but this, all pleasures fancies be.     *5*

If ever any beauty I did see,

Which I desired, and got, 'twas but a dream of thee.


And now good-morrow to our waking souls,

Which watch not one another out of fear;

For love, all love of other sights controls,     *10*

And makes one little room an every where.

Let sea-discoverers to new worlds have gone,

Let maps to others, worlds on worlds have shown,

Let us possess one world, each hath one, and is one.


My face in thine eye, thine in mine appears,     *15*

# 鄧約翰 (1572-1631)*

## oio. 良晨 ❶

真叫人納悶，你我先前究竟做了什麼

才彼此相愛起來？那時尚未斷奶？

只是乳臭未乾便吸吮野趣❷？

或在七睡人山洞里，❸ 我們曾酣睡？

就算如此，可種種樂趣無非層層迷幻，

倘若說我見過任何美，

我所欲所得，不外乎夢見你。

此刻你我靈魂醒來，但願共享良晨，

靈魂對靈魂無須惶恐相覷，

因為情愛統帥聲色之愛，

弄個小洞房，遍布浩瀚廣宇。

讓他們出海發現新世界，

讓地圖❹ 給別人展示天外雲天，

讓你我各自擁有一個世界，再合為一。

我在你眼裏，你在我心裏，

And true plain hearts do in the faces rest;

Where can we find two better hemispheres,

Without sharp north, without declining west?

Whatever dies, was not mixed equally;

If our two loves be one, or, thou and I    20

Love so alike, that none do slacken, none can die.

兩心誠摯，臉上就會流露心跡，❺
兩個半球要想更好──既無北極寒，
又無西天傾，舍此何處尋覓？❻
染色之物必死，只緣和合不均；❼
假如兩心合一，我與你
同樣深愛，就不會洩氣無死期。❽

# THE FLEA

Mark but this flea, and mark in this,
How little that which thou deniest me is ;
It suck'd me first, and now sucks thee,
And in this flea our two bloods mingled be.
Thou know'st that this cannot be said                         5
A sin, or shame, or loss of maidenhead ;
   Yet this enjoys before it woo,
    And pamper'd swells with one blood made of two ;
    And this, alas ! is more than we would do.

Oh stay, three lives in one flea spare,                       10
Where we almost, yea, more than married are.
This flea is you and I, and this
Our marriage bed, and marriage temple is.
Though parents grudge, and you, we're met,
And cloister'd in these living walls of jet.                  15
   Though use make you apt to kill me,
    Let not to that self-murder added be,

## 011. 跳蚤

小小跳蚤，此處做個標記，
不起眼，你對我同樣睥睨；
跳蚤吸人血，先叮我後叮你，
你我血相融，融在跳蚤肚子裏。
懺悔時，這不能稱為罪孽，
亦非羞恥，或失了貞潔；
　　可它未求愛先享艷福，
肚子漲鼓鼓，陰陽血合二為一；
此等情事，啊呀呀！比我們更出格！

呀，且住，一隻跳蚤三條命，
命中勝卻你我連理枝上棲。
小小跳蚤容納你我，於中應有
鴛鴦床，陰陽和合大殿宇。
儘管父母憤懣你抱怨，我們還是邂逅，
幽居烏黑四牆裏，卻充滿生氣。
　　雖然舊俗使你起殺心，
　　可此刻正是修道時，他殺亦自殺，

And sacrilege, three sins in killing three.

Cruel and sudden, hast thou since

Purpled thy nail in blood of innocence?                    *20*

In what could this flea guilty be,

Except in that drop which it suck'd from thee?

Yet thou triumph'st, and say'st that thou

Find'st not thyself nor me the weaker now.

   'Tis true, then learn how false, fears be ;          *25*

   Just so much honour, when thou yield'st to me,

   Will waste, as this flea's death took life from thee.

加上瀆神就是三重罪。

殘忍事，突然來，你真的
染紅指甲把手伸進血泊裏？
請問，跳蚤何罪之有——
除了它從你身上吸了幾滴血？
你是贏家，並且揚言說，
尚未發現你我因失血而虛弱。
　　真如此，就得明白此乃一場虛驚；
　　當你來就我，宛如掐死跳蚤這件小事，
　　多多聲譽只會破費些許。

# Ben Jonson (1573-1637)

## Echo's Song

Slow, slow fresh fount, keep time with my salt tears;

Yet slower, yet; O faintly gentle springs:

List to the heavy part the music bears,

Woe weeps out her division, when she sings.                    5

    Droop herbs and flowers;

    Fall grief in showers;

    Our Beauties are not ours;

      O, I could still,

    Like melting snow upon some craggy hill,                    10

      Drop, drop, drop, drop,

Since nature's pride is, now, a wither'd daffodil.

# 本・瓊生 (1573-1637)*

## 012. 回聲之歌●

水悠悠，恨悠悠，一股清泉和淚流。

悠悠泉水慢些兒走，

樂音沉痛難忍受。

她聲聲唱出心頭怨，

花草落地，陣雨澆憂愁。

人之美，非私有。

唉，我癡情如舊，

恰似積雪消融在野山溝，

點點滴滴滴不盡，

只緣天性高傲化水仙，

此刻枯萎低垂著頭。

# The Noble Nature

It is not growing like a tree
In bulk, doth make man better be;
Or standing long an oak, three hundred year,
To fall a log at last, dry, bald, and sere:
A lily of a day                                                                5
Is fairer far in May,
Although it fall and die that night;
It was the plant and flower of light.
In small proportions we just beauties see;
And in short measures, life may perfect be.                   10

## 013. 高貴品格❶

人之向善趨美

不像樹幹挺立；

也不像橡樹苟延三百年，

一旦傾倒只剩朽木一堆。

百合純潔豔麗，

堪稱五月奇葩，

清晨吐蕊黃昏零落，

卻有一日燦爛光輝。

尺幅之內可見多彩之美；

短暫里程亦能臻於完美。

# Robert Herrick (1591-1674)

## To the Virgins, to Make Much of Time

Gather ye rosebuds while ye may,
Old Time is still a-flying:
And this same flower that smiles to-day
To-morrow will be dying.

The glorious lamp of heaven, the sun,　　　　　　　5
The higher he's a-getting,
The sooner will his race be run,
And nearer he's to setting.

That age is best which is the first,
When youth and blood are warmer,　　　　　　　10
But being spent, the worse, and worst
Times still succeed the former.

Then be not coy, but use your time,
And while ye may, go marry:
For having lost but once your prime,　　　　　　　15
You may for ever tarry.

# 羅伯特·赫里克 (1591-1674)*

## 014. 勸女及時采薔薇❶

勸女及時采薔薇，
韶光如過翼：
今朝微笑花一枝，
明日即枯淒。

朝暾燦爛點天燈，
高昇復高攀，
驕陽競走愈疾行，
愈怯近西殘。

最佳花期是初開，
熱流青春血，
一旦耗損漸衰敗，
移晷無停歇。

及時綻蕾莫羞澀，
于歸擇郎君：
良辰一過佳期失，
興許誤終生。

# Richard Lovelace (1618-1657)

## To Althea, from Prison

When Love with unconfinèd wings
  Hovers within my gates,
And my divine Althea brings
  To whisper at the grates;

When I lie tangled in her hair                   5
  And fetter'd to her eye,
The birds that wanton in the air
  Know no such liberty.

When flowing cups run swiftly round
  With no allaying Thames,               10
Our careless heads with roses bound,
  Our hearts with loyal flames;

When thirsty grief in wine we steep,
  When healths and draughts go free —

# 理查・拉夫羅斯 (1618-1657)*

## 015. 獄中致阿爾西亞❶

愛情鼓翼長空，
輕盈飛入牢囚，
阿爾西亞聖女來，
細語與我分憂。

當我斜倚秀髮，
鐐銬鎖住明眸，
空中飛鳥鬧紛紛，
不解此種自由。

流觴輕輕轉動，
權當澆愁清流❷，
你我頭繞赤薔薇，
情焰熾烈心頭。

兩情沉浸如酒，
對飲千盅解愁，

Fishes that tipple in the deep

Know no such liberty.


When, like committed linnets, I

With shriller throat shall sing

The sweetness, mercy, majesty,

And glories of my King;


When I shall voice aloud how good

He is, how great should be,

Enlargèd winds, that curl the flood,

Know no such liberty.


Stone walls do not a prison make,

Nor iron bars a cage;

Minds innocent and quiet take

That for an hermitage;


If I have freedom in my love

And in my soul am free,

Angels alone, that soar above,

Enjoy such liberty.

深水暢遊魚皆醉，
不知此種自由。

我心定如紅雀，
欲啟亮麗歌喉，
贊美陛下之榮光，
吾王仁慈寬厚。

當我高聲吟誦，
偉哉一代王侯，
大風起兮洪波湧，
不知此種自由。

石牆並非囹圄，
鐵窗不作籠囚，
心中泰然無罪愆，
隱居騷客風流。

愛中得此自由，
靈魂自在悠遊，
獨有天使翔廣宇，
享有此種自由。

# Abraham Cowley (1618-1667)

## SWALLOW

Foolish prater, what dost thou

So early at my window do?

Cruel bird, thou'st ta'en away

A dream out of my arms to-day;

A dream that ne'er must equall'd be                    5

By all that waking eyes may see.

Thou this damage to repair

Nothing half so sweet and fair,

Nothing half so good, canst bring,

Tho' men say thou bring'st the Spring.                 10

# 亞伯拉罕・考利 (1618-1667)*

## 016. 燕子 虞美人❶

逗情語燕飛來早，

當戶啼清曉。

忍心驚夢入懷中，

銜去如泥轉眼杳無蹤。


朦朧睡意今猶在，

只怕夢園改，

風流一失半難求，

枉自喚來春色賦閒愁。

# John Milton (1608-1674)

## ON HIS BLINDNESS

When I consider how my light is spent

  E're half my days, in this dark world and wide,

  And that one Talent which is death to hide,

  Lodg'd with me useless, though my Soul more bent

To serve therewith my Maker, and present           *5*

  My true account, lest he returning chide,

  'Doth God exact day-labour, light deny'd ?'

  I fondly ask; But Patience to prevent

That murmur, soon replies, 'God doth not need

  Either man's work or his own gifts, who best       *10*

  Bear his mild yoke, they serve him best, his State

Is Kingly — thousands at his bidding speed

  And post o're Land and Ocean without rest:

  They also serve who only stand and waite.'

# 約翰·密爾頓 (1608-1674)*

## 017. 光之殤❶

費思量，身處黑暗世界一片茫然，

　　年日不足一半❷，晴光空耗費，

　　一個特倫埋起來好比進了死人堆，

　　給我卻不用❸，可我心懷宏願，

渴望盡心為造物主服事，以便

　　跟他結算一筆實賬❹，將來好脫罪。

　　「上帝要人做日工❺，卻不賜我明慧？」

　　我癡情發問。「堅忍」❻在心間

迅速作答，叫我勿怨懟：上帝

　　無須人做日工，也無須回饋天賦：

　　誰套緊他那柔和之軛❼，即服事之義人。

神之王國遼闊——萬千天使遵命馳驅，

　　奔波於陸地海洋上，從不停步，

　　耐心等候站得穩，也是服事神。❽

# LYCIDAS

*In this Monody the author bewails a learned friend, unfortunately drowned*
*in his passage from Chester on the Irish Seas, 1637. And by occasion*
*foretells the ruin of our corrupted clergy, then in their height.*

Yet once more, O ye laurels, and once more,
Ye myrtles brown, with ivy never sere,
I come to pluck your berries harsh and crude,
And with forced fingers rude
Shatter your leaves before the mellowing year.                    5
Bitter constraint,and sad occasion dear,
Compels me to disturb your season due:
For Lycidas is dead, dead ere his prime,
Young Lycidas, and hath not left his peer.
Who would not sing for Lycidas? he knew                           10
Himself to sing, and build the lofty rhyme.
He must not float upon his watery bier
Unwept, and welter to the parching wind,
Without the meed of some melodious tear.

# 018. 利西達[1]

借此輓歌，作者哀悼一位博學詩友，他不幸於 1637 年沉溺於愛爾蘭海域從徹斯特啟程之水路。借此際遇，作者同時預言：當今腐敗教士必盛極而衰，淪為糞土。[2]

余哀悼而重來兮，見諸尊之次第，
月桂香而桃金娘黃兮，常春藤耐寒而不枯，[3]
既來之而依樹兮，余伸手而采擷，
罔顧生果之青澀兮，采采而捋之，
惜豐年之未臨兮，搖屢弱之嫩葉。
因辛酸之脅迫兮，失知音之傷楚，
余獨步而前來兮，擾汝輩之花季；
傷君子之謝世兮，謝於未盛開之際，
青春雖枯萎兮，未遠離其朋侶。
誰不為利西達而歌兮？死者亦有其靈知，
其生前之歌喉兮，奠定崇高之韻律。
其漂泊之孤魂兮，不見於澤國靈臺，[4]
無守靈之哀歌兮，海風起而枯澀，
無豐饒之回報兮，無彈落之詩淚。

Begin then, Sisters of the sacred well                    15

That from beneath the seat of Jove doth spring,

Begin, and somewhat loudly sweep the string.

Hence with denial vain,and coy excuse,

So may some gentle Muse

With lucky words favour my destined urn,                    20

And as he passes turn,

And bid fair peace be to my sable shroud.


For we were nursed upon the self-same hill,

Fed the same flock, by fountain, shade, and rill.

Together both, ere the high lawns appeared                    25

Under the opening eyelids of the morn,

We drove afield, and both together heard

What time the grey-fly winds her sultry horn,

Battening our flocks with the fresh dews of night,

Oft till the star that rose at evening bright                    30

Toward heaven's descent had sloped his westering wheel.

Meanwhile the rural ditties were not mute,

Temper'd to the oaten flute;

Rough Satyrs danced, and Fauns with cloven heel,

From the glad sound would not be absent long,                    35

請靈泉之姊妹兮，啟歌喉而淺唱，
汨汨之湧泉兮，源自王座之下方，❺
其初韻何低昂兮，繼以琴瑟之高亢。
知婉拒之無用兮，切勿作態而推諉，
其溫情之繆思兮，動靈感而啟冥想，
余命中之骨甕兮，亦好悼亡之吉言，❻
繼君子之謝世兮，輪迴而有常，
願黑貂之屍布兮，裹余安詳之死相。

因少年之你我兮，養育於同一山嶺，
於泉邊樹間之溪谷兮，放牧同一圈羊羣。
憶吾輩之共游兮，漫步於高地草坪，
見旭日之開眼兮，棲身於朝暉之下，
同驅步於牧場兮，聽天籟之音韻，
聞曷神之角笳兮，隨過翼而吹奏，
以清新之夜露兮，催肥吾輩之牲畜，
常早出而晚歸兮，望天際之金星，
向西天而沉落兮，映如燒之日輪。❼
聞鄉間之歌謠兮，此起而彼伏，
與潘神之牧笛❽兮，唱和而親昵，
鄙羊人之狂舞兮，林間精靈之跟進，❾
歡娛之歌聲兮，未曾久歇而不聞，

And old Damætas loved to hear our song.

But O the heavy change, now thou art gone,
Now thou art gone, and never must return!
Thee, Shepherd, thee the woods and desert caves,
With wild thyme and the gadding vine o'ergrown,                    40
And all their echoes mourn.
The willows and the hazel copses green
Shall now no more be seen
Fanning their joyous leaves to thy soft lays.
As killing as the canker to the rose,                             45
Or taint-worm to the weanling herds that graze,
Or frost to flowers that their gay wardrobe wear,
When first the white thorn blows:
Such, Lycidas, thy loss to shepherd's ear.

Where were ye, Nymphs, when the remorseless deep                  50
Closed o'er the head of your lov'd Lycidas?
For neither were ye playing on the steep
Where your old bards, the famous Druids, lie,
Nor on the shaggy top of Mona high,
Nor yet where Deva spreads her wizard stream.                     55
Ay me! I fondly dream,

有長者之光臨兮，聽吾輩之歌吟。❿

悲沉重之變故兮，君抽身而離去，
嗟步履之匆匆兮，一去而不回顧！
望牧人之森林兮，荒山之洞窟，
覆之以百里香兮，繞之以葡萄藤。
聽空谷之回聲兮，皆哀泣而不已。
依依之楊柳兮，青青之榛樹，
枝搖搖而尋歡兮，不見君之蹤影，
葉沙沙而欲語兮，不聞君之歌吟。
如尺蠖之啃噬兮，置玫瑰於死地，
如蠕蟲之羣起兮，犯吃草之羊羣，
如寒霜之逼視兮，侵盛裝之花神，
此夕何夕兮，恰逢山楂初紅之時：
利西達之靈歌兮，舍牧人而誰聽？

悲深水之無情兮，陷友人於滅頂，
愛才之水澤仙姝兮，可曾戲水於海濱？
不見於詩人之高崗兮，不聞汝等嬉鬧之語，
不見於高僧之故園兮，不聞汝等酣睡之聲，
莫奈之高聳兮，唯山峰挺而壁立，⓫
狄河之激流兮，唯神女噴其巫水。⓬
嗚呼！依余夢中之幻見兮，汝等現身於現場。

Had ye been there!--for what could that have done?

What could the Muse herself that Orpheus bore,

The Muse herself, for her enchanting son,

Whom universal nature did lament,                    60

When by the rout that made the hideous roar

His gory visage down the stream was sent,

Down the swift Hebrus to the Lesbian shore?


Alas! what boots it with uncessant care

To tend the homely, slighted shepherd's trade,        65

And strictly meditate the thankless Muse?

Were it not better done, as others use,

To sport with Amaryllis in the shade,

Or with the tangles of Neaera's hair?

Fame is the spur that the clear spirit doth raise      70

(That last infirmity of noble mind)

To scorn delights and live laborious days;

But the fair guerdon when we hope to find,

And think to burst out into sudden blaze,

Comes the blind Fury with the abhorrèd shears,         75

And slits the thin-spun life. "But not the praise,"

Phoebus replied, and touch'd my trembling ears:

'Fame is no plant that grows on mortal soil,

可曾盡救援之力兮，免君子於滅頂？
念奧菲斯之生母兮，豈不枉為詩神？
目睹親子之劫難兮，束手而無能？
憶山川之多情兮，無不致哀而傷心，
歌手之慘痛兮，身首裂而異處，
當年之血汙兮，至今而不忘，
托頭顱之激流兮，送歌喉至海濱。❸

以終日之勞頓兮，經營家常之牧業，
嘔心而瀝血兮，奉不知回報之繆思，
其盈利何菲薄兮，豈能比之於別業？
卻自得其樂兮，與彼岸花❹嬉戲於樹蔭，
見交際花之鬈髮兮，興起而撫弄。❺
問榮名何所似兮，如提昇精神之鞭策，
初而令人亢奮兮，繼而墮高尚之心性，

小覷日常之樂兮，每日操勞而不已；
吾輩之所尋覓兮，乃求美之所應得，
或作非非之想兮，盼驀然怒放於廣庭，
厭狂女之瞎來兮，揮剪刀而逼近，
斷其脆弱之生命兮，不置片言以贊美，❻
聽佛布斯❼之解惑兮，其箴言發聾而振瞶：
凡俗之薄田兮，非榮名之沃土，

Nor in the glistering foil

Set off to the world, nor in broad rumour lies,                80

But lives and spreads aloft by those pure eyes

And perfect witness of all-judging Jove:

As he pronounces lastly on each deed,

Of so much fame in Heaven expect thy meed.'


O fountain Arethuse, and thou honoured flood,                85

Smooth-sliding Mincius, crowned with vocal reeds,

That strain I heard was of a higher mood.

But now my oat proceeds,

And listens to the Herald of the Sea,

That came in Neptune's plea.                                           90

He asked the waves, and asked the felon winds,

'What hard mishap hath doom'd this gentle swain?'

And questioned every gust of rugged wings

That blows from off each beaked promontory —

They knew not of his story,                                             95

And sage Hippotades their answer brings,

That not a blast was from his dungeon strayed;

The air was calm, and on the level brine

Sleek Panope with all her sisters played.

It was that fatal and perfidious bark,                              100

榮名之為用兮，不作寶石之扶葉，❶

遠離於塵世兮，不棲於謠諑之地，

以德行而處世兮，蒙天眼之眷顧，

作完美之見證兮，聽主神❶而定是非：

無善行或劣跡兮，能免於最後裁決，

君所期之榮名兮，天國之獎掖有期。


西西里之古泉兮，水洪亮而噴射，

明秀河之清流兮，冠以沙沙蘆葦，

余聞其旋律兮，其詩情高下有別：❷

可此刻所吟詠兮，乃余販運燕麥之所得，

見大海之使者兮，聞螺號之清脆，

其傳號之見證兮，免海王之權責。❷

借彼之喉舌兮，余質問風波之詭譎，

此事故何艱澀兮，何陷君子於劫數？

又問矯健之羽翼兮，何以煽風而生事，

風起於海角之尖兮，其尖峭銜鳥喙之毒？

怪萬籟皆無聲兮，無一知其故事，

唯明智之風神❷兮，吹來八方之回復，

曰風窩之地牢兮，無賊風開溜而肇事，

風閑定而不動兮，波平和而不起，

好靜之水仙❷兮，邀姊妹而戲水。

此乃命運之乖張兮，罪在失信之舟楫，

Built in the eclipse, and rigged with curses dark,
That sunk so low that sacred head of thine.

Next Camus, reverend sire, went footing slow,
His mantle hairy, and his bonnet sedge,
Inwrought with figures dim, and on the edge                          *105*
Like to that sanguine flower inscribed with woe.
'Ah! who hath reft,' quoth he, 'my dearest pledge?'
Last came, and last did go,
The Pilot of the Galilean lake;
Two massy keys he bore of metals twain                               *110*
(The golden opes, the iron shuts amain).
He shook his mitred locks, and stern bespake:
'How well could I have spared for thee, young swain,
Enow of such as for their bellies' sake
Creep and intrude, and climb into the fold?                          *115*
Of other care they little reckoning make
Than how to scramble at the shearers' feast
And shove away the worthy bidden guest.
Blind mouths! that scarce themselves know how to hold
A sheep-hook, or have learn'd aught else the least                   *120*
That to the faithful herdman's art belongs!
What recks it them? What need they? They are sped;

造船於月食之日兮，載黑暗之咒語，
哀沉舟於深水兮，淹聖潔之貴體。


劍河㉔之新秀兮，步履穩重而緩慢，
水波何幽深兮，河岸之莎草迷離，
其邊緣之刺繡兮，圖像昏昏而不彰，
風信子之喪服兮，鐫刻以哀辭。㉕
嗚呼！問誰人為劫賊兮，劫人生之信賴？
其最後之來人兮，亦最後而離去，
加利利湖水清兮，舟搖搖而漁父出，
其攜帶之鑰匙兮，光閃閃而顯眼，
以金鑰匙開啟兮，以鐵鑰匙關閉，㉖
搖大主教之門鎖兮，出嚴詞以苛責，
君何幸之有兮，屬免責之青年，
余皆為饕餮之徒兮，刮民脂而自肥，
趁羊圈之虛兮，或匍匐或強闖以入，㉗
懷貪欲之鬼胎兮，無他事令其眷顧，
唯垂涎羊毛之盛宴兮，伸黑手而劫掠，
屑小而爭上座兮，擠貴賓於一隅。
其瞎吞之盆口兮，懵然而不自知，
既不知持羊杖兮，又無起碼之通識，
更無誠摯之心兮，焉能嫻熟牧人之長技！
問其心何所思兮？問其人何所需？

And when they list their lean and flashy songs
Grate on their scrannel pipes of wretched straw,
The hungry sheep look up, and are not fed,                    *125*
But swoln with wind and the rank mist they draw,
Rot inwardly, and foul contagion spread;
Besides what the grim wolf with privy paw
Daily devours apace, and nothing said,
But that two-handed engine at the door                        *130*
Stands ready to smite once, and smite no more.'

Return, Alpheus,the dread voice is past
That shrunk thy streams; return, Sicilian Muse,
And call the vales and bid them hither cast
Their bells and flowerets of a thousand hues.                 *135*
Ye valleys low, where the mild whispers use
Of shades and wanton winds, and gushing brooks,
On whose fresh lap the swart star sparely looks,
Throw hither all your quaint enamelled eyes,
That on the green turf suck the honied showers                *140*
And purple all the ground with vernal flowers.
Bring the rathe primrose that forsaken dies,
The tufted crow-toe, and pale jessamine,
The white pink, and the pansy freaked with jet,

其屈指而細數兮，皆鄙俗之歌謠，
其嘔啞嘈雜之聲兮，出自蕪雜之麥管。
望賑災之餓羊兮，乏喂養之人，
餐冷風而吞毒霧兮，病鼓脹而可憐，
其內臟之腐爛兮，噴臭氣而傳染。
可憎之野狼兮，舞黑爪而呲踞牙，
日啖羊羔而不厭兮，夜吐不出人言，
觀門庭之所懸兮，雙刃劍㉘何其鋒利，
待時機而重擊兮，從此入鞘而收斂。


清泉勿再鄒面兮，白水追獵之聲已逝，㉙
魂兮歸來兮，西西里之詩神，
喚海島之溪谷兮，請山澗之精靈，
拋咩咩之羊鈴兮，鋪菲菲之花卉。
多情之耳語兮，常聒噪於谷地，
風習習而散漫兮，水澹澹而入夜，
下有新鮮之地裙兜兮，上有璀璨之天狼星，
其古雅之明眸兮，閑拋於山頭水濱，
親茵茵之草地兮，飲涓涓之蜜露，
聞羣芳之馨香兮，戀花仙之春意。
早熟之鮮果兮，遭遺棄而褪色。
風信子之簇簇兮，茉莉花之淡淡，
粉紅而透白兮，三色堇多美人斑㉚。

The glowing violet, 145

The musk-rose, and the well attired woodbine,

With cowslips wan that hang the pensive head,

And every flower that sad embroidery wears.

Bid amaranthus all his beauty shed,

And daffadillies fill their cups with tears, 150

To strew the laureate hearse where Lycid lies.

For so to interpose a little ease,

Let our frail thoughts dally with false surmise.

Ay me! Whilst thee the shores and sounding seas

Wash far away, where'er thy bones are hurled, 155

Whether beyond the stormy Hebrides,

Where thou perhaps under the whelming tide

Visit'st the bottom of the monstrous world,

Or whether thou, to our moist vows denied,

Sleep'st by the fable of Bellerus old, 160

Where the great Vision of the guarded mount

Looks toward Namancos and Bayona's hold:

Look homeward Angel, now, and melt with ruth;

And, O ye dolphins, waft the hapless youth.


Weep no more, woeful shepherds, weep no more, 165

For Lycidas, your sorrow, is not dead,

紫羅蘭之灼熱兮，赤炎炎而欲燃，

麝香薔薇之芬芳兮，金銀花之盛裝，

淡雅之櫻草兮，佩戴於沉思之首領[31]，

願普天之花卉兮，繡哀婉之辭章：

請不謝之仙葩[32]兮，綻多彩之美艷，

多情之水仙兮，淚盈盈而滿杯盞。

為利西達之靈柩兮，撒束束之月桂。

亡靈之安息兮，乃生者之所祈願，

嘆神思何貧乏兮，難臆測君之所適。

悲乎! 海浪何洶湧兮，卷貴體而遠去，

望煙波之浩渺兮，問遺骨落於何處，

或隨波而上下兮，越風雨羣島[33]之彼岸。

念君身之所棲兮，或溺於波濤而不死，

正出訪於澤國兮，見海底之奇觀；

憶淚染之盟誓兮，而今君已忘卻？

夢中君所聽聞兮，皆地角[34]之寓言，

彼處之勝景兮，在警戒之山巒，

天使之登高兮，常遠眺西班牙之城垣，

可此刻之望眼兮，見鄉關而節哀。[35]

願吉祥之海豚兮，[36]護送不幸之青年。


勸哀傷之牧人兮，請從此而節哀，

君所悲之故人兮，乃不死之精靈，

Sunk though he be beneath the watery floor;

So sinks the day-star in the ocean bed,

And yet anon repairs his drooping head,

And tricks his beams, and with new spangled ore          170

Flames in the forehead of the morning sky:

So Lycidas sunk low, but mounted high,

Through the dear might of him that walked the waves,

Where, other groves and other streams along,

With nectar pure his oozy locks he laves,          175

And hears the unexpressive nuptial song,

In the blest kingdoms meek of joy and love.

There entertain him all the Saints above,

In solemn troops, and sweet societies,

That sing, and singing in their glory move,          180

And wipe the tears for ever from his eyes.

Now, Lycidas, the shepherds weep no more:

Henceforth thou art the Genius of the Shore,

In thy large recompense, and shalt be good

To all that wander in that perilous flood.          185


Thus sang the uncouth swain to the oaks and rills,

雖沉溺於河床兮，臥澤國而不醒，

如西沉之落日兮，以海底為枕席，

待明朝之破曉兮，復抬頭而昇起，

刷新其光束兮，亮新敷之金珀，

光燁燁而燦爛兮，照曉天之眉宇：

利西達之低沉兮，欲攀高而退卻，

借行於波濤之人兮，效祂之神跡；❸❼

彼處別有洞天兮，林茂而水清，

有神露之甘醇兮，可潔身而濯纓，

其戀歌之悅耳兮，有難說之情韻，

居福樂之王國兮，溫柔眷戀之故里。

有聖人居其上兮，賜君心以歡欣，

有莊嚴之天兵兮，有和睦之社羣，

步履何壯觀兮，歌聲此起而彼伏，

滿面之淚痕兮，請擦乾而收淚。❸❽

為利西達之死兮，牧人勿再傷悲不已；

從此以降兮，君即海濱之精靈❸❾，

君之厚德兮，獲大獎之報償，

凡洪災之迷津兮，有救度之指引。


亂曰


對橡樹與清溪兮，歌無名之青年，

While the still morn went out with sandals grey;

He touched the tender stops of various quills,

With eager thought warbling his Doric lay.

And now the sun had stretched out all the hills,    *190*

And now was dropped into the western bay;

At last he rose, and twitch'd his mantle blue:

To-morrow to fresh woods, and pastures new.

見黎明之神兮，著灰涼鞋而復出，

見葦管之吹口兮，❹伸聖手而撫弄，

以奔放之神思兮，哼鄉間之小曲。❹

見旭日之東昇兮，臨羣山而鍍金，

朝霞之點滴兮，滲入西海之灣。

沉睡而復起之人兮，抖一抖湛藍之披風，

邁向新生之山林兮，步入新生之牧場。

# Alexander Pope (1688-1744)

## NOT WITH MORE GLORIES, IN TH' ETHEREAL PLAIN

Not with more glories, in the ethereal plain,

The sun first rises o'er the purpled main,

Than, issuing forth, the rival of his beams

Launch'd on the bosom of the silver Thames.

Fair nymphs, and well-dress'd youths around her shone,     *5*

But every eye was fix'd on her alone.

On her white breast a sparkling cross she wore,

Which Jews might kiss, and infidels adore.

Her lively looks a sprightly mind disclose,

Quick as her eyes, and unfix'd as those:     *10*

Favours to none, to all she smiles extends;

Oft she rejects, but never once offends.

Bright as the sun, her eyes the gazers strike,

And, like the sun, they shine on all alike.

Yet graceful ease, and sweetness void of pride,     *15*

Might hide her faults, if belles had faults to hide;

If to her share some female errors fall,

Look on her face, and you'll forget them all.

# 亞歷山大‧蒲伯 (1688-1744)*

## 019. 太空何靈異，難攀此華榮❶

太空❷何靈異，難攀此華榮，
苒苒朝暾昇，臨水照紫紅，❸
金光燁煜時，兩美攀比中，
朗照泰晤士，銀波蕩酥胸。❹
嫣嫣眾仙姝，少年繞裙風，
遊目不轉移，膠著在花容。
貼胸十字架，璀璨亂人心，
猶太人想吻，異教徒想親。❺
花瓣初綻時，才情露芳容，
明眸顧盼時，輕捷若流鶯：
逢人百媚笑，不拋一縷情。
屢拒君之意，不侮君之心。
灼熱如驕陽，逼退不轉睛，
溫和亦如日，同仁無偏心。
天香解人意，妍態不驕嗔，
美人有微瑕，巧掩不露真。
即便缺婦德，即便乏女功，
但看芳容笑，百愁可銷融。

# Thomas Gray ( 1716-1771)

## Elegy Written in a Country Churchard

The curfew tolls the knell of parting day,

The lowing herd winds slowly o'er the lea,

The ploughman homeward plods his weary way,

And leaves the world to darkness and to me.


Now fades the glimmering landscape on the sight,            5

And all the air a solemn stillness holds,

Save where the beetle wheels his droning flight,

And drowsy tinklings lull the distant folds:


Save that from yonder ivy-mantled tower

The moping owl does to the moon complain            10

Of such as, wandering near her secret bower,

Molest her ancient solitary reign.


Beneath those rugged elms, that yew-tree's shade,

Where heaves the turf in many a mouldering heap,

# 托瑪斯·格雷 (1716-1771)*

## 020. 鄉村墓園哀歌❶

敲晚鐘而報喪兮，白日入夜而為安，

聽牛羣之低哞兮，蜿蜒於草場之上，

望耕夫之倦歸兮，荷鋤犁而步緩緩，

棄四野於夜幕兮，唯我獨對幽惶。


暮色之沉沉兮，晚景入眼而朦朧，

萬籟皆肅穆兮，念天地之蒼茫。

唯火蟲之螢光兮，旋飛而語嗡嗡，❷

引歸欄之遠路兮，頭羊之鈴聲叮噹。❸


望離離之藤蔓兮，遮遠處之高塔臺樹，

聽鴞鳥之嘔啞兮，鬱鬱然怨懟皓月，

問浪步之流光兮，何故窺女皇私舍，

其君臨之悠久兮，豈容蟾兔凌越？❹


見粗礪之榆樹兮，下有濃蔭之紫杉，

蒿草之蓬蓬兮，搖曳於腐土堆上。

Each in his narrow cell for ever laid, 15

The rude Forefathers of the hamlet sleep.

The breezy call of incense-breathing morn,

The swallow twittering from the straw-built shed,

The cock's shrill clarion, or the echoing horn,

No more shall rouse them from their lowly bed. 20

For them no more the blazing hearth shall burn,

Or busy housewife ply her evening care:

No children run to lisp their sire's return,

Or climb his knees the envied kiss to share,

Oft did the harvest to their sickle yield, 25

Their furrow oft the stubborn glebe has broke;

How jocund did they drive their team afield!

How bowed the woods beneath their sturdy stroke!

Let not Ambition mock their useful toil,

Their homely joys, and destiny obscure; 30

Nor Grandeur hear with a disdainful smile

The short and simple annals of the Poor.

想陋室之侷促兮，逝者羈身其間，❺
哀永夜之漫漫兮，棲祖先之原鄉。

微風之細細兮，攜花香而拂晨露，
燕語之呢喃兮，出草棚而飛翔，
雞鳴之咯咯兮，如獵號之催促，
喚不醒之亡靈兮，黯然仰臥於冥床。

念身後之淒景兮，無壁爐之溫馨，
日無家務之煩兮，夜無妻室之怨，
盼父歸之幼兒兮，語牙牙而誰聽：
無繞膝之親吻兮，無他人之妒羨。

憶豐年之鐮刀兮，常上下而揮舞，
犁鑵之深耕兮，開旱田而破硬土；
其樂之融融兮，驅牛羊於原野！
樹紛紛而折腰兮，服膺其開山利斧！

笑「野心」❻之淺薄兮，何不屑有益之苦工，
農家自有其樂兮，縱然命乖而運舛；
看「富麗」之奢侈兮，露其輕蔑之笑容，
何孤陋而寡聞兮，不知凡夫之窮年。

The boast of heraldry, the pomp of power,
And all that beauty, all that wealth e'er gave,
Awaits alike the inevitable hour: —                    35
The paths of glory lead but to the grave.

Nor you, ye Proud, impute to these the fault
If Memory o'er their tomb no trophies raise,
Where through the long-drawn aisle and fretted vault
The pealing anthem swells the note of praise.          40

Can storied urn or animated bust
Back to its mansion call the fleeting breath?
Can Honour's voice provoke the silent dust,
Or Flattery soothe the dull cold ear of Death?

Perhaps in this neglected spot is laid                  45
Some heart once pregnant with celestial fire;
Hands, that the rod of empire might have swayed,
Or waked to ecstasy the living lyre:

But Knowledge to their eyes her ample page,
Rich with the spoils of time, did ne'er unroll;        50
Chill Penury repressed their noble rage,

笑紋章❼之虛飾兮，縟禮何足以渲染，
不自知其歸宿兮，眾美與財富同塚，
有天眼之同仁兮，時來而不可逆轉：❽
獵名之山道兮，榮耀登極即墳塋。

勸盲目之「傲慢」兮，莫以儉樸為謬錯，
莫笑其墓室之上兮，無「紀念」之光顧，
薄鄉村而厚教堂兮，乃向來之偏頗，
雕長廊而繪拱頂兮，奏贊歌而獻詩賦。

觀史筆之古甕兮，畫像栩栩如生，❾
其徒勞之造作兮，能喚回流年死鬼？
「榮譽」之聲張兮，能激起死寂凝塵？
「阿諛」之浮華兮，能撫慰死者冷灰？

哀無名之薄地兮，英名埋沒而不揚，
其心本燦爛兮，亦可竊天國之火星，
其性本善良兮，亦可持帝國之權杖，
其才本潛在兮，亦可操狂喜之詩琴。

「知識」何吝嗇兮，不在眾人眼前開卷，
一頁復一頁兮，任時間損耗不休。
恨「赤貧」之猖獗兮，辱高貴之青年，

And froze the genial current of the soul.


Full many a gem of purest ray serene
The dark unfathomed caves of ocean bear:
Full many a flower is born to blush unseen,                55
And waste its sweetness on the desert air.


Some village-Hampden, that with dauntless breast
The little tyrant of his fields withstood,
Some mute inglorious Milton here may rest,
Some Cromwell, guiltless of his country's blood.          60


The applause of listening senates to command,
The threats of pain and ruin to despise,
To scatter plenty o'er a smiling land,
And read their history in a nation's eyes,


Their lot forbad: nor circumscribed alone                65
Their growing virtues, but their crimes confined;
Forbad to wade through slaughter to a throne,
And shut the gates of mercy on mankind,


The struggling pangs of conscious truth to hide,

壓抑其熱望兮，凍結其靈府暖流。

念彼村夫兮，有赤純之珍寶閃爍，
藏海底之洞穴兮，戲水者渾然不知。
聞幽谷有蘭草兮，無心於花開花落，
如荒野之殊香兮，虛擲而無人賞識。

憶鄉野之匹夫兮，漢普頓英勇而無懼，
巍然獨立於曠野兮，敢與暴君抗衡，
或長眠於此兮，如密爾頓之無語；
或無疚於戰亂兮，如克倫威爾之英魂。❿

無戀於掌聲兮，不慕元老之權位，
雖救厄於一時兮，撒甘霖於旱地，
雖留名於青史兮，儼然如眾望之所歸，
王道之輝煌兮，異於蓬蓽之野趣。⓫

既遠離於大善兮，亦不妄為小惡，
有德行之滋長兮，大罪不臨庶人，
以民為魚肉兮，霸道萬萬不可，
借殺戮而登基兮，將革出仁愛之教門。

愛真理之清明兮，忌真實之隱瞞，

To quench the blushes of ingenuous shame,                              70

Or heap the shrine of Luxury and Pride

With incense kindled at the Muse's flame.


Far from the madding crowd's ignoble strife,

Their sober wishes never learned to stray;

Along the cool sequestered vale of life                                75

They kept the noiseless tenour of their way.


Yet even these bones from insult to protect

Some frail memorial still erected nigh,

With uncouth rhymes and shapeless sculpture decked,

Implores the passing tribute of a sigh.                                80


Their name, their years, spelt by the unlettered Muse,

The place of fame and elegy supply:

And many a holy text around she strews,

That teach the rustic moralist to die.


For who, to dumb Forgetfulness a prey,                                 85

This pleasing anxious being e'er resigned,

Left the warm precincts of the cheerful day,

Nor cast one longing lingering look behind?

因過失而蒙羞兮，則供認而不諱，
慕繆思之火花兮，鄙「奢華」與「傲慢」，
焚詩壇之清香兮，豈供兩霸之神壇？！

見爭鬥而遠避兮，惡狂徒之頑愚，
持中庸之尺度兮，不偏離於正道；
親溪穀之小徑兮，遠塵囂之通衢，
寄真情於山水兮，守貧賤之清高。

立碑銘以紀念兮，以免遺骨遭褻瀆，
其墓園之寒磣兮，難追殿堂之豐碑，
其錯訛之韻律兮，雜以粗糙之雕刻，
路人見而興歎兮，令人撫今而追昔。

念鄉野之偏遠兮，亦有初通文墨之人，
得繆思❶❷之濡染兮，記死者之名字，
錄年事與籍貫兮，賦挽歌而哀吟，
託聖言❶❸以教化兮，頌德譽之直死。

「遺忘」雖喑啞兮，猛如獵人之出擊，
誰願被其追捕兮，作無名之獵物？
人生之悲歡兮，屢屢交織而來，
拋卻生前之樂景兮，誰不回首當初？

On some fond breast the parting soul relies,

Some pious drops the closing eye requires; 90

Even from the tomb the voice of Nature cries,

Even in our ashes live their wonted fires.


For thee, who, mindful of the unhonoured dead,

Dost in these lines their artless tale relate;

If chance, by lonely contemplation led, 95

Some kindred spirit shall inquire thy fate, —


Haply some hoary-headed swain may say,

Oft have we seen him at the peep of dawn

Brushing with hasty steps the dews away,

To meet the sun upon the upland lawn; 100


'There at the foot of yonder nodding beech

That wreathes its old fantastic roots so high.

His listless length at noontide would he stretch,

And pore upon the brook that babbles by.


'Hard by yon wood, now smiling as in scorn, 105

Muttering his wayward fancies he would rove;

念斷魂之無儔兮，思親情之溫馨，
雖善終而瞑目兮，盼友人之淚落；
雖久眠於墓室兮，大自然悲聲可聞，
雖骨灰已寒徹兮，盼陽世之紅火。

君❶殫思而極慮兮，哀村夫死無榮名，
以素樸之詩章兮，鋪陳其本真故事，
若天假以良機兮，以幽思為牽引，
後世之同仁兮，將追尋君之足跡。

待來年之機緣兮，野翁將話說當初：
「經年而累月兮，見他於熹微晨光，
步匆匆而前行兮，晨露紛紛而讓路，
情切切而上山兮，席草地而迎太陽。

「山毛櫸之高枝兮，垂濃蔭而下顧，
見其蒼老之深根兮，見獨倚樹幹之人，
人疲憊而稍息兮，逢正午而舒四肢，
望清清之溪流兮，聽潺潺之水聲。

「樹木然見其人兮，或會心而訕笑，❶
乘幻想而馳騁兮，徘徊於烏有之鄉，

Now drooping, woeful wan, like one forlorn,
Or crazed with care, or crossed in hopeless love.

'One morn I missed him on the customed hill,
Along the heath, and near his favourite tree;                    110
Another came; nor yet beside the rill,
Nor up the lawn, nor at the wood was he;

'The next with dirges due in sad array
Slow through the church — way path we saw him borne, —
Approach and read (for thou canst read) the lay                  115
Graved on the stone beneath yon aged thorn.'

## THE EPITAPH

Here rests his head upon the lap of Earth
A youth to Fortune and to Fame unknown.
Fair Science frowned not on his humble birth,
And Melacholy marked him for her own.

Large was his bounty, and his soul sincere,                      5
Heaven did a recompense as largely send:
He gave to Misery all he had, a tear,

或戚戚而垂首兮，影煢煢而孑立，
或恍惚而迷茫兮，或失戀而憂傷。

「一日晨起而上山兮，余不見其身影，
游目於四野兮，觀其獨好之佳樹，
樹空等其倚靠兮，水空等其濯纓，
草地不聞其足音兮，森林痛失其朋侶。

「明日復明日兮，眾人早起而列隊，
經教堂之小徑兮，步緩緩而送遺骨，
無不著喪服兮，無不哀歌而噓唏，
其碑銘之依稀兮，撥開野荊即可辨讀。」

## 碑銘

地母有情，以膝鋪枕，
青年寡欲，無權無名。
出生寒門，「科學」尊重，
「憂鬱」同情，引為知心。

一生慷慨，靈魂至誠，
上蒼獎拔，同樣豐盛：
傾囊扶困，揾淚憫農，

He gained from Heaven ('twas all he wished) a friend.

No farther seek his merits to disclose,
Or draw his frailties from their dread abode           10
(There they alike in trembling hope repose),
The bosom of his Father and his God.

天國如願，得一友人。

德行自彰，無須溢美，
微瑕難免，詆訶審慎，
安息之望，人所共有，
天父懷中，寄託清魂。

# William Black ( 1757-1827)

## THE LAMB

Little Lamb, who made thee
Does thou know who made thee
Gave thee life & bid thee feed.
By the stream & o'er the mead;
Gave thee clothing of delight,                                  5
Softest clothing woolly bright;
Gave thee such a tender voice.
Making all the vales rejoice!
Little Lamb who made thee
Does thou know who made thee                                    10

Little Lamb I'll tell thee,
Little Lamb I'll tell thee!
He is called by thy name,
For he calls himself a Lamb:
He is meek & he is mild,                                        15
He became a little child:

# 威廉・布萊克 (1757-1827)*

## 021. 羊羔❶




小小羊羔，是誰創造？

你可知道，是誰創造？

給你生命，餵你食糧，

清溪岸邊，芳草地上，

為你高興，給你衣裳，

衣裳柔和，絨絨明亮;

給你聲音，溫柔親昵，

羣山溪谷，草木欣喜。

小小羊羔，是誰創造？

你可知道，是誰創造？


小小羊羔，聽我絮語，

小小羊羔，聽我絮語！

你的名字，與他一致，❷

他以羊羔，自稱自詡：

他真溫順，他真和煦，

道成肉身，化為童子：

I a child & thou a lamb,

We are called by His name,

    Little Lamb God bless thee,

    Little Lamb God bless thee.          20

你是小羊，我亦童子，
你我共享，他的名字。
小小羊羔，上帝佑你。
小小羊羔，上帝佑你。

# THE TIGER

Tiger, tiger, burning bright
In the forest of the night,
What immortal hand or eye
Could Frame thy fearful symmetry?

In what distant deeps or skies          5
Burnt the fire of thine eyes?
On what wings dare he aspire?
What the hand dare seize the fire?

And what shoulder and what art
Could twist the sinews of thy heart?          10
And, when thy heart began to beat,
What dread hand and what dread feet?

What the hammer? what the chain?
In what furnace was thy brain?
What the anvil? what dread grasp          15

## 022. 老虎[1]

老虎老虎！燦爛燃燒，
黑夜林莽，虎視朗照，
駭人勻稱，誰之聖手，
永恆天眼，為爾鍛造？

爾之雙眼，熊熊火炬，
深淵昊天，何處燒製？
何種羽翼，助他高舉？
何種手掌，攫火無炙？

何種膂力，何種絕技，
為爾搓捏，心臟肌肉？
爾之心跳，協以音律，
恐懼之美，何種舞步？

虎頭虎腦，熔爐鍛製？
鐵砧之上，錘擊鏈繫，
其形若何？想其怪異，

Dare its deadly terrors clasp?

When the stars threw down their spears,
And watered heaven with their tears,
Did he smile his work to see?
Did he who made the lamb make thee? 20

Tiger, tiger, burning bright
In the forests of the night,
What immortal hand or eye
Dare frame thy fearful symmetry?

何種手掌，敢於擺布？

星辰敗北，擲其長矛，❷
以其淚珠，澆灌天照，
主神見爾，可曾微笑？
造爾之前，先造羊羔？

老虎老虎！燦爛燃燒，
黑夜林莽，虎視朗照，
駭人勻稱，誰之聖手，
永恆天眼，為爾鍛造？

# A POISON TREE

I was angry with my friend:
I told my wrath, my wrath did end.
I was angry with my foe:
I told it not, my wrath did grow.

And I watered it in fears                          5
Night and morning with my tears;
And I sunned it with smiles,
And with soft deceitful wiles.

And it grew both day and night,
Till it bore an apple bright.                       10
And my foe beheld it shine,
And he knew that it was mine,

And into my garden stole,
When the night had veiled the pole;
In the morning glad I see                           15
My foe outstretched beneath the tree.

# 023. 一株毒樹 ❶

我對朋友生氣，
一把明火，燒了就熄滅。
我對敵人生氣，
一團暗火，越悶越熾烈。

心懷驚懼播種，
日夜淚水澆樹苗；
綻開笑容作日照，
溫和背後夾花招。

小樹天天長大，
結出蘋果真艷麗。
敵人見它光閃閃，
知道是我栽的樹。

夜幕遮了北斗，❷
竊賊入園偷蘋果；
天剛亮時我起身，
喜見敵人倒在樹下僵臥。

# Robert Burns (1759-1796)

## LOVE IN THE GUISE OF FRINDSHIP

Talk not of love, it gives me pain,
  For love has been my foe;
He bound me in an iron chain,
  And plung'd me deep in woe.

But friendship's pure and lasting joys,             5
  My heart was form'd to prove;
There, welcome win and wear the prize,
  But never talk of love.

Your friendship much can make me blest,
  O why that bliss destroy?                        10
Why urge the only, one request
  You know I will deny?

Your thought, if Love must harbour there,
  Conceal it in that thought;
Nor cause me from my bosom tear             15
  The very friend I sought.

# 羅伯特‧彭斯 (1759-1796)*

## 024. 友誼偽裝之愛 憶江南（雙調）二首

枉說愛，令我痛難當，
情愛竟然成敵寇，
一條鐵鏈縛心房，
深處塞悲傷。

談友誼，純潔又欣歡。
心意鑄成能檢驗，
君來領獎掛胸前，
愛勿再奢談。

情誼久，令我樂悠悠。
極樂焉能摧毀掉？
我將拒絕作情儔，
何故再強求？

君若想，愛港泊情舟，
此念望君能隱匿，
我心不想帶淚流。
但願覓詩儔，

# Phillis the Queen o' the fair
## Tune-'the muckin o' geordie's byre.'

Adown winding Nith I did wander,
　To mark the sweet flowers as they spring;
Adown winding Nith I did wander,
　Of Phillis to muse and to sing.

Chorus. — Awa' wi' your belles and your beauties,　　　5
　They never wi' her can compare,
Whaever has met wi' my Phillis,
　Has met wi' the queen o' the fair.

The daisy amus'd my fond fancy,
　So artless, so simple, so wild;　　　10
Thou emblem, said I, o' my Phillis,
　For she is Simplicity's child.

The rose-bud's the blush o' my charmer,

## 025. 美后菲莉絲之歌❶

彎彎尼斯河畔行，❷
春日踏青尋芳心。
彎彎尼斯河畔行，
一曲歌謠思芳心。

合唱——
遠遜你那麗質，
眾美難為侶儔。
誰與芳心相邂逅，
如見純美皇后！

清新激蕩神思，
素心散發野氣：
眼前所見皆芳心，
她是素心兒女。❸

玫紅羞我臉頰，

Her sweet balmy lip when 'tis prest:
How fair and how pure is the lily!                    15
But fairer and purer her breast.

Yon knot of gay flowers in the arbour,
  They ne'er wi' my Phillis can vie:
Her breath is the breath of the woodbine,
  Its dew-drop o' diamond her eye.                 20

Her voice is the song of the morning,
  That wakes thro' the green-spreading grove,
When Phoebus peeps over the mountains,
  On music, and pleasure, and love.

But Beauty, how frail and how fleeting,               25
  The bloom of a fine summer's day!
While worth in the mind o' my Phillis,
  Will flourish without a decay.

甘甜銜她皓齒。
百合花開美且純，
遜她酥胸雪白。

涼亭羣芳妍姿，
無一能與她比：
吐納金花❹含淚珠，
宛如鑽石滴露。

歌喉亮如黎明，
喚醒沉睡翠林，
朝陽冉冉上山嶺，
戀歌怡悅人心。

可憐美景易逝，
夏花紛謝一時！
但願芳心情意深，
永駐不老青枝。

# Samuel Rogers (1763-1855)

## THE SLEEPING BEAUTY

Sleep on, and dream of Heaven awhile —
Tho' shut so close thy laughing eyes,
Thy rosy lips still wear a smile
And move, and breathe delicious sighs!

Ah, now soft blushes tinge her cheeks                    5
And mantle o'er her neck of snow:
Ah, now she murmurs, now she speaks
What most I wish — and fear to know!

She starts, she trembles, and she weeps!
Her fair hands folded on her breast:                     10
— And now, how like a saint she sleeps!
A seraph in the realms of rest!

Sleep on secure! Above controul
Thy thoughts belong to Heaven and thee:
And may the secret of thy soul                           15
Remain within its sanctuary!

# 塞繆爾・羅傑斯 (1763-1855)*
## 026. 睡美人

沉沉入睡，今宵天國夢中——
歡笑眼波已收攏，
微笑雙唇依舊綻玫紅，
數聲嬌喘香氣濃！

雙頰柔潤含羞，
頸上雪映披風，
美人喃喃低語時，
我之所願所懼，誰知情？！

朱唇欲啟又止，顫動，流淚！
纖纖素手撫酥胸，
宛如聖女安睡！
又如六翼天使飛入凡花叢！

睡意濃，夢繞無羈自由風！
風吹思緒入天國，縷縷繫汝心。
汝之靈魂有隱衷，
含而不露藏匿深閨中！

# William Wordsworth (1770-1850)

## She Dwelt Among the Untrodden Ways

She dwelt among the untrodden ways
  Beside the springs of Dove,
A Maid whom there were none to praise
  And very few to love:

A violet by a mossy stone                    5
  Half hidden from the eye!
— Fair as a star, when only one
  Is shining in the sky.

She lived unknown, and few could know
  When Lucy ceased to be;                    10
But she is in her grave, and, oh,
  The difference to me!

# 威廉・華茲華斯 (1770-1850)*

## 027. 她幽居於鄉野之間❶

寂寞鴿泉邊，❷
野徑罕足音，
深閨無人題詩篇，
無人寄深情。

石邊紫羅蘭，
蒼苔半掩映，
美在天邊光閃閃，
昏曉第一星。❸

露西在人寰，
生死兩無名，
而今托體墓室眠，
與我隔幽明！

# To a Butterfly I

Stay near me — do not take thy flight!
A little longer stay in sight!
Much converse do I find in thee,
Historian of my infancy!
Float near me; do not yet depart!                    5
Dead times revive in thee:
Thou bring'st, gay creature as thou art!
A solemn image to my heart,
My father's family!

Oh! pleasant, pleasant were the days,                10
The time, when, in our childish plays,
My sister Emmeline and I
Together chased the butterfly!
A very hunter did I rush
Upon the prey: — with leaps and springs             15
I followed on from brake to bush;
But she, God love her! feared to brush
The dust from off its wings.

## 028. 致蝴蝶 之一·天香[1]

請勿飛離，翩然靠近，
我欲多多看汝！
促膝相談，
幻中史話，
點點童年花絮！
莫言辭別，飛近我！
死中生趣，
勾起莊嚴意象，
回眸祖先家府。

韶華縱情喜度，
好時光，幾多童趣，
兄妹同追蝴蝶，
宛如弓弩
追獵逃亡狡兔，
蹦而跳，
藏身樹叢處。
上帝憐她，
吹塵刷羽。

# To a Butterfly II

I've watched you now a full half-hour;
Self-poised upon that yellow flower
And, little Butterfly! indeed
I know not if you sleep or feed.
How motionless! — not frozen seas                     5
More motionless! and then
What joy awaits you, when the breeze
Hath found you out among the trees,
And calls you forth again!

This plot of orchard-ground is ours;                    10
My trees they are, my Sister's flowers;
Here rest your wings when they are weary;
Here lodge as in a sanctuary!
Come often to us, fear no wrong;
Sit near us on the bough!                               15
We'll talk of sunshine and of song,
And summer days, when we were young;
Sweet childish days, that were as long
As twenty days are now.

## 029. 致蝴蝶 之二 · 聲聲慢

觀花賞蝶，蝶落黃花，
神思恍恍惚惚。
靜靜悄悄良久，
不知飛蝶，
安然收翼入睡，曉夢迷，
或吸花汁？
汝不動，
若冰河，
醒悟待風吹拂。

綠樹黃花園圃，
吾亦有，
歡迎汝來投宿。
妹妹栽花，果樹自家種植。
安全港如聖地，
遠塵囂，
好待貴客。
話舊事，
旭日夏歌
忒短促！

# THE DAFFODILS

I wander'd lonely as a cloud
That floats on high o'er vales and hills,
When all at once I saw a crowd,
A host, of golden daffodils;
Beside the lake, beneath the trees,         5
Fluttering and dancing in the breeze.

Continuous as the stars that shine
And twinkle on the Milky Way,
They stretch'd in never-ending line
Along the margin of a bay:         10
Ten thousand saw I at a glance,
Tossing their heads in sprightly dance.

The waves beside them danced; but they
Out-did the sparkling waves in glee:
A poet could not but be gay,         15
In such a jocund company:

# 030. 詠水仙[1]

我如片雲獨自飄，
漫過翠谷青山腰，
山頭忽見花色濃，
金黃水仙一叢叢。
碧湖邊，綠樹下，
隨風起舞花莖斜。

複如繁星泛銀波，
河漢滾動光閃爍，
點點繽紛牽成線；
連綿不斷到海灣，
望眼下，千萬朵，
昂首搖莖舞婆娑。

花邊波光亦起舞，
粼粼不及花楚楚，
如此良朋助詩興，
詩人焉能不動情！

I gazed — and gazed — but little thought

What wealth the show to me had brought:

For oft, when on my couch I lie

In vacant or in pensive mood,                          20

They flash upon that inward eye

Which is the bliss of solitude;

And then my heart with pleasure fills,

And dances with the daffodils.

只顧看，少思索，
美景帶來財富多。

閒暇屢在臥榻躺，
茫然四顧或冥想；
心扉窗眼花影動，
縱然獨處樂融融；
心歡喜，喜無邊，
水仙伴我舞翩躚。

# Samuel Taylor Coleridge (1772-1834)

## Kubla Khan

In Xanadu did Kubla Khan

A stately pleasure-dome decree:

Where Alph, the sacred river, ran

Through caverns measureless to man

Down to a sunless sea.                                          *5*

So twice five miles of fertile ground

With walls and towers were girdled round:

And there were gardens bright with sinuous rills,

Where blossomed many an incense-bearing tree;

And here were forests ancient as the hills,        *10*

Enfolding sunny spots of greenery.


But oh! that deep romantic chasm which slanted

Down the green hill athwart a cedarn cover!

A savage place! as holy and enchanted

As e'er beneath a waning moon was haunted       *15*

By woman wailing for her demon-lover!

# 賽繆爾・泰勒・柯爾律治 (1772-1834)*

## 031. 忽必烈汗❶

忽必烈汗立上都，

詔令建造金碧輝煌安樂宮。

神河阿爾佛❷，訇然穿岩洞，

奔流直下，深不可測，

匯入不見天日地下海洋中。

方圓十哩，一片沃野，

樓臺亭閣，輔以城闉。

溪流穿花園，蜿蜒閃光澤，

溪邊植香木，鮮花開不謝；

四山拱衛壽比丘壑林間樹

環抱明媚大草地，一片青蔥色。


噫噓嚱！驀見天崩地開裂，急轉直下青山側，

上有濃蔭覆蓋之水松，下有幽深莫測之罅隙。

其險也如此，其神也難說——

但聞寒月下，神出鬼沒一女郎

只緣情人化魔怪，淚汪汪。

And from this chasm, with ceaseless turmoil seething,
As if this earth in fast thick pants were breathing,
A mighty fountain momently was forced:
Amid whose swift half-intermitted burst                    20
Huge fragments vaulted like rebounding hail,
Or chaffy grain beneath the thresher's flail:
And 'mid these dancing rocks at once and ever
It flung up momently the sacred river.

Five miles meandering with a mazy motion                   25
Through wood and dale the sacred river ran,
Then reached the caverns measureless to man,
And sank in tumult to a lifeless ocean:
And 'mid this tumult Kubla heard from far
Ancestral voices prophesying war!                          30

The shadow of the dome of pleasure
Floated midway on the waves;
Where was heard the mingled measure
From the fountain and the caves.
It was a miracle of rare device,                           35
A sunny pleasure-dome with caves of ice!

又聞罅隙一片喧囂騰烈焰。

仿佛大地不堪地衣緊，氣喘喘。

一股地泉，洶湧噴射，

巨石碎沙，騰上雲天，

或如列缺霹靂之中冰雹之倒落，

或如農夫連枷之下稻穀之反彈。

龐然大岩石，飛舞何蹣跚！

神河夾石出深淵，倒流上青山。


聖水流過峽谷穿森林，

迷迷茫茫，蜿蜒五哩長，

直入深不可測岩洞間，

一片喧囂沉入死寂大海洋。

喧囂間，忽必烈汗遙聞祖先

吐真言，預見一場大惡戰。


雕樑畫棟之殿堂，

水中倒影泛波瀾；

詭祕迷幻之交響，❸

來自岩洞和地泉。

奇乎怪哉！鬼斧神工，世所罕見，

陽光映照逍遙宮，閃爍冰窟間！

A damsel with a dulcimer

In a vision once I saw:

It was an Abyssinian maid,

And on her dulcimer she played, 40

Singing of Mount Abora.

Could I revive within me

Her symphony and song,

To such a deep delight 'twould win me,

That with music loud and long, 45

I would build that dome in air,

That sunny dome! those caves of ice!


And all who heard should see them there,

And all should cry, Beware! Beware!

His flashing eyes, his floating hair! 50

Weave a circle round him thrice,

And close your eyes with holy dread,

For he on honey-dew hath fed,

And drunk the milk of Paradise.

憶昔朦朧生幻象，

飄然飛來一女郎，

自言本為異邦女，❹

蝴蝶古琴❺抱身上，

為我一揮手，天音飄神山❻。

松風交響，從此不再聞，

和諧歌吟，而今在何方？

若能摹寫銷魂之仙曲，

定能以樂音之悠遠高揚，

重建霧裏樓臺，雲中仙邦，

陽光燦爛逍遙宮，聳立冰窟上！


如此海外奇談，凡能耳聞目睹者，

定然高聲呼喊：提防！提防！

他那眼光閃亮，他那髮絲飄蕩！❼

織一圓環，繞他三匝，

心懷神聖恐懼，閉上雙眼，

只緣他朝食人間蜜露

夕飲天國乳漿。❽

# Metrical Feet: Lesson for a Boy

Trochee trips from long to short;
From long to long in solemn sort
Slow Spondee stalks, strong foot!, yet ill able
Ever to come up with Dactyl's trisyllable.
Iambics march from short to long.                    5
With a leap and a bound the swift Anapests throng.
One syllable long, with one short at each side,
Amphibrachys hastes with a stately stride —
First and last being long, middle short, Amphimacer
Strikes his thundering hoofs like a proud high-bred Racer.    10

If Derwent be innocent, steady, and wise,
And delight in the things of earth, water, and skies;
Tender warmth at his heart, with these meters to show it,
With sound sense in his brains, may make Derwent a poet —
May crown him with fame, and must win him the love        15
Of his father on earth and his father above.
   My dear, dear child!
Could you stand upon Skiddaw, you would not from its whole ridge
See a man who so loves you as your fond S.T. Colerige.

# 032. 詩律啟蒙：示兒❶

揚抑格從長跳到短；
揚揚格從長走到長，
步履莊重而緩慢；音韻多鏗鏘！
揚抑抑格三音步，慎用方見技藝強。
抑揚格從短走到長。
一跳一躍多敏捷，喚作抑抑揚；
中間長，兩頭短，喚作抑揚抑，
步履穩健行色甚匆忙——
兩頭長，中間短，動步起風雷，
宛如訓練有素競走者，喚作揚抑揚。

倘若吾兒本天真，步沉穩，眼明亮，
逸興登山觀湖景，壯思上天摘星光；
溫情蓄內美，詩律作皮囊，
心智圓通有識力，造就詩人有指望。
他年若想名播遐邇戴桂冠，
須得塵寰乃翁愛，天父垂愛在上蒼。
　　稚子稚子聽端詳：
佇立山頭❷放眼望，誰人愛汝如乃翁？
柯爾律治家傳詩書香。

# George Gordon Byron (1788-1824)

## BEAR WITNESS, GREECE!

Such is the aspect of this shore;

'Tis Greece, but living Greece no more!

So coldly sweet, so deadly fair,

We start, for soul is wanting there.

Hers is the loveliness in death,                                    5

That parts not quite with parting breath;

But beauty with that fearful bloom,

That hue which haunts it to the tomb,

Expression's last receding ray,

A gilded halo hovering round decay,                                10

The farewell beam of Feeling pass'd away!

Sparks of that flame, perchance of heavenly birth,

Which gleams, but warms no more its cherished earth!


Clime of the unforgotten brave!

Whose land from plain to mountain-cave                             15

Was Freedom's home, or Glory's grave!

# 喬治・戈登・拜倫 (1788-1824)*

## 033. 希臘的見證❶

海岸風光如昔——

希臘啊，希臘不再充滿活力！

如此冷峻的甜美，如此死寂的晴明，

我們出發吧，因為靈魂正在丟失。

她的愛心是死亡中的麗質，

辭行後落氣了卻不會完全離去；

留下那夾帶恐怖的花卉之美，

落英周遭縈繞不散的色彩滲入墓室，

情感是最後撤退的光束，

金色光環在四合的潰敗中盤旋，

那是激情消失前告別的光束！

那烈焰的火花，也許在天庭釀生，

寒光閃閃，再也不能溫暖它珍愛的大地！


令人難忘的勇武之鄉！

廣袤的土地，從平原到山崗

原本自由的家園，壯觀的陵園——

Shrine of the mighty! can it be
That this is all remains of thee?
Approach, thou craven crouching slave:
Say, is not this Thermopylae?                    20
These waters blue that round you lave,
Oh servile offspring of the free —
Pronounce what sea, what shore is this?
The gulf, the rock of Salamis!
These scenes, their story not unknown,           25
Arise, and make again your own;
Snatch from the ashes of your sires
The embers of their former fires;
And he who in the strife expires
Will add to theirs a name of fear                30
That Tyranny shall quake to hear,
And leave his sons a hope, a fame,
They too will rather die than shame:
For Freedom's battle once begun,
Bequeath'd by bleeding Sire to Son,              35
Though baffled oft is ever won.


Bear witness, Greece, thy living page,
Attest its many a deathless age!

威嚴的聖壇！豈能只剩下

你這一片斷壁殘垣？

來吧，你這卑賤的奴隸：

請問，難道這不是塞莫皮萊山關❷？

不是懷抱你為你洗濯的碧水綠瀾？

自由之魂的不肖子孫——

這是一片怎樣的海域，怎樣的海岸？

看那海灣，薩拉米❸的岩石！

壯美的風光及其故事不再傳揚。

起來，自強不息的兒郎，

從歷代帝王縱火過後的灰燼中

奪回昔日烈焰的星火；

在抗爭中獻身的英傑

將給帝王添加一個可怕的名字，

暴君一聽就會坐立不安，

英名將給子孫留下希望和榮光，

他們同樣會寧死不屈：

因為自由的抗爭一旦發端，

霸王的後裔就會繼承帝業，

儘管受挫的英雄屢敗屢戰。


充當見證吧，希臘，你生命的詩頁！

向世人證明一個不死的時代！

While kings, in dusty darkness hid,

Have left a nameless pyramid, 40

Thy heroes, though the general doom

Hath swept the column from their tomb,

A mightier monument command,

The mountains of their native land!

There points thy Muse to stranger's eye 45

The graves of those that cannot die!

'Twere long to tell, and sad to trace,

Each step from splendour to disgrace:

Enough — no foreign foe could quell

Thy soul, till from itself it fell; 50

Yes! Self — abasement paved the way

To villain — bonds and despot sway.


What can he tell who treads thy shore?

No legend of thine olden time,

No theme on which the muse might soar, 55

High as thine own in days of yore,

When man was worthy of thy clime.

The hearts within thy valleys bred,

The fiery souls that might have led

Thy sons to deeds sublime, 60

當王侯在甚囂塵上的黑暗中隱匿，

留下一個無名的金字塔時，

你的英雄，儘管不斷遇劫，

可那墓穴來風正在吹拂，

一個更宏偉的紀念碑高聳俯瞰

故國的峰巒絕壁！

你的詩神給外邦人迷茫的眼神，

指點那不能死去的墳墓！

一個悠長的故事，說起來令人傷悲，

從榮光到恥辱的每一步；

夠了——沒有外敵能夠鎮壓

你的精神，除非靈魂自己倒地；

是的！自暴自棄鋪平一條道路

通向罪惡的牢籠和專制統治。


他能把什麼告訴在你的海岸徘徊的人？

不是你往古的傳說故事，

不是往昔像騰飛的你自己一樣

盤旋其上的詩神顧盼的主題。

那時的人們配得上你的風土。

你在山谷中哺育的萬眾之心，

那火熱的靈魂也許曾牽引

你的子孫去建樹崇高的事業，

Now crawl from cradle to the grave,

Slaves ─ nay, the bondsmen of a slave,

nd callous, save to crime;

Stain'd with each evil that pollutes

Mankind, where least above the brutes;      65

Without even savage virtue blest,

Without one free or valiant breast.

Still to the neighbouring ports they waft

Proverbial wiles, and ancient craft;

In this the subtle Greek is found,      70

For this, and this alone, renown'd.

In vain might Liberty invoke

The spirit to its bondage broke,

Or raise the neck that courts the yoke:

No more her sorrows I bewail,      75

Yet this will be a mournful tale,

And they who listen may believe,

Who heard it first had cause to grieve.

此刻卻從搖籃到墳墓一路匍匐，

奴隸們——不，一個奴隸的奴隸們，❹

冷酷無情，除了犯罪之外，

還要用各種邪惡的腐蝕劑

汙染人類，缺德到近乎禽獸的地步；

甚至缺乏四夷初純的聖德，❺

不見一個獨立而勇敢的胸懷，

只有吹向鄰國港灣的惡臭之氣

輸出臭名昭著的花招和古老的權術；

在這裏，敏銳的希臘現身了，

因此，寄望這唯一的聲譽。

也許自由之神會徒勞地呼喚

打破束縛靈魂的桎梏，

昂起脖子上套著枷鎖的頭顱：

我不再為她的憂患嘆息，

可這詩章將成為一個哀婉的故事，

正在聆聽的人們會相信，

最早聽完故事的人會不勝噓唏。

# SHE WALKS IN BEAUTY

She walks in beauty, like the night
Of cloudless climes and starry skies,
And all that's best of dark and bright
meets in her aspect and her eyes,
Thus mellowed to that tender light                    5
Which heaven to gaudy day denies.

One shade the more, one ray the less,
Had half impaired the nameless grace
Which waves in every raven tress,
Or softly lightens o'er her face,                     10
Where thoughts serenely sweet express
How pure, how dear their dwelling place.

And on that cheek, and o'er that brow,
So soft, so calm, yet eloquent,
The smiles that win, the tints that glow,             15
But tell of days in goodness spent,
A mind at peace with all below,
A heart whose love is innocent!

# 034. 她步入美 ❶

她步入美，宛如
無雲之夜，閃爍星空，
光與影之精彩萬匯
聚於瑰態明眸，
柔光圓融，勝卻白日浮豔，
天姿淡雅，無意現身晴空。❷

添一絲陰影略嫌暗，
添一束光線欠朦朧，
難言神韻甚而半折損，❸
黑髮波動，溫柔照亮芳容，
甜美思緒牽情絲，
靜悄悄出了純淨閨宮。

香腮眉宇如此柔靜，
無言百意，雄辯如流水淙淙，
微笑動人，淡色閃亮，
道盡了一片善意，悠悠歲月，
平和心態與萬物融洽，
一顆愛心，天真如兒童！

# LIVE NOT THE STARS AND MOUNTAINS?
## FROM THE ISLAND: CANTO II. XVI

Live not the Stars and Mountains? Are the Waves

Without a spirit? Are the dropping caves

Without a feeling in their silent tears?


No, no; — they woo and clasp us to their spheres,

Dissolve this clog and clod of clay before       5

Its hour, and merge our soul in the great shore.

## 035. 星辰山岳，悄然寂滅？少年游[1]

星辰山岳，悄然寂滅？

波浪少精神？野洞幽深，

水珠滴落，無語淚無情？

何須問：有靈之物，求愛解人心。

孽土銷形，此身歸去，

魂魄入洪溟。

# Percy Bysshe Shelley (1792-1822)
## ENGLAND IN 1819

An old, mad, blind, despised, and dying King,

Princes, the dregs of their dull race, who flow

Through public scorn, — mud from a muddy spring,

Rulers who neither see nor feel nor know,

But leechlike to their fainting country cling,                    *5*

Till they drop, blind in blood, without a blow,

A people starved and stabbed in the untilled field,

An army, whom liberticide and prey

Makes as a two-edged sword to all who wield;

Golden and sanguine laws which tempt and slay;                    *10*

Religion Christless, Godless — a book sealed;

A senate, Time's worst statute, unrepealed,

Are graves from which a glorious Phantom may

Burst, to illumine our tempestuous day.

# 珀西·比希·雪萊 (1792-1822)*
## 036. 一八一九年的英格蘭❶

老朽瘋狂盲目，人所共棄的垂死之王，❷

王子孽孫，庸碌王族的沉渣，❸穿過

鄙夷王侯的人流時泛起的泥漿，

無見無察無知的統治者——

附麗於積弱之邦的螞蟥，

終將無需一擊暈血墜地的黨賊，

曠野挨餓廣場遇劫的黎庶，❹

砍殺自由四處擄掠的大軍——

一柄雙刃劍下流血的無辜，

拜金分紅誘人犯罪借法殺人的法庭，

無基督無上帝的宗教——一本塵封的經書，

一個參議院，苟延一時的酷法條律❺——

一切如荒塚，一個壯麗幻影也許從中

一躍而起，為風雨如晦的時代啟蒙。

# ODE TO THE WEST WIND

*I*

O wild West Wind, thou breath of Autumn's being,

Thou from whose unseen presence the leaves dead

Are driven, like ghosts from an enchanter fleeing,


Yellow, and black, and pale, and hectic red,

Pestilence-stricken multitudes: O thou                    5

Who chariotest to their dark wintry bed


The wingèd seeds, where they lie cold and low,

Each like a corpse within its grave, until

Thine azure sister of the Spring shall blow


Her clarion o'er the dreaming earth, and fill            10

(Driving sweet buds like flocks to feed in air)

With living hues and odours plain and hill:


Wild Spirit, which art moving everywhere;

Destroyer and preserver; hear, O hear!

## 037. 西風頌[1]

一.

啊，狂野的西風，你這秋神的浩氣，[2]
吞吐呼嘯無形跡，抖落滿地枯萎，
猶如巫師念咒語，羣鬼紛紛逃逸，

蠟黃，潮紅，蒼白，鐵灰，
四處潰散，一大批瘟邪病毒。
你駕長車，滿載良種翼果插翅飛，

漫天撒落，任憑寒凝凍土
長夜冬眠，恰似僵屍臥墓穴。
待到你青翠的陽春妹妹再次吹拂，

沉睡的大地響起醒世號角，
催促蓓蕾吸清氣，如驅趕羊羣
覓食新綠，到處瀰滿生香活色。[3]

狂野的精靈，吹遍山山嶺嶺，
你這破壞者保護者，[4]聽呵，聽！

## II

Thou on whose stream, 'mid the steep sky's commotion,    *15*

Loose clouds like earth's decaying leaves are shed,

Shook from the tangled boughs of heaven and ocean,


Angels of rain and lightning: there are spread

On the blue surface of thine airy surge,

Like the bright hair uplifted from the head    *20*


Of some fierce Mænad, even from the dim verge

Of the horizon to the zenith's height,

The locks of the approaching storm. Thou dirge


Of the dying year, to which this closing night

Will be the dome of a vast sepulchre,    *25*

Vaulted with all thy congregated might


Of vapours, from whose solid atmosphere

Black rain, and fire, and hail, will burst: oh, hear!


## III

Though who didst waken from his summer dreams

二.

海天糾結為樹，亂雲翻飛為葉，

你湧上高天險關，沖落敗葉撼大樹，

豈容這蒼老古木盤根錯節！


你這雨電的天使漫天散布，

你翻湧的碧空颯然驚裂，

墨雲裏動一顆頭顱，


宛如酒神的狂女鬈髮散披，❺

從大地到天頂，烏亮青絲

昭示正在逼近的暴雨。


你是殘年的挽歌怨詩，

今宵的天穹恰似一座墳塋，

陰霾凝聚拱起龐大墓室，


卻擋不住電火噴射，黑雨傾盆，

夾著冰雹的奇襲：啊，聽！


三.

蔚藍的地中海睡眼朦朧，

The blue Mediterranean, where he lay,                    *30*

Lull'd by the coil of his crystàlline streams,


Beside a pumice isle in Baiæ's bay,

And saw in sleep old palaces and towers

Quivering within the wave's intenser day,


All overgrown with azure moss, and flowers

So sweet, the sense faints picturing them! Thou

For whose path the Atlantic's level powers


Cleave themselves into chasms, while far below

The sea-blooms and the oozy woods which wear

The sapless foliage of the ocean, know                    *40*


Thy voice, and suddenly grow grey with fear,

And tremble and despoil themselves: oh, hear!


*IV*

If I were a dead leaf thou mightest bear;

If I were a swift cloud to fly with thee;

A wave to pant beneath thy power, and share            *45*

碧波是它甜美的催眠曲。
你驚破它夏日的迷夢——

它夢見巴延灣外浮石島嶼，❻
瞥見古老的殿堂樓臺，夕照金輝
層層倒影搖曳著一灣澄碧，

到處青翠苔蘚甜美花卉
遙想堪使人醉！聲獵獵，
你一路俯衝，大西洋潮湧浪飛，

劈開海面，道道濠隙驚裂，
直搗海底，撼動水國叢林，
閒花枯葉聞聲震懾，

霎時慘然變色，淒零零
飄落多少枝葉：啊，聽！❼

四.
我願為一片枯葉與你同飄零，
我願為一片疾雲隨你共飛越，
你強勁無比匯聚洪波待出征，

The impulse of thy strength, only less free

Than thou, O uncontrollable! if even

I were as in my boyhood, and could be


The comrade of thy wanderings over heaven,

As then, when to outstrip thy skiey speed              50

Scarce seem'd a vision; I would ne'er have striven


As thus with thee in prayer in my sore need.

Oh, lift me as a wave, a leaf, a cloud!

I fall upon the thorns of life! I bleed!


A heavy weight of hours has chain'd and bow'd         55

One too like thee: tameless, and swift, and proud.


V

Make me thy lyre, even as the forest is:

What if my leaves are falling like its own!

The tumult of thy mighty harmonies


Will take from both a deep, autumnal tone,            60

Sweet though in sadness. Be thou, Spirit fierce,

My spirit! Be thou me, impetuous one!

我願為一個浪頭沖向最前列。
你來去自由難追難駕馭，
若還我少年狂氣熱血，

願與你結伴遨游到天宇，
騰空直上興許比你輕疾，
不難飛近願景；可我從未如此焦慮，

苦求你助我脫塵羈。
哦，卷我去也，如雲飄落葉葉逐清波！
我跌落人生荊棘叢，鮮血滴！

豈容時世沉重的鎖鏈束縛手腳，
你我原本酷似：傲岸，狂放，漂泊。

五.
請把我煉為你的詩琴，❽即便入寒林
又何妨同心飄落葉，
你狂飆一曲有和諧的雄渾，

請揉進這深秋的蕭瑟，
甜美的悲切。烈焰般的精靈，哦，
願你我同燃燒同寂滅！

Drive my dead thoughts over the universe

Like wither'd leaves to quicken a new birth!

And, by the incantation of this verse,

Scatter, as from an unextinguish'd hearth

Ashes and sparks, my words among mankind!

Be through my lips to unawaken'd earth

The trumpet of a prophecy! O Wind,

If Winter comes, can Spring be far behind? 70

吹散我思想的冷灰向遠天揚播，
像片片枯葉催生嫩蘗新樹！
憑這詩韻的符咒將我的新歌

一字字傳遍人世寰宇，
如尚未熄滅的爐頭火星撒落莽原！
啟用我的喉舌向沉睡的大地

吹響預言的號角！❾啊，西風卷，
當寒冬來臨，春天豈會遙遠？

# A Song

A widow bird sate mourning for her Love
  Upon a wintry bough;
The frozen wind crept on above,
  The freezing stream below.

There was no leaf upon the forest bare,         5
  No flower upon the ground,
And little motion in the air
  Except the mill — wheel's sound.

## 038. 哀歌 ❶

霜枝寒，鳥影孤，
喪偶哀歌啼血。
上有凍風躡足行，
下有冬溪凝不發。

野林枯，殘葉稀，
荒原不見花色。
唯聞吱呀水磨聲，
散入虛空更清寂。

# MUSIC, WHEN SOFT VOICES DIE

Music, when soft voices die,

Vibrates in the memory,

Odours, when sweet violets sicken,

Live within the sense they quicken.

Rose leaves, when the rose is dead,                     5

Are heaped for the beloved's bed;

And so thy thoughts, when thou art gone,

Love itself shall slumber on.

## 039. 音樂輕柔曲散時 七絕二首❶

音樂輕柔曲散時，
餘波瀲灩成追思。
紫羅蘭謝花魂斷，
撲鼻清香心上棲。

紅潤薔薇零落時，
戀花人共芳魂棲。
他年君若身先死，
情愛將隨劫夢飛。❷

# THE WORLD'S WANDERERS

Tell me, thou Star, whose wings of light
Speed thee in thy fiery flight,
In what cavern of the night
  Will thy pinions close now?

Tell me, Moon, thou pale and grey          5
Pilgrim of Heaven's homeless way
In what depth of night or day
  Seekest thou repose now?

Weary Wind, who wanderest
Like the world's rejected guest,          10
Hast thou still some secret nest
  On the tree or billow?

## 040. 世界游子❶

星辰之光，燦若亮翅，
鼓翼欲燃，君飛迅疾。
問君何時，倦收雙臂？
何方山洞，供君夜宿？

今宵月色，一臉蒼白，
天庭香客，無家之旅。
白日黑夜，各有深邃，
君之求索，無意稍息？

長風漂泊，零落倦客，
人世厭客，拒君門外。
問君歸宿，家在何處？
樹間浪下，可有密穴？

# John Keats (1795-1821)

## LA BELLE DAM SANS MERCI

O what can ail thee, knight at arms,

    Alone and palely loitering?

The sedge has wither'd from the lake,

    And no birds sing.


O what can ail thee, knight at arms,                  5

    So haggard and so woe-begone?

The squirrel's granary is full,

    And the harvest's done.


I see a lily on thy brow,

    With anguish moist and fever dew,           10

And on thy cheeks a fading rose

    Fast withereth too.


I met a lady in the meads,

    Full beautiful — a faery's child;

# 約翰·濟慈 (1795-1821)*

## 041. 美女薄情仙 添字畫堂春六首❶

持矛騎士獨傷悲，

　　問君何事徘徊？

湖邊葦草影淒淒，

　　不見鳥兒啼。


騎士愁腸九轉！

　　為何憔悴傷懷？

窩邊松鼠食糧堆，

　　收獲正逢時。


眉間百合若飄蓬，

　　濡濡熱露愁容，

玫紅雙頰色衰中，

　　君老太匆匆！


我有林間艷遇，

　　花容絕代仙蹤，

Her hair was long, her foot was light,                    *15*

And her eyes were wild.


I made a garland for her head,

And bracelets too, and fragrant zone;

She look'd at me as she did love,

And made sweet moan.                                      *20*


I set her on my pacing steed,

And nothing else saw all day long,

For sidelong would she bend, and sing

A faery's song.


She found me roots of relish sweet,                       *25*

And honey wild, and manna dew,

And sure in language strange she said —

"I love thee true."


She took me to her elfin grot,

And there she wept and sigh'd full sore,                  *30*

And there I shut her wild wild eyes

With kisses four.

飄飄長髮步輕鬆，
　　野氣凝明瞳。

為她我織一花環，
　　又編手鐲香鬘，
美人顧盼意綿綿，
　　嘆息亦甘甜。

我攜她騎駿馬，
　　整天兩兩相看，
斜倚低唱妙歌鮮，
　　深入我心田。

芳心素手採仙根，
　　甘霖野蜜❷溫馨，
她操仙語啟丹唇：
　　「我愛你情真。」

攜我進她仙洞，
　　見她落淚悲鳴，
明眸野氣攝人心，
　　四次吻情深。

And there she lulled me asleep
And there I dreamed — Ah! woe betide!
The latest dream I ever dream'd                                    35
On the cold hill side.

I saw pale kings and princes too,
Pale warriors, death-pale were they all;
They cried — "La Belle Dam Sans Merci
Hath thee in thrall!"                                              40

I saw their starv'd lips in the gloom
With horrid warning gaped wide,
And I awoke and found me here
On the cold hill's side.

And this is why I soujourn here                                    45
Alone and palely loitering,
Though the sedge is wither'd from the lake,
And no birds sing.

她逗弄我得安眠，
　　突然噩夢聯翩！
依稀夢裏透心寒，
　　在那冷山邊。

但見王公王子，
　　蒼蒼武士堪憐，
齊呼：「美女薄情仙
　　誘你入籬樊！」

情囚焦渴黯然時，
　　大聲卜告艱危，
幡然醒悟我心知，
　　在那冷山隈。

因此我身客居，
　　愴然獨自徘徊，
任他湖畔草淒淒，
　　不見鳥兒啼。

# ODE ON MELANCHOLY

*I*

No, no, go not to Lethe, neither twist

Wolf's-bane, tight-rooted, for its poisonous wine;

Nor suffer thy pale forehead to be kiss'd

By nightshade, ruby grape of Proserpine;

Make not your rosary of yew-berries,           5

Nor let the beetle, nor the death-moth be

Your mournful Psyche, nor the downy owl

A partner in your sorrow's mysteries;

For shade to shade will come too drowsily,

And drown the wakeful anguish of the soul.           10

*II*

But when the melancholy fit shall fall

Sudden from heaven like a weeping cloud,

That fosters the droop-headed flowers all,

And hides the green hill in an April shroud;

Then glut thy sorrow on a morning rose,           15

## 042. 憂鬱頌[1]

一.

莫莫莫，莫去遺忘河[2]，莫挖山金車，

根莖榨得狼毒酒，安能解乾渴，[3]

龍葵好比冥后園裏紅葡萄，[4]

君之蒼白眉宇[5]與此劇毒親不得，

莫用水松球果[6]作念珠，

莫近甲蟲，莫近致命飛蛾，

以免蟲化靈魂悲戚戚，[7]莫讓夜梟

陪君消磨難解之寂寞，

因為陰影對陰影令人昏昏，

濁浪蓋頂，堪使靈魂劇痛難察覺。[8]

二.

憂鬱驟然襲來時，

好比一塊愁雲帶淚從天落，

讓人間花卉無不垂首，

以一塊暮春屍布遮蓋青山坡，

勸君愁腸朝餐晨光玫瑰，

Or on the rainbow of the salt sand-wave,

Or on the wealth of globed peonies;

Or if thy mistress some rich anger shows,

Emprison her soft hand, and let her rave,

And feed deep, deep upon her peerless eyes.                    20


*III*

She dwells with Beauty- Beauty that must die;

And Joy, whose hand is ever at his lips

Bidding adieu; and aching Pleasure nigh,

Turning to Poison while the bee-mouth sips:

Ay, in the very temple of Delight                              25

Veil'd Melancholy has her sovran shrine,

Though seen of none save him whose strenuous tongue

Can burst Joy's grape against his palate fine;

His soul shall taste the sadness of her might,

And be among her cloudy trophies hung.                         30

夕吞多彩長虹，品味海浪苦澀，
饜足牡丹富貴花色；
君切記，倘若情人怨懟，
讓她傾訴，但請執手相看，
以君之慧眼，深入她那明眸清波。❾


三.
她❿與美同在，美必有一死，
歡樂之手每往唇間塞，
笑語道別，痛中有愉悅，⓫
一旦蜜蜂吮吸，便化為毒汁。
逍遙宮裏，憂鬱有膜拜之神位，⓬
面紗遮顏，遮不住憂鬱傷心語，
塞進歡樂葡萄裏，脹得甘甜變酸味，
歡樂之魂飽嘗她那悲情之力，
被她掠為戰利品，黯然掛在陰霾裏。⓭

# To Autumn

*I*

Season of mists and mellow fruitfulness,
Close bosom-friend of the maturing sun;
Conspiring with him how to load and bless
With fruit the vines that round the thatch-eves run;
To bend with apples the moss'd cottage-trees,          5
And fill all fruit with ripeness to the core;
To swell the gourd, and plump the hazel shells
With a sweet kernel; to set budding more,
And still more, later flowers for the bees,
Until they think warm days will never cease,          10
For Summer has o'er-brimm'd their clammy cells.

*II*

Who hath not seen thee oft amid thy store?
Sometimes whoever seeks abroad may find
Thee sitting careless on a granary floor,

# 043. 致秋君 ❶

一.

應景季節，一身霧氣，掛滿碩果，

太陽成熟了，與他結為同夥，

共謀如何如何把串串珠球

綴滿簷下葡萄藤，叫累累蘋果

往那屋前老樹背上馱，❷

讓熟透氣味滲進果心，

讓葫蘆脹大，讓一顆甜核

鼓起榛子殼，讓嫩芽重發

花蕾再綻，更多更多，

讓花期為蜜蜂延長，拖一拖，

讓花卉以為日子終年暖和，

只因炎夏早已灌滿微濕蜂窩。


二.

誰不見君穀倉邊常現身

田頭地裏常落腳？

或在打麥場上席地坐，

Thy hair soft-lifted by the winnowing wind;                     15

Or on a half-reap'd furrow sound asleep,

Drows'd with the fume of poppies, while thy hook

Spares the next swath and all its twined flowers:

And sometimes like a gleaner thou dost keep

Steady thy laden head across a brook;                           20

Or by a cyder-press, with patient look,

Thou watchest the last oozings hours by hours.


*III*

Where are the songs of Spring? Aye, where are they?

Think not of them, thou hast thy music too, ─

While barred clouds bloom the soft-dying day,                   25

And touch the stubble plains with rosy hue;

Then in a wailful choir the small gnats mourn

Among the river sallows, borne aloft

Or sinking as the light wind lives or dies;

And full-grown lambs loud bleat from hilly bourn;               30

Hedge-crickets sing; and now with treble soft

The red-breast whistles from a garden-croft;

And gathering swallows twitter in the skies.

鬈髮隨著簸穀風輕輕飄過，

或為罌粟花香沉醉不已，

當田壟半已收獲，君就地倒臥，

讓鐮刀花下歇息，靜待下次收割，

或像拾穗人，越過溪流，

背負穀袋，君之倒影亂清波，

或在榨果架下小憩片刻，

閑看酒漿徐徐滴落。


三.

春之歌飄落何處？別作他想，

君有雙手自編音樂——

當那雲浪映晚照，

殘梗碎落田野上，胭紅任情塗抹，

河柳下，一羣小蟲飛來，

宛如小小唱詩班，唱起輓歌，

歌聲陣陣隨風起落；

山坡上畜欄裏，羊羔咩咩；

籬間蟋蟀，雄唧唧，雌默默，❸

庭園裏，紅脯鳥❹叫喳喳；

燕子呢喃，結隊從天邊掠過。

# William Howitt (1792-1879)

## DEPARTURE OF THE SWALLOW

And is the swallow gone?
Who beheld it?
Which way sail'd it?
Farewell bade it none?

No mortal saw it go:                                      5
But who doth hear
Its summer cheer
As it flitteth to and fro?

So the freed spirit flies!
From its surrounding clay                                 10
It steals away
Like the swallow from the skies.

Whither? wherefore doth it go?
'T is all unknown:
We feel alone                                             15
That a void is left below.

# 威廉・豪易特 (1792-1879)

## 044. **離燕** 河傳❶

離燕？
誰見？
孤帆飄遠？
誰送它行？

有無凡眼？
啼鳥鬧夏
誰聞？
去來

瀟灑魂！
塵寰隱逸
如歸燕。
花季晚？

底事尋他岸？
竟無人曉，
高瞰寂寞空枝，
夢魂飛。

# Thomas Hood (1799-1845)

## THE WATER LADY

Alas, the moon should ever beam
To show what man should never see!
I saw a maiden on a stream,
And fair was she!

I stayed awhile, to see her throw     5
Her tresses back, that all beset
The fair horizon of her brow
With clouds of jet.

I stayed a little while to view
Her cheek, that wore in place of red     10
The bloom of water, tender blue,
Daintily spread.

I stayed to watch, a little space,
Her parted lips if she would sing;

# 托馬斯·胡德 (1799-1845)*

## 045. 水娘 西江月三首❶

明月常臨溪澗，

照覽罕見風觀，

驀然瞥見水中仙，

瑋態瑰姿驚艷！


我看水娘神韻，

滿頭黑髮披肩，

繚繞拋甩宇眉間，

雲影紛紛攪亂。


仔細近前觀賞，

見她雙頰紅妍，

波光嫩綠水花鮮，

盡興鋪延翻卷。


再假須臾詳察，

見她唇齒微綻，

The waters clos'd above her face 15
With many a ring.

And still I stayed a little more:
Alas, she never comes again!
I throw my flowers from the shore,
And watch in vain. 20

I know my life will fade away,
I know that I must vainly pine,
For I am made of mortal clay,
But she's divine!

歌喉欲啟水波翻，
把那芳容遮掩。

良久悵然空等，
水娘不再回還，
拋花入水逐微瀾，
倦收神思知返。

了悟年華憔悴，
行吟澤畔尋歡，
只緣我本濁泥團，
羨慕清流神眷！

# Ralph Waldo Emerson (1803-1882)
## THE RHODORA

*On being asked, Whence is the flower?*

In May, when sea-winds pierced our solitudes,

I found the fresh Rhodora in the woods,

Spreading its leafless blooms in a damp nook,

To please the desert and the sluggish brook.

The purple petals, fallen in the pool,                    5

Made the black water with their beauty gay;

Here might the red-bird come his plumes to cool,

And court the flower that cheapens his array.

Rhodora! if the sages ask thee why

This charm is wasted on the earth and sky,               10

Tell them, dear, that if eyes were made for seeing,

Then Beauty is its own excuse for being:

Why thou wert there, O rival of the rose!

I never thought to ask, I never knew:

But, in my simple ignorance, suppose                     15

The self-same Power that brought me there brought you.

# 拉爾夫‧沃爾多‧愛默生 (1803-1882)*

## o46. 紫杜鵑❶

或問花從哪裏來，以此作答

五月海風穿透人心寂寞，
見林間鮮美杜鵑，
潮濕處葉未綻花先開，❷
情動野地激起寒溪微瀾。
落英亂紫入池塘，
幽暗春水潋灩生香；
紅雀或飛來濯羽納涼，
羨花容壯色膽亮翅求歡。
紫杜鵑，若有聖賢發問：
何以天地間空耗嬌艷？
甜心，請回答：天生雙眼為觀看，
美之為美，乃自身存在之情理。
堪與玫瑰媲美，為何花開荒原？
我無意細究，不明真諦，
卻以初念冒昧揣測，❸
是同源自力攜你我邂逅林間。❹

# Concord Hymn

*Sung at the Completion of the Battle Monument, April 19, 1836*

By the rude bridge that arched the flood,
Their flag to April's breeze unfurled,
Here once the embattled farmers stood
And fired the shot heard round the world.

The foe long since in silence slept;                    5
Alike the conqueror silent sleeps;
And Time the ruined bridge has swept
Down the dark stream which seaward creeps.

On this green bank, by this soft stream,
We set to-day a votive stone;                          10
That memory may their deed redeem,
When, like our sires, our sons are gone.

# 047. 康科特讚歌[1]

1836年4月19日戰役紀念碑落成時唱頌

洪波拱起陌橋側，
旗卷四月風拂拂；
卸去農裝披戎衣，
一聲槍響震世界。

敗將勝手今安在？
雙方沉寂臥墓穴。
斷橋已隨逝水去，
暗流幽深向海發。

綠岸柔水今又是，
一塊石碑掩遺骨，
先人後輩皆過客，
不朽功績昭日月。

Spirit, that made those heroes dare

To die, and leave their children free,

Bid Time and Nature gently spare                    15

The shaft we raise to them and thee.

誰使英雄敢戰死，
兒孫自由得恩澤？
但願時空勤呵護，
豎旗敬神祭先烈。

# THE APOLOGY

Think me not unkind and rude
That I walk alone in grove and glen;
I go to the god of the wood
To fetch his word to men.

Tax not my sloth that I                          5
Fold my arms beside the brook;
Each cloud that floated in the sky
Writes a letter in my book.

Chide me not, laborious band,
For the idle flowers I brought;                  10
Every aster in my hand
Goes home loaded with a thought.

There was never mystery,
But 'tis figured in the flowers;
Was never secret history,                        15

## 048. 辯白 ●

雅士莫嗤我鄙俗，
獨穿荆莽過野溪；
我去拜謁林中神，
為君傳來春消息。

勞者莫斥我懶惰，
行吟澤畔覓新詩，
天際飄來一朵雲，
是我書中一行字。

繭手莫嗟我閒適，
引臂採擷野花枝，
朵朵翠菊寄深情，
攜回書齋化妙思。

欲求空靈奇異物，
且待鮮花盛開日；
欲知祕密隱諱事，

But birds tell it in the bowers.


One harvest from thy field
Homeward brought the oxen strong;
A second crop thine acres yield,
Which I gather in a song.                    20

且聽小鳥私語時。

農夫豐年收五穀，
車載牛馱回家去，
撒落稻穗或麥秸，
讓我拾來賦新曲。

# Elizabeth Barrett Browning (1806-1861)
## HIRAM POWERS'S GREEK SLAVE

They say Ideal beauty cannot enter

The house of anguish. On the threshold stands

An alien image with enshackled hands,

Called the Greek Slave! as if the artist meant her

(That passionless perfection which he lent her,                5

Shadowed not darkened where the sill expands.)

To so confront man's crimes in different lands

With man's ideal sense. Pierce to the centre,

Art's fiery finger! and break up ere long

The serfdom of this world. Appeal, fair stone,                10

From God's pure heights of beauty against man's wrong!

Catch up in thy divine face, not alone

East griefs but west, and strike and shame the strong,

By thunders of white silence, overthrown.

# 伊莉莎白·芭蕾特·勃朗寧 (1806-1861)*

## 049. 希倫·包爾斯的希臘奴隸❶

他們說理想美不能進入

苦難之家。在門口佇立的

是一個銬住雙手的異邦形象，

雕塑家把她稱為「希臘奴隸」

（他賦予她的那種缺乏激情的完美，

沒有遮蔽基石拓展的黑暗空間）

就這樣在不同國度以人類的理想

直面人類的罪惡。觸及心靈的

火焰般的藝術手指! ——世界的奴隸制

即將崩潰! 呼籲吧，公正的石頭，

從上帝的純美高度抗衡人類的謬誤！

捕獲在你聖潔面容上的，是東方的

也是西方的悲哀——以沉默的白色雷霆

撞擊強權，辱沒強權，把它顛覆！

# The Soul's Expression

With stammering lips and insufficient sound
I strive and struggle to deliver right
That music of my nature, day and night
With dream and thought and feeling interwound
And inly answering all the senses round                    5
With octaves of a mystic depth and height
Which step out grandly to the infinite
From the dark edges of the sensual ground.
This song of soul I struggle to outbear
Through portals of the sense, sublime and whole,          10
And utter all myself into the air:
But if I did it, — as the thunder — roll
Breaks its own cloud, my flesh would perish there,
Before that dread apocalypse of soul.

# 050. 靈魂的表現❶

以結巴的嘴唇貧乏的聲音
盡力準確地表現
我人性的音樂，白日和夜晚，
夢、思想和情感相互交織，
內心在回答周遭感受的一切，
以神祕深淵和高峰的八度音階
從感官基地的黑暗邊緣
莊嚴邁向無限的領域。
我努力噴射的靈魂之歌
經由感官的入口，崇高而完整，
把我全身心吐進空中：
可是，一旦我這樣做，就會像滾雷
撕裂它自己的烏雲一樣，我的肉體
會在靈魂可怕的啟示之前當場毀滅。

# Henry Wadsworth Longfellow (1807-1882)

## A PSALM OF LIFE

### WHAT THE HEART OF THE YOUNG MAN SAID
### TO THE PSALMIST

Tell me not, in mournful numbers,
  Life is but an empty dream!
For the soul is dead that slumbers,
  And things are not what they seem.

Life is real! Life is earnest!           *5*
  And the grave is not its goal;
Dust thou art, to dust returnest,
  Was not spoken of the soul.

Not enjoyment, and not sorrow,
  Is our destined end or way;        *10*
But to act, that each to-morrow
  Find us farther than to-day.

Art is long, and Time is fleeting,
  And our hearts, though stout and brave,
Still, like muffled drums, are beating     *15*

# 亨利·沃茲沃恩·朗費羅 (1807-1882)*

## 051. 人生禮讚
## ——年輕人心靈對歌者所言❶

勸君切勿放悲聲：
「人生虛無如幻夢！」
靈魂酣睡若死寂，
虛相真髓兩不同。

人生真！人生誠！
人生歸宿非墳塋；
「來於塵，歸於土」❷，
言者無意指靈魂。

或逸樂，或悲痛，
均非天定在命中；
從今起，重行動，
明朝喜見日久功。

藝術長，光陰飛，❸
青年壯志多恢弘，
揮動鼙鼓陣陣催，

Funeral marches to the grave.

In the world's broad field of battle,
  In the bivouac of Life,
Be not like dumb, driven cattle!
  Be a hero in the strife! 20

Trust no Future, howe'er pleasant!
  Let the dead Past bury its dead!
Act, — act in the living Present!
  Heart within, and God o'erhead!

Lives of great men all remind us 25
  We can make our lives sublime,
And, departing, leave behind us
  Footprints on the sands of time;

Footprints, that perhaps another,
  Sailing o'er life's solemn main, 30
A forlorn and shipwrecked brother,
  Seeing, shall take heart again.

Let us, then, be up and doing,
  With a heart for any fate;
Still achieving, still pursuing, 35
  Learn to labor and to wait.

慷慨悲歌到荒塚。❹

大千世界一戰場，
人生軍旅常出征，
任人驅策是牛馬，
抗爭方能見英雄！

莫望明天樂融融，
掩埋昨日尺寸功，
當下行動重今日，
上帝懸鏡照心胸！

前輩偉人啟後人，
崇高亦可是吾身，
人生征途如飛鴻，
時代沙灘留印痕。

或見孤鴻掠大海，
波飛浪湧任飄蓬，
檣傾楫摧拋沙灘，
見我足跡整雄風。

我輩奮起快行動，
命乖運舛亦從容；
不斷建樹多求索，
勤勉堅忍奏奇功。

# THE BRIDGE

I stood on the bridge at midnight,

   As the clocks were striking the hour,

And the moon rose o'er the city,

   Behind the dark church-tower.


I saw her bright reflection               5

   In the waters under me,

Like a golden goblet falling

   And sinking into the sea.


And far in the hazy distance

   Of that lovely night in June,          10

The blaze of the flaming furnace

   Gleamed redder than the moon.


Among the long, black rafters

   The wavering shadows lay,

And the current that came from the ocean     15

## 052. 橋 巫山一斷雲七首❶

午夜橋頭立，
鐘聲擊塔樓。
一輪皓月上城頭，
尖頂影幽幽。

腳下清清水，
微波映月浮。
金觥傾酒入江流，
向海去悠悠。

薄霧天穹遠，
良宵六月中。
熔爐赤焰正熊熊，
月染幾分紅。❷

水漲梁椽傾，
波搖暗影空，
海流托舉挾懷中，

Seemed to lift and bear them away;

As, sweeping and eddying through them,
   Rose the belated tide,
And, streaming into the moonlight,
   The seaweed floated wide.        20

And like those waters rushing
   Among the wooden piers,
A flood of thoughts came o'er me
   That filled my eyes with tears.

How often, oh, how often,        25
   In the days that had gone by,
I had stood on that bridge at midnight
   And gazed on that wave and sky!

How often, oh, how often,
   I had wished that the ebbing tide        30
Would bear me away on its bosom
   O'er the ocean wild and wide!

For my heart was hot and restless,

卷去杳無蹤。

向晚洪波起，
強風掀浪頭，
大川推擁月華流，
萍藻漫江浮。

流水匆匆洗，
淋淋木碼頭，
如潮思緒上心頭，
珠淚若泉流。

故地心常繫，
年年春復秋，
孑然午夜立橋頭，
獨見水天愁！

故地心常繫，
遙看追遠舟，
退潮挾我共洪流，
海闊騁情遊！

焦躁縈心頭，

And my life was full of care,
And the burden laid upon me 35
Seemed greater than I could bear.

But now it has fallen from me,
It is buried in the sea;
And only the sorrow of others
Throws its shadow over me. 40

Yet whenever I cross the river
On its bridge with wooden piers,
Like the odor of brine from the ocean
Comes the thought of other years.

And I think how many thousands 45
Of care-encumbered men,
Each bearing his burden of sorrow,
Have crossed the bridge since then.

I see the long procession
Still passing to and fro, 50
The young heart hot and restless,
And the old subdued and slow!

平生有所求，
沉沉負擔壓肩頭，
我亦若駝牛。

此刻輕裝上，
煩憂付海流。
他人尚有斷腸愁，
擲影我心舟。

每每河邊走，
橫橋木碼頭，
宛如海浪苦鹹浮，
往事上心頭。

千萬傷心客，
精於名利謀，
熙來攘往負憂愁，
倉促過橋頭。

我見人流湧，
來回動不休。
壯心灼熱意難收，
到老氣如秋！

And forever and forever,

    As long as the river flows,

As long as the heart has passions,          55

    As long as life has woes;


The moon and its broken reflection

    And its shadows shall appear,

As the symbol of love in heaven,

    And its wavering image here.          60

思念無終日，
悠長如水流，
恰如心上有情儔，
人世有離愁。

滿地流光碎，
朦朧月影浮。
天堂之愛露徵候，
意象蕩荒洲。

# The Prelude to Evangeline

This is the forest primeval. The murmuring pines and the hemlock,

Bearded with moss, and in garments green, indistinct in the twilight,

Stand like Druids of eld, with voices sad and prophetic,

Stand like harpers hoar, with Beards that rest on their bosoms.


Loud from its rocky caverns, the deep-voiced neighboring ocean          5

Speaks, and in accents disconsolate answers the wail of the forest.

This is the forest primeval; but where are the hearts that beneath it

Leaped like the roe, when he hears in the woodland the voice of the huntsman

Where is the thatch-roofed village, the home of Acadian farmers —

Men whose lives glided on like rivers that water the woodlands,          10


Darkened by shadows of earth, but reflecting an image of heaven?

Waste are those pleasant farms, and the farmers forever departed!

Scattered like dust and leaves, when the mighty blasts of October

Seize them, and whirl them aloft, and sprinkle them far o'er the ocean


Naught but tradition remains of the beautiful village of Grand-Pre.

## 053. 〈伊芳吉琳〉序曲 玉蝴蝶慢[1]

望處野林縹緲，沙沙松柏，地老天荒。
絲髯苔衣，昏黯夾帶悽惶。
似高僧[2]，肅然並立，卜後事，不勝悲涼。
豎琴張，撥弦抒臆，鬢髮秋霜。

低昂，潮頭擊岸，
伴松風哭，
徹夜林殤，樹下離魂，
獵槍驚起跳如獐。
草堂村，誰知何處？指故園，稼穡田莊——
水流長，浮生涓滴，灌溉林場。

大地黯然磷影，是何意象，照見天堂？
快活田園，虛度了結一場！
散如塵，飄如落葉，十月裏，雨驟風狂，
遇強梁，斷魂安在？煙水茫茫。

難忘，煙雲散盡，尚餘芳美，

Ye who believe in affection that hopes, and endure, and is patient,   15
Ye who believe in the beauty and strength of woman's devotion,
List to the mournful tradition still sung by the pines of the forest;
List to a Tale of Love in Acadie, home of the happy.

小小村莊❸，萬壑松濤，

誄辭悲曲意蒼涼。

寄希望，韌而不折，化育中，巾幗剛強。

賦新章，史詩懷抱，幸福家鄉。❹

# RETRIBUTION

Though the mills of God grind slowly,
    Yet they grind exceeding small;
Though with patience He stands waiting,
    With exactness grinds He all.

# 054. 神的正義❶

上帝獨立磨坊，
　萬千水輪悠揚，
轉呀轉，耐心等候細細磨，
　把人間的不平磨成祂的天堂。

# Edgar Allan Poe (1809-1849 )

## THE BELLS

*I*

Hear the sledges with the bells,

   Silver bells!

What a world of merriment their melody foretells!

   How they tinkle, tinkle, tinkle,

      In the icy air of night!                                    *5*

   While the stars, that oversprinkle

   All the heavens, seem to twinkle

      With a crystalline delight;

      Keeping time, time, time,

      In a sort of Runic rhyme,                                   *10*

To the tintinnabulation that so musically wells

   From the bells, bells, bells, bells,

      Bells, bells, bells —

   From the jingling and the tinkling of the bells.

# 愛德格・愛倫・坡 (1809-1849)*
## 055. 鐘鈴

一.

欣聞雪橇響鈴聲，

　　　銀鈴聲！

鳴琴響，預示環球喜樂情！

　　叮鈴叮鈴響叮鈴，

　　散入冰清夜空中！

　　星星高高頭上掛，

　　佈滿天，亮晶晶，

　　　閃閃爍爍如水晶。

　　守時守時守時辰

　　押的韻是呂那韻，❶

音韻和諧配銀鈴，

　　銀鈴銀鈴響銀鈴，

　　響銀鈴——

叮鈴叮鈴響叮鈴。

*II*

Hear the mellow wedding bells, 15

    Golden bells!

What a world of happiness their harmony foretells!

    Through the balmy air of night

    How they ring out their delight!

      From the molten-golden notes, 20

        And all in tune,

      What a liquid ditty floats

To the turtle-dove that listens, while she gloats

      On the moon!

      Oh, from out the sounding cells, 25

What a gush of euphony voluminously wells!

      How it swells!

      How it dwells

    On the Future! how it tells

    Of the rapture that impels 30

   To the swinging and the ringing

   Of the bells, bells, bells,

  Of the bells, bells, bells, bells,

    Bells, bells, bells —

To the rhyming and the chiming of the bells! 35

二.

欣聞婚禮響鐘聲，

　　金鐘聲！

多和諧，預示世界真幸運！

　　夜氣溫馨傳鐘聲，

　　聲聲入耳多歡欣！

　　　音符可以爍黃金，

　　　不離譜，

　　歌如清流涓涓聲。

斑鳩喜，聆聽偷窺

　　在月宮！❷

　　呀，從那喧嘩小室中，

歡歌汩汩如泉湧！

　　　多洶湧！

　　　多洶湧！

　　看未來！──說故事，

　　狂喜疊來步步推，

多姿多彩如金鐘，

　　　金鐘金鐘敲金鐘──

　　　金鐘金鐘敲金鐘，

　　　金鐘金鐘敲金鐘──

配上韻律與和聲！

*III*

Hear the loud alarum bells,

    Brazen bells!

What a tale of terror, now, their turbulency tells!

    In the startled ear of night

    How they scream out their affright!        40

      Too much horrified to speak,

      They can only shriek, shriek,

        Out of tune,

In a clamorous appealing to the mercy of the fire,

In a mad expostulation with the deaf and frantic fire,     45

      Leaping higher, higher, higher,

      With a desperate desire,

    And a resolute endeavor

    Now—now to sit or never,

  By the side of the pale-faced moon.       50

    Oh, the bells, bells, bells!

    What a tale their terror tells

      Of Despair!

    How they clang, and clash, and roar!

    What a horror they outpour       55

On the bosom of the palpitating air!

    Yet the ear it fully knows,

三.

惡聞尖聲響警鐘——
　　　黃銅聲!
騷亂聲,夜色深深灌滿耳,
　　故事恐怖狂風勁!
　　警鐘發出驚叫聲!
　　　想要細說太可怕,
　　　只好驚叫叫不停,
　　　　沒調門,
吵吵嚷嚷懇求大火發善心,
狂亂聲中勸告聾啞烈火停,
　　　烈焰昇,更昇高昇更高昇,
　　　鋌而走險不顧身,
　　　決意肆虐不近情,
　　　坐立不安兩難中,
　　蒼白月亮作背景。
　　　呀,警鐘警鐘敲警鐘!
　　　故事恐怖多絕望,
　　　　太難聽!
　　磕碰撞響大聲吼!
　　鐘聲傾瀉大恐怖,
空氣心中也震驚!
　　耳朵悉聽全知情,

By the twanging

And the clanging,

How the danger ebbs and flows;                                    60

Yet the ear distinctly tells,

In the jangling

And the wrangling,

How the danger sinks and swells, ─

By the sinking or the swelling in the anger of the bells,         65

Of the bells,

Of the bells, bells, bells, bells,

Bells, bells, bells ─

In the clamor and the clangor of the bells!


*IV*

Hear the tolling of the bells,                                    70

Iron bells!

What a world of solemn thought their monody compels!

In the silence of the night

How we shiver with affright

At the melancholy menace of their tone!                           75

For every sound that floats

From the rust within their throats

Is a groan.

聲聲撞

砰砰響，

潮頭起伏多險情；

耳朵也在講不停，

刺耳聲

叫嚷聲，

險情沉落復昇騰，

沉落昇騰都是警鐘怨懟聲——

敲警鐘——

警鐘警鐘敲警鐘，

警鐘警鐘敲警鐘——

警鐘喧鬧煩人心！


四.

忽聞鐘聲緩緩敲——

黑鐵聲！

悲戚戚，世界肅穆輓歌近！

夜無聲，

我們顫抖多害怕

鐘聲陣陣訴悲聲！

每一聲，漂浮來

來自喉嚨鐵銹中

哀怨聲。

And the people — ah, the people,

They that dwell up in the steeple, *80*

 All alone,

And who tolling, tolling, tolling,

 In that muffled monotone,

Feel a glory in so rolling

On the human heart a stone — *85*

They are neither man nor woman,

They are neither brute nor human,

 They are Ghouls:

And their king it is who tolls;

And he rolls, rolls, rolls, *90*

 Rolls

 A paean from the bells;

And his merry bosom swells

 With the paean of the bells,

And he dances, and he yells:

Keeping time, time, time,

In a sort of Runic rhyme,

 To the paean of the bells,

 Of the bells:

Keeping time, time, time, *100*

In a sort of Runic rhyme,

人啊人，人啊人——
住在尖塔上，
　　孤零零，
他們敲鐘敲呀敲，
　　聲音單調又沉悶，
卻有美景寓其中
　　奈何心上一塊石——
他們非男亦非女——
不算惡鬼不算人——
　　他們就是盜屍人：
　　盜屍王在敲喪鐘；
　　敲呀敲呀敲呀敲，
　　敲呀敲，
一支贊歌出鐘聲！
他的酒意大膨脹，
　　醉態伴著贊歌聲！
他舞蹈，他叫嚷：
守時守時守時辰，
跟著喪鐘贊美聲
　　押著歡喜呂那韻——
　　敲喪鐘：
守時守時守時辰，
跟著喪鐘震顫聲，

To the throbbing of the bells,

Of the bells, bells, bells —

  To the sobbing of the bells;

Keeping time, time, time,                  105

  As he knells, knells, knells,

In a happy Runic rhyme,

To the rolling of the bells,

  Of the bells, bells, bells:

  To the tolling of the bells,            110

Of the bells, bells, bells, bells,

    Bells, bells, bells —

To the moaning and the groaning of the bells.

押著古雅呂那韻——

喪鐘喪鐘敲喪鐘——

　　配著喪鐘啜泣聲：

守時守時守時辰，

　　就像喪鐘喪鐘聲，

押著歡喜呂那韻，

喪鐘敲——

　　喪鐘喪鐘敲喪鐘：

　　喪鐘敲，

喪鐘喪鐘敲喪鐘——

　　　喪鐘喪鐘敲喪鐘——

喪鐘聲聲在悲吟。

# Alfred, Lord Tennyson (1809-1892)

## TEARS, IDLE TEARS

Tears, idle tears, I know not what they mean,

Tears from the depth of some divine despair

Rise in the heart, and gather to the eyes,

In looking on the happy autumn-fields,

And thinking of the days that are no more.      *5*

Fresh as the first beam glittering on a sail,

That brings our friends up from the underworld,

Sad as the last which reddens over one

That sinks with all we love below the verge;

So sad, so fresh, the days that are no more.      *10*

Ah, sad and strange as in dark summer dawns

The earliest pipe of half-awaken'd birds

To dying ears, when unto dying eyes

The casement slowly grows a glimmering square;

So sad, so strange, the days that are no more.      *15*

# 阿爾弗雷德・丁尼生 (1809-1892)*

## 056. 滴滴無端淚❶

滴滴無端淚，不解此中意味，
來自神聖絕望深處，
心頭湧起，凝聚眼眶裏，
眺望歡暢秋野時，
似水年華，情牽縷縷思緒。

鮮如出海後，晴光初閃帆桅，
攜來冥土百侶相聚，
淒如晚劫，殘霞銷盡時，
人寰情愛溺天底──
似水年華，如此新鮮含悲意。

悲涼而詭異，宛如夏日晨曦，
鳥兒半醒暗中初啼，
彌留之人，眼耳開復閉，
但見窗櫺光微微──
似水年華，如此悲涼又詭異。

Dear as remembered kisses after death,

And sweet as those by hopeless fancy feigned

On lips that are for others; deep as love,

Deep as first love, and wild with all regret;

O Death in Life, the days that are no more.　　　　*20*

親如歷劫後，回味最後吻別，
此刻奢望夢中甜蜜，
初戀深情，雙唇如急雨，
種種遺恨帶狂野——
似水年華，生命蘊含死氣。

# THE EAGLE

He clasps the crag with crooked hands;
Close to the sun in lonely lands,
Ring'd with the azure world, he stands.

The wrinkled sea beneath him crawls;
He watches from his mountain walls,                                    5
And like a thunderbolt he falls.

# 057. 雄鷹 攤破浣溪沙 ❶

利爪雙鉤扣絕崗，
蠻荒孤影近斜陽，
天界周身一環套，色蒼蒼。

腳底海波蠢豸動，
居高雄視立山墻，
雲端俯衝雷暴落，野茫茫。

# THE HARRIER

She drapes the drops with dripping wings
Dreams a'load on the flapping being
Zooms across the wave froth, she sings
The sea expands beyond the rain
Gliding afar her tilt un-gained                    5
At dusk, a butterfly she lands

## 058. 海鷗

雙翅滴雨，肩披淒淒風雨
拍擊長空，背負非非幻夢
一曲驪歌，穿越浪花泡沫
大海浩蕩，沖向暴雨他鄉
遠征滑行，巾幗一無所擒
悵望暮色，捕獲一只蝴蝶❶

# William Makepeace Thackeray (1811-1863)
## A Tragic Story

There lived a sage in days of yore

And he a handsome pigtail wore;

But wondered much and sorrowed more,

Because it hung behind him.


He mused upon this curious case,                                                5

And swore he'd change the pigtail's place,

And have it hanging at his face,

Not dangling there behind him.


Says he, 'The mystery I've found, —

I'll turn me round,' —                                                          10

He turned him round;

But still it hung behind him.


Then round, and round, and out and in,

All day the puzzled sage did spin;

# 威廉・梅克比斯・薩克萊 (1811-1863)*

## 059. 一個悲劇故事❶

從前有個聖人

紮一條漂亮的辮子；

可他十分驚詫又悲傷

因為辮子掛在背後。


他琢磨這樁怪事

發誓要讓辮子換個地方，

要讓它掛在臉皮面前，

不讓它搖搖擺擺拖在背後。


他說：「個中奧祕我已發現——

我要打一個轉轉。」——

他開始轉呀轉；

可辮子仍然掛在背後。


於是轉呀轉，轉出轉進，

這個迷惑的聖人整天都在紡線線；

In vain — it mattered not a pin —
The pigtail hung behind him.


And right, and left, and round about,
And up, and down, and in, and out,
He turned; but still the pigtail stout
Hung steadily behind him.


And though his efforts never slack,
And though he twist, and twirl, and tack,
Alas! still faithful to his back,
The pigtail hangs behind him.

白費力氣——一點也不管用——
辮子仍然掛在背後。

右轉，左轉，轉個大圓圈，
轉上轉下轉進轉出，
他轉呀轉；可辮子仍然結結實實
穩穩當當掛在後面。

雖然他的努力從來沒有鬆懈，
雖然他轉來轉去，不斷調整方向，
唉！依附他背脊的辮子
始終掛在背後。

# Robert Browning (1812-1889)

## HOME-THOUGHTS, FROM ABROAD

Oh, to be in England

Now that April 's there,

And whoever wakes in England

Sees, some morning, unaware,

That the lowest boughs and the brushwood sheaf          5

Round the elm-tree bole are in tiny leaf,

While the chaffinch sings on the orchard bough

In England — now!


And after April, when May follows,

And the whitethroat builds, and all the swallows!          10

Hark, where my blossom'd pear-tree in the hedge

Leans to the field and scatters on the clover

Blossoms and dewdrops — at the bent spray's edge —

That 's the wise thrush; he sings each song twice over,

Lest you should think he never could recapture          15

The first fine careless rapture!

# 羅伯特・勃朗寧 (1812-1889)*

## 060. 海外鄉思❶

憶英倫，

此時是四月。

故國春眠曉起時，

誰不喜見晨曦？

誰不貪看灌木叢中榆樹碧？

低枝嫩葉棲鳴禽，

振翼果園自在啼，

英倫好時節！


匆匆四月去，五月來時，

流鶯築巢，飛燕成羣呢喃語，

梨花一樹繞籬棘，

斜靠田園，撫弄三葉草，

撒上花瓣和露珠，枝頭一畫眉，

鳥亦多慧心，一唱三疊，

生怕人大意，

不知初試歌喉多愜意！

And though the fields look rough with hoary dew,

All will be gay when noontide wakes anew

The buttercups, the little children's dower

—— Far brighter than this gaudy melon-flower!          20

田野白露帶寒氣，興許不解情，
日正午時，萬物重新添暖意。
金鳳花開，少女好嫁奩，
比那爭俏甜瓜花，更豔更亮麗！

# Henry David Thoreau (1817-1862)

## ON FIELDS O'ER WHICH THE REAPER'S HAND HAS PASS'D

On fields o'er which the reaper's hand has pass'd
Lit by the harvest moon and autumn sun,
My thoughts like stubble floating in the wind
And of such fineness as October airs,

There after harvest could I glean my life                    5
A richer harvest reaping without toil,
And weaving gorgeous fancies at my will
In subtler webs than finest summer haze.

# 亨利・戴維・梭羅 (1817-1862)*

## 061. 麥田上 鵲橋仙

麥田繭手,收鐮去了,

月滿年豐日暮,

點燃思緒穗花揚,

十月裏,微風和煦。


農忙過後,心田拾穗,

輕得幻中豐富。

神思結網順心時,

勝卻那朦朧夏霧。

# SMOKE

Light-winged Smoke, Icarian bird,
Melting thy pinions in thy upward flight,
Lark without song, and messenger of dawn,
Circling above the hamlets as thy nest;
Or else, departing dream, and shadowy form                    5
Of midnight vision, gathering up thy skirts;
By night star-veiling, and by day
Darkening the light and blotting out the sun;
Go thou my incense upward from this hearth,
And ask the gods to pardon this clear flame.                  10

## 062. 煙❶

羽翼輕盈，因風裊裊，一只黑鳥
飛得高，蠟翅點點熔化了。❷
一隻雲雀，不亮歌喉只把黎明報，
別了村舍，仍在窩邊上空繞。
一縷夢魂，影影綽綽，
夜半幻見，撩起裙裾高高飄，
撲向星空塗鴉，
抹黑晨曦日照。
你呀你，寒舍壁爐一柱香，
請登天求神，饒了人間明火高！

# THE MOON

*Time wears her not; she doth his chariot guide;*
*Mortality below her orb is placed.*
　— *Raleigh*


The full-orbed moon with unchanged ray
Mounts up the eastern sky,　　　　　　　　　　　5
Not doomed to these short nights for aye,
But shining steadily.

She does not wane, but my fortune,
Which her rays do not bless,
My wayward path declineth soon,　　　　　　　　10
But she shines not the less.

And if she faintly glimmers here,
And paled is her light,
Yet alway in her proper sphere
She's mistress of the night.　　　　　　　　　　15

# 063. 月亮

時間磨損不了她的玉容；她牽引時間戰車；
寒月下，屍骨層層堆砌。
　　——羅利❶


流光不變，一輪滿月
東昇上天闕，
並非命薄如短夜，
她那明輝常在，多皎潔。


月正圓時我虧缺，
命中難得清光惜，
任性野徑，窮年日日疾行，
她卻亮如昨夜。


儘管偶爾現幽光，
臉色一時慘白，
她卻運行有常，
夜夫人，陪她夫君永夜。

# Walt Whitman (1819-1892)

## A CLEAR MIDNIGHT

This is thy hour O Soul, thy free flight into the wordless,

Away from books, away from art, the day erased, the lesson done,

Thee fully forth emerging, silent, gazing, pondering the themes thou

    lovest best.

Night, sleep, death and the stars.                5

# 瓦爾特·惠特曼 (1819-1892)*
## 064. 明朗的子夜❶

魂兮魂兮，此刻乃君之良辰，

自由飛入無言處，遠離書本，遠離藝術，

白日勾銷，功課完畢，真體內充，寂然外浮，

　　凝視，深思君所青睞之主題。

夜入睡，星沉寂。

# Ernest Jones (1819-1869)

## PRISON BARS

Ye scowling prison bars
That compass me about,
I'll forge ye into armour
To face the world without.

Bold Aspiration's furnace                                      5
Shall fuse ye with its heat,
And stern Resolve shall fashion
With steady iron beat.

Experience' solid anvil
The burning mass shall hold;                                   10
And Patience' bony fingers
Each groove exactly mould.

Then with my modern armour
Above my ancient scars,
I'll march upon my foemen                                      15
And strike with prison bars.

# 艾內斯特・鐘斯 (1819-1869)*

## 065. 鐵窗吟❶

你這鐵窗欄杆
怒目相向把我圍困，
我要把你鍛成頭盔
直面外界的崢嶸。

我這雄心的熔爐
升騰的烈焰將把你銷鎔，
堅定的意志
將以穩健的錘擊造型。

經驗的穩固鐵鉆
承受鐵塊的燃燒。
堅忍的瘦削手恉
精確地澆鑄彈道。

身披現代鎧甲，
掩護古老的傷痕，
我將步步進逼，
揮舞鐵條奇襲敵軍。

# Matthew Arnold (1822-1888)

## DOVER BEACH

The sea is calm to-night.

The tide is full, the moon lies fair

Upon the straits; on the French coast the light

Gleams and is gone; the cliffs of England stand;

Glimmering and vast, out in the tranquil bay.                    5

Come to the window, sweet is the night air!


Only, from the long line of spray

Where the sea meets the moon-blanch'd land,

Listen! you hear the grating roar

Of pebbles which the waves draw back, and fling,        10

At their return, up the high strand,

Begin, and cease, and then again begin,

With tremulous cadence slow, and bring

The eternal note of sadness in.


Sophocles long ago

# 麥修‧阿諾德 (1822-1888)*

## o66. 多佛海灘❶

今宵大海平靜。

潮漲水滿，中天皓月

徘徊於峽口之上；彼岸燈塔

顯隱於法蘭西海域❷；英格蘭危崖壁立；

光迷離，影森森，港灣無語相對。❸

請臨窗晚眺，夜氣馥郁！


看！海岸線上白浪初起，

海空天地交匯處，遍染月色如乳。

聽！聽那洪濤沖擊高灘卷卵石，

挾回浪心又重擲，

滿地碎石，碰碰磕磕砰然吼，❹

一次又一次，隨波起伏，

顫巍巍揚抑抑，萬古悲吟

徐徐傳來入靈府。


追憶當年，索福克勒斯

Heard it on the Aegean, and it brought 15
Into his mind the turbid ebb and flow
Of human misery; we
Find also in the sound a thought,
Hearing it by this distant northern sea.

The Sea of Faith 20
Was once, too, at the full, and round earth's shore
Lay like the folds of a bright girdle furl'd.
But now I only hear
Its melancholy, long, withdrawing roar,
Retreating, to the breath 25
Of the night-wind, down the vast edges drear
And naked shingles of the world.

Ah, love, let us be true
To one another! for the world, which seems
To lie before us like a land of dreams, 30
So various, so beautiful, so new,
Hath really neither joy, nor love, nor light,
Nor certitude, nor peace, nor help for pain;
And we are here as on a darkling plain
Swept with confused alarms of struggle and flight, 35
Where ignorant armies clash by night.

愛琴島上聽海，夜挽黃流灌悲劇，

落潮混濁，

滿腹人間苦楚；❺

今人愁緒遙牽古人幽思，

偏遠北海，依舊秋聲淒切。


信仰之海

也曾漲潮，水漫大地四野，

如亮麗衣裙卷舒折疊。❻

此刻但聞

濤聲悲鳴悠長，如人寰號哭，

散入夜空隨風飄去，

消弭於無涯幽暗天際，

混跡於紅塵裸體砂石。


喚聲心上人，願你我

真誠相對！眼前濁世

恰似那夢中幻境，

看來浮華多彩夜夜新，

卻並無歡娛真情，無光無色，

無信無和諧，無解苦良劑。

你我在世，好比佇立黑暗荒原，

烽煙因風亂，疏散警號催，

沙場黑夜無明軍旅鏖戰急！❼

# REQUIESCAT

Strew on her roses, roses,
   And never a spray of yew!
In quiet she reposes;
   Ah, would that I did too!

Her mirth the world required;           5
   She bathed it in smiles of glee.
But her heart was tired, tired,
   And now they let her be.

Her life was turning, turning,
   In mazes of heat and sound.        10
But for peace her soul was yearning,
   And now peace laps her round.

Her cabin'd, ample spirit,
   It flutter'd and fail'd for breath.
To-night it doth inherit          15
   The vasty hall of death.

# 067. 安魂曲❶

送她一程，撒些兒薔薇薔薇，
千萬別撒勁松枝！❷
芳魂歸去，但求芳心安睡：
他年我心終相隨！

世界求歡，她報以微笑微笑；
滋潤了紅塵旱苗。
芳容憔悴，芳心也倦了倦了，
此刻已無人驚擾。

畢其一生，迷失於輪迴輪迴，
間以興奮與喧囂。
和平生活，是她內心熱望，
和平已將她擁抱。

鳥魂富麗，束縛於樊籬樊籬，
嬌喘微微難呼吸。
承襲家風，今宵她已安息，
安息於死亡廣廈裏。

# PHILOMELA

Hark! ah, the nightingale !
The tawny-throated!
Hark, from that moonlit cedar what a burst!
What triumph! hark! — what pain!

O wanderer from a Grecian shore,                    5
Still, after many years, in distant lands,
Still nourishing in thy bewilder'd brain
That wild, unquench'd, deep-sunken, old-world pain —

Say, will it never heal?
And can this fragrant lawn                           10
With its cool trees, and night,
And the sweet, tranquil Thames,
And moonshine, and the dew,
To thy rack'd heart and brain
Afford no balm?                                     15

## o68. 菲洛美拉①

聽！啊，夜鶯！
黃褐色的咽喉！
聽！突然一聲血啼，來自月下雪松枝頭！
聽！怎樣的勝利！怎樣的哀愁！

啊，你這來自希臘海岸的遊魂，
千百年後，仍然在遠方漂流，
仍然以你勾魂的智慧澆灌
荒野上撲不滅陷得深的舊世界的哀愁——

請問，那創傷永遠不能癒合嗎？
這片馨香的草地
能否以涼爽的樹蔭、良宵、
芳草、寧靜的泰晤士碧流、
月色和露珠當作一塊香膏
為你劇痛的心靈和神智
敷貼傷口？

Dost thou to-night behold,

Here, through the moonlight on this English grass,

The unfriendly palace in the Thracian wild?

Dost thou again peruse

With hot cheeks and sear'd eyes                                        20

The too clear web, and thy dumb Sister's shame?

Dost thou once more assay

Thy flight, and feel come over thee,

Poor fugitive, the feathery change

Once more, and once more seem to make resound        25

With love and hate, triumph and agony,

Lone Daulis, and the high Cephissian vale?

Listen, Eugenia —

How thick the bursts come crowding through the leaves!

Again — thou hearest?                                                     30

Eternal Passion!

Eternal Pain!

今宵此地，你

透過朗照英格蘭草坪的流光

同樣看到了色雷斯荒原❷上敵意的宮殿？

你是否再一次

以灼熱的臉頰和雙眼審讀

那明麗的錦繡，回眸你喑啞的姊姊如何蒙羞？

你是否再一次試圖

飛離，體驗渾身的感受？

可憐的流亡者，你添翼變形後，

也要叫苦不迭，滿懷

愛和恨，凱旋和劇痛，為的是讓普世知曉

那孤絕的道里斯，險峻的塞菲秀河谷山溝❸？

聽，丁香花──

透過枝枝葉葉密集怒放！

再一次 ──你聽見！

千秋激憤

萬古愁！

# Dante Gabriel Rossetti (1828-1882)

## SUDDEN LIGHT

I have been here before,
　But when or how I cannot tell:
I know the grass beyond the door,
　The sweet keen smell,
The sighing sound, the lights around the shore.　　5

You have been mine before, —
　How long ago I may not know:
But just when at that swallow's soar
　Your neck turned so,
Some veil did fall, — I knew it all of yore.　　10

Then, now, — perchance again! ...
　O round mine eyes your tresses shake!
Shall we not lie as we have lain
　Thus for Love's sake,
And sleep, and wake, yet never break the chain?　　15

# 但丁·加百列·羅塞蒂 (1828-1882)*

## 069. 閃光❶

舊地望中猶記，
　　忘卻何時何故，
但知門外芬芳，
　　濃郁鋒利刺鼻，
海歎息，燈影繞岸迷離。

君曾光顧我處，
　　日久年月失憶，
恰好燕子飛來，
　　君顧盼時大意，
面紗落，舊事我全知悉。

眼前風光如昔，
　　君之長髮飄逸，
不再就地同臥，
　　為了愛之目的？
睡復醒，循環鏈條永固？

# Venus Verticordia

She hath the apple in her hand for thee,
Yet almost in her heart would hold it back;
She muses, with her eyes upon the track
Of that which in thy spirit they can see.
Haply, 'Behold, he is at peace,' saith she;          5
'Alas! the apple for his lips, — the dart
That follows its brief sweetness to his heart, —
The wandering of his feet perpetually!'

A little space her glance is still and coy,
But if she give the fruit that works her spell,     10
Those eyes shall flame as for her Phrygian boy.
Then shall her bird's strained throat the woe foretell,
And her far seas moan as a single shell,
And through her dark grove strike the light of Troy.

## 070. 維納斯・心靈的轉化者❶

她為你手捧蘋果，
卻差點把它收回她心裏；
她在冥想，雙眼凝視
你靈魂中可以窺見的痕跡。
也許，「看，他不分心」，她說，
「呀！湊近他嘴唇的蘋果——瞄準
他心口的瞬間甜蜜的箭矢，——
他沒有盡頭的流浪的腳步！」


她瞥見的小塊地盤靜謐而偏遠，
可是，假如她惠贈魔力釀成的禁果，
那些眼睛會像佛里吉亞少年❷一樣著火。
然後她背後敵意的鳥喉將預告人寰悲愴，
她的遠海將呻吟，像一枚孤獨的貝殼，
穿越她的黑色森林襲擊特洛伊之光。

# Christina Georgina Rossetti (1830-1894)

## A CHILL

What can lambkins do
All the keen night through?
Nestle by their woolly mother
The careful ewe.

What can nestlings do
In the nightly dew?
Sleep beneath their mother's wing
Till day breaks anew.

If in a field or tree
There might only be
Such a warm soft sleeping-place
Found for me!

# 克莉絲蒂娜・喬治娜・羅塞蒂 (1830-1894)*

## 071. 寒意吟 八六子❶

夜如刀，小羊羔嫩，

何堪骨冷通宵？

見幼崽依偎母腹，

母羊鋪蓋絨衣，悉心護調。

隻隻雛雀心焦，怎耐夜來寒露？

鋪開母鳥絨毛，

羽翼下，安然睡他一覺，

避開風口，盼來晨照。

須知野外難尋大樹，

人心同盼良宵，

落荒郊，

何處得一暖巢？！

# Emily Dickinson (1830-1886)

## HOPE

'Hope' is the thing with feathers —

That perches in the soul —

And sings the tune without the words —

And never stops — at all —


And sweetest — in the Gale — is heard —                    5

And sore must be the storm —

That could abash the little Bird

That kept so many warm —


I've heard it in the chillest land —

And on the strangest Sea —                                 10

Yet, never, in Extremity,

It asked a crumb — of Me.

# 艾密莉・狄金森 (1830-1886)*

## 072. 希望 漁歌子三首

靈羽牽魂領意飛，

無詞歌闋每相隨，

長守望，不離枝，

多情最是勁風時。


急雨催人節節愁，

鳥兒難耐劍霜秋，

情切切，恨悠悠，

絲絲暖意上心頭。


地老荒原寂寞身，

天涯滄海陌生人，

危境裏，妙歌聞，

無求粒米作盤飧。

# THE BATTLEFIELD

They dropped like flakes, they dropped like stars,
Like petals from a rose,
When suddenly across the June
A wind with fingers goes.

They perished in the seamless grass, —
No eye could find the place;
But God on his repealless list
Can summon every face.

## 073. **戰場** 搗練子二首

飄似雪，墜如星，
豔麗玫紅化落英。
六月陣風揮手指，
忽然穿越折哀兵。

花密密，草茵茵，
望眼無處見離魂。
上帝展開花卉錄，
逐一傳喚入天門。

# I Taste A liquor Never Brewed

I taste a liquor never brewed —
From Tankards scooped in Pearl —
Not all the vats upon the Rhine
Yield such an Alcohol!

Inebriate of air — am I —                                   5
And Debauchee of dew —
Reeling — through endless summer days —
From inns of molten Blue —

When 'Landlords' turn the drunken Bee
Out of the Foxglove's door —                                10
When Butterflies — renounce their 'drams' —
I shall but drink the more!

Till Seraphs swing their snowy Hats —
And Saints — to windows run —
To see the little Tippler                                   15
Leaning against the — sun!

# 074. 細品味，此酒無人釀

細品味，此酒無人釀，
珍珠掏空作酒盅，
流出涓涓瓊漿。
萊茵河上酒桶多
難得此種醇香！

我之所醉在空氣，
樂與露水放蕩，
踉踉蹌蹌，夏日不落，
藍天銷融作酒館。

直到房東攆醉蜂
出了酒壺花❶門檻，
直到蝴蝶棄酒盅，
我依舊豪飲海量！

直到天使手搖雪帽❷叫停，
直到聖徒破窗而入
見識我這小酒鬼，
我依舊斜靠太陽！

# A Long, Long Sleep, A Famous Sleep

A long — long Sleep — A famous — Sleep —
That makes no show for Morn —
By Strech of Limb — or stir of Lid —
An independent One —

Was ever idleness like This?                                    5
Within a Bank of Stone
To bask the Centuries away —
Nor once look up — for Noon?

# 075. 快哉長夜濃睡

快哉長夜濃睡，
不見黎明催，
四肢不伸被不移❶——
床頭人影孤。

試問懶散之狀
可曾與此相似？——
石屋避光千百年，
從不見日午？

# Algernon Charles Swinburne (1837-1909)

## A MATCH

If love were what the rose is,
And I were like the leaf,
Our lives would grow together
In sad or singing weather,
Blown fields or flowerful closes                    *5*
Green pleasure or gray grief ;
If love were what the rose is,
And I were like the leaf.

If I were what the words are,
And love were like the tune,                         *10*
With double sound and single
Delight our lips would mingle,
With kisses glad as birds are
That get sweet rain at noon ;
If I were what the words are,                        *15*
And love were like the tune.

# 阿爾加儂·查理斯·斯溫伯恩 (1837-1909)*

## 076. 伉儷❶

若把愛情比玫瑰，
我是一片葉青翠，
你我人生同滋長，
無論春歌秋聲悲。
無論野風花徑裏，
灰色添愁綠愜意。
若把愛情比玫瑰，
我是一片葉青翠。

若把我來比歌詞，
愛情是首好歌曲，
對唱獨唱皆歡欣，
嘴唇相對融為一，
親吻好比鳥啼春，
日正午時得喜雨。
若把我來比歌詞，
愛情是首好歌曲。

If you were life, my darling,

And I your love were death,

We 'd shine and snow together

Ere March made sweet the weather                     *20*

With daffodil and starling

And hours of fruitful breath ;

If you were life, my darling,

And I your love were death.


If you were thrall to sorrow,                        *25*

And I were page to joy,

We 'd play for lives and seasons

With loving looks and treasons

And tears of night and morrow

And laughs of maid and boy ;                         *30*

If you were thrall to sorrow,

And I were page to joy.


If you were April's lady,

And I were lord in May,

We 'd throw with leaves for hours                    *35*

And draw for days with flowers,

假如甜心是生命，
我既是愛又是死，
同在陽光冰雪裏，
直到三月好天氣，
水仙花開八哥啼，
芬芳碩果累累時。
假若甜心是生命，
我既是愛又是死。

假如你被愁緒縛，
歡心派我做奴僕，
不管四季朝復暮，
我將表演悲喜劇，
或作歡顏或背叛，
亦男亦女笑或哭。
假如你被愁緒縛，
歡心派我做奴僕。

假如你是四月婦，
我做五月好丈夫，
伉儷時拋翠綠葉，
采來鮮花作畫圖，

Till day like night were shady
And night were bright like day ;
If you were April's lady,
And I were lord in May.                              40

If you were queen of pleasure,
And I were king of pain,
We 'd hunt down love together,
Pluck out his flying-feather,
And teach his feet a measure,                        45
And find his mouth a rein ;
If you were queen of pleasure,
And I were king of pain.

直到日落夜沉沉，
夜亦光明如日出。
假如你是四月婦，
我做五月好丈夫。

假如你是歡喜后，
我就是個痛苦主，
國王王后同出獵，
追上愛情大亡逋，
拔其羽毛銬住腳，
嘴套韁繩好駕馭。
假如你是歡喜后，
我就是個痛苦主。

# Emma Lazarus (1849-1887 )

## The New Colossus

Not like the brazen giant of Greek fame,

With conquering limbs astride from land to land;

Here at our sea-washed, sunset gates shall stand

A mighty woman with a torch, whose flame

Is the imprisoned lightning, and her name                 5

Mother of Exiles. From her beacon-hand

Glows world-wide welcome; her mild eyes command

The air-bridged harbor that twin cities frame.

'Keep, ancient lands, your storied pomp!' cries she

With silent lips. 'Give me your tired, your poor,         10

Your huddled masses yearning to breathe free,

The wretched refuse of your teeming shore.

Send these, the homeless, tempest-tost to me,

I lift my lamp beside the golden door!'

# 埃瑪·拉扎勒斯 (1849-1887)*

## 077. 自由女神塑像❶

不像希臘顯赫魯莽無恥的青銅巨人

以雄霸的雙腿橫跨兩片土地，❷

在這浪湧霞飛的大門，將屹立一位

英姿女郎，她高擎的熊熊火炬

是凝固的閃電，她的名字

是流亡者之母，伸開燈塔般的巨臂

熱忱接引八方來客，她柔和的目光

俯瞰雲天下毗連雙城的海港。❸

「古老之鄉，保持你歷史的壯觀！」

她靜穆的雙唇呼喊：「把你的疲憊、貧困，

把廣大民眾對自由呼吸的嚮往，

把豐饒海岸給不幸難民的庇護，

把風雨顛簸中失落的家園，統統交給我吧：

我高擎明燈守望在黃金門廊！」

# Alfred Edward Housman (1859-1936)

## BRING, IN THIS TIMELESS GRAVE TO THROW

Bring, in this timeless grave to throw,

No cypress, sombre on the snow;

Snap not from the bitter yew

His leaves that live December through;

Break no rosemary, bright with rime       5

And sparkling to the cruel clime;

Nor plod the winter land to look

For willows in the icy brook

To cast them leafless round him: bring

No spray that ever buds in spring.       10


But if the Christmas field has kept

Awns the last gleaner overstept,

Or shrivelled flax, whose flower is blue

A single season, never two;

Or if one haulm whose year is o'er       15

Shivers on the upland frore,

# 阿爾福雷德·愛德華·豪斯曼 (1859-1936)*
## o78. 柏枝壓霜雪❶

柏枝壓霜雪，勸君慎勿折，
拋入墓穴中，幽冥永相隔❷；
水松味苦辛❸，勸君慎勿折，
松葉耐風雨，堪度十二月；
莫采迷迭香❹，霜枝性高潔，
寒冬嚴相逼，依舊閃光澤；
莫涉冰溪水，歲暮氣凜冽，
折來殘柳枝❺，安能繞身側；
願以歲寒心，珍惜歲寒枝，
越冬發新芽，蓓蕾添春色。

倘若農舍女，拾穗到田家，
時已過聖誕，枯穗地下撒；
抑或見胡麻，夏季開青花，
一旦枯乾後，不再發新葩；
抑或見豆莢，委棄在山崖；
高地霜寒重，殘梗結冰花，

— Oh, bring from hill and stream and plain

Whatever will not flower again,

To give him comfort: he and those

Shall bide eternal bedfellows                              20

Where low upon the couch he lies

Whence he never shall arise.

或在山之隈，或在水之涯，
或無重開日，一一采回家，
願以零落意，撫慰零落花：
落花通人性，伴君度年華。
人死歸塵土，托體同山窪，
落花共君眠，安息黃泉下。

# George Santayana (1863-1952)

# To W. P.

*I*

Calm was the sea to which your course you kept,

Oh, how much calmer than all southern seas!

Many your nameless mates, whom the keen breeze

Wafted from mothers that of old have wept.

All souls of children taken as they slept                    5

Are your companions, partners of your ease,

And the green souls of all these autumn trees

Are with you through the silent spaces swept.

Your virgin body gave its gentle breath

Untainted to the gods. Why should we grieve,              10

But that we merit not your holy death?

We shall not loiter long, your friends and I;

Living you made it goodlier to live,

Dead you will make it easier to die.

# 喬治・桑塔耶納 (1863-1952)*

## 079. 給 W.P.❶

一.

海浪平息，諸君相伴出海去，

不知那海域比南海❷平靜幾許！

卻難料微風陡然疾行，把多少無名伙伴

從年邁慈母淚眼裏一一奪去。

赤子靈魂熟睡時，遭此劫數，

一個個快樂朋友天界團聚，

一株株嘉樹綠魂飄如浮萍，

海空靜觀，悄然無語。

童真遺體斷了最後一口清氣，

無染面對神明。何故再傷悲？

豈不知其死乃聖潔之死？

死者安息，生者不會久徘徊，

借君一生，生活煥然添美好，

借君一死，死亡從此更容易。

*II*

With you a part of me hath passed away;                    15

For in the peopled forest of my mind

A tree made leafless by this wintry wind

Shall never don again its green array.

Chapel and fireside, country road and bay,

Have something of their friendliness resigned;            20

Another, if I would, I could not find,

And I am grown much older in a day.

But yet I treasure in my memory

Your gift of charity, your mellow ease,

And the dear honour of your amity;                        25

For these once mine, my life is rich with these.

And I scarce know which part may greater be, —

What I keep of you, or you rob of me.


*III*

Your bark lies anchored in the peaceful bight

Until a kinder wind unfurl her sail;                      30

Your docile spirit, wingèd by this gale,

Hath at the dawning fled into the light.

And I half know why heaven deemed it right

Your youth, and this my joy in youth, should fail;

二.

我心破碎，碎片帶血隨君飛，

只因我意林中友人如樹，

君茂盛時不敵冬日風急，

葉飄零，再難重披綠衣。

教堂爐邊，山路水隈，

當年親昵已辭退，

舊情新景，不知何處覓，

晚來對鏡，秋霜一日染青絲。

望中猶記心田裏，

勞君惠贈輕盈童心和善意，

親切友愛即榮譽，

厚禮添我人生富裕。

我珍藏君之所饋，

君擄去我心碎片，孰多孰少難知。


三.

君已拋錨繫心舟，靜待港灣裏，

直到和風催帆再度出海去，

大風為君插翅，護送靈魂

乘著黎明翱翔，融入碧天清輝。

無情卻有情？天意半解半疑。

君之韶華伴我歡娛，枯萎有日，

God hath them still, for ever they avail,                    35
Eternity hath borrowed that delight.
For long ago I taught my thoughts to run
Where all the great things live that lived of yore,
And in eternal quiet float and soar;
There all my loves are gathered into one,                    40
Where change is not, nor parting any more,
Nor revolution of the moon and sun.


## IV

In my deep heart these chimes would still have rung
To toll your passing, had you not been dead;
For time a sadder mask than death may spread             45
Over the face that ever should be young.
The bough that falls with all its trophies hung
Falls not too soon, but lays its flower-crowned head
Most royal in the dust, with no leaf shed
Unhallowed or unchiselled or unsung.                         50
And though the after world will never hear
The happy name of one so gently true,
Nor chronicles write large this fatal year,
Yet we who loved you, though we be but few,
Keep you in whatsoe'er is good, and rear                     55
In our weak virtues monuments to you.

上帝令其安息，賜予恆久恩惠，
當年樂景，永生已借去。
但憶舊時我教神思起飛，
飛向今昔鴻圖棲身之地，
生命永恆不熄，靜靜飄忽高飛，
瞥見彼岸我所愛，萬千合為一，
不見生變易，不再恨別離，
不見日出日落月盈虧。


四.

心底鐘聲和諧，長鳴不已，
為君報喪，即使嘉樹尚未死去。
因為時間如面具，遮蓋當年青春容顏，
興許比死亡面具更令人悲戚。
且看那枝條，掛滿碩果易脫落，
倘若枝頭只有花冠，便難摧折。
幾多貴冑化塵埃，恰如枯樹無片葉，
身後汙濁，無人銘記無人獻詩。
相比之下，君乃真誠赤子，
儘管後世難知君之嘉名，
史筆不會大書災年事故，
卻有稀少知音，眷戀摯友生前行跡，
無論何時長相憶。吾輩德行不厚，
願以內美為君樹立紀念碑。

# Rudyard Kipling (1865-1936)

## THE WHITE MAN'S BURDEN

Take up the White Man's burden —
Send forth the best ye breed —
Go, bind your sons to exile
To serve your captives' need;
To wait in heavy harness                                    5
On fluttered folk and wild —
Your new-caught sullen peoples,
Half devil and half child.


Take up the White Man's burden —
In patience to abide,                                       10
To veil the threat of terror
And check the show of pride;
By open speech and simple,
An hundred times made plain,
To seek another's profit                                    15
And work another's gain.

# 魯德亞德・吉卜林 (1865-1936)*
## 080. 白人的負擔❶

肩負白人的負擔——

派遣你們養育的菁英——

走吧，把你們的孩子綁在流亡中，

為你們的俘虜的需要效命；

在蠢蠢欲動的野性的人們身上

披上沉重的盔甲——

你們新捕獲的鬱悶的人民

半是魔鬼半是孩子。❷


肩負白人的負擔——

忍耐地遵守，

遮蓋恐懼的威脅

抑制驕傲的表情；

通過公開演說和蠢事

一千次創造平原

去尋找他人的福祉，

去工作讓他人贏利。

Take up the White Man's burden —

The savage wars of peace —

Fill full the mouth of Famine,

And bid the sickness cease;                                        20

And when your goal is nearest

The end for others sought,

Watch Sloth and heathen Folly

Bring all your hope to nought.


Take up the White Man's burden —                                   25

No tawdry rule of kings,

But toil of serf and sweeper —

The tale of common things.

The ports ye shall not enter,

The roads ye shall not tread,                                      30

Go make them with your living,

And mark them with your dead!


Take up the White Man's burden —

And reap his old reward:

The blame of those ye better,                                      35

The hate of those ye guard —

肩負白人的負擔——

和平的野蠻戰爭——

填滿饑餓的嘴巴

讓疾病銷聲匿跡；

當你們的目的最接近

別人的終點也就找到，

看看異教徒的懶惰和愚昧

把你們的一切希望化為零。


肩負白人的負擔——

不要王侯俗麗的原則

只要農奴和清道夫的辛勤——❸

尋常事物的故事。

那些港口你們將進不去，

那些道路你們將不能踏足，❹

用你們的生活方式來打造它們，

用你們的死亡給它們打上印記！


肩負白人的負擔——

收穫那舊時的獎賞：

你們所改進的那些人的譴責，

你們所保護的那些人的憎恨——

The cry of hosts ye humour

(Ah, slowly!) toward the light: —

"Why brought ye us from bondage,

Our loved Egyptian night?"                                    40


Take up the White Man's burden —

Ye dare not stoop to less —

Nor call too loud on freedom

To cloak your weariness.

By all ye cry or whisper,                                          45

By all ye leave or do,

The silent sullen peoples

Shall weigh your God and you.


Take up the White Man's burden —

Have done with childish days —                               50

The lightly proffered laurel,

The easy, ungrudged praise.

Comes now, to search your manhood

Through all the thankless years,

Cold-edged with dear-bought wisdom,                       55

The judgment of your peers!

你們所調理的那些人的哭號

（啊，慢！）轉向光明：——

「你為什麼把我們從束縛中

從我們喜歡的埃及之夜帶領出來？」❺


肩負白人的負擔——

你既不敢稍微彎一下腰——

也不敢高聲呼喊自由

來掩飾你們的勞倦；

憑你們所有的喊叫或耳語，

憑你們所有的告別或行動，

那些沉默的鬱悶的人們

將把你們的神與你們自己估量。


肩負白人的負擔——

在幼稚的日子裏的所作所為——

那輕盈的令人青睞的月桂，

那舒心的令人滿意的讚賞。

來吧，去搜尋你們的男子漢氣概，

經由所有那些費力不討好的歲月，

寒光閃閃的代價高昂的智慧的刀刃，

接受你們同輩人的評判！

# BLUE ROSES

Roses red and roses white
Plucked I for my love's delight.
She would none of all my posies —
Bade me gather her blue roses.

Half the world I wandered through,                          5
Seeking where such flowers grew.
Half the world unto my quest
Answered me with laugh and jest.

Home I came at wintertide,
But my silly love had died,                                10
Seeking with her latest breath
Roses from the arms of Death.

It may be beyond the grave
She shall find what she would have.
Mine was but an idle quest —                               15
Roses white and red are best!

# 081. 藍玫瑰 ❶

玫瑰紅，玫瑰白，
采呀采，為我情人喜悅。
她不要我一朵花，
只愛藍玫瑰，催我去采擷。

尋找藍玫花鄉，
走遍半個世界，
問遍半個世界，
人人笑我出格。

冬天回到家裏，
情人命薄氣絕。
尋她最後一縷香魂，
懷裏玫瑰已凋謝。

也許在她墳塋那邊，
她能找到彼岸花色。
我的尋找了無意義——
玫紅玫白就是最佳花色！

# William Butler Yeats (1865-1939)

## THE PRIEST OF PAN

If the melancholy music of the spheres

Ever be perplexing to his mortal ears,

He flies unto the mountain

And sitting by some fountain

That in a beam of coolness from a mossy rock                    5

Plunges in a pool all bubbling with its shock,

There he hears in the sound of the water falling

The sweet-tongued oriads to each other calling

Secrets that for years

Have escaped his ears.                                          10

# 威廉・巴特勒・葉慈 (1865-1939)*
## 082. 牧神的祭司❶

假若周遭管絃愁煞人

亂了他浮生之聽

他會插翅入山林

棲身泉邊

但聽蒼苔危巖一股涼意

跌落清潭驚起水花

飛瀑聲中山阿之間若有人❷

舌端吐蜜相與托出

山林祕密，那神韻已多年

逃離他雙耳清聽

# HE TELLS OF THE PERFECT BEAUTY

O cloud-pale eyelids, dream-dimmed eyes,
The poets labouring all their days
To build a perfect beauty in rhyme
Are overthrown by a woman's gaze
And by the unlabouring brood of the skies:          5
And therefore my heart will bow, when dew
Is dropping sleep, until God burn time,
Before the unlabouring stars and you.

# 083. 他講述完美 **❶**


眼臉如雲潔白，雙眸若夢迷離，
詩人苦吟一世，格律堆成完美。
頃刻間，掀翻彩箋詩筆——
輸給美女顧盼著穹天韻。
詩心不禁幾鞠躬，
仰望無念之星共爾汝，
清露點點滴，沉沉入睡，
直到上帝一把火，時間劫後餘灰。

# The Sorrow of Love I

The quarrel of the sparrows in the eaves,

The full round moon and the star-laden sky,

And the loud song of the ever-singing leaves

Had hid away earth's old and weary cry.

And then you came with those red mournful lips,　　　　5

And with you came the whole of the world's tears,

And all the sorrows of her labouring ships,

And all burden of her myriad years.

And now the sparrows warring in the eaves,

The crumbling moon, the white stars in the sky,　　　　10

And the loud chanting of the unquiet leaves,

Are shaken with earth's old and weary cry.

(First Printed Version, 1892)

## o84. 情殤 之一 · 八六子 ❶

雀羣飛，繞檐爭嘴，
星河皓月同輝，
聽草葉高歌永在，
濁塵哀泣稀聞，匿聲片時。

朱唇❷來兮銜悲，
為爾普天流淚，
帆船苦聚愁思，
數百載，肩頭重荷同哭。

此時禾雀，舊年兵戈，
星天低掛蟾宮冷寂，
高吟衰草迷離，
盡含悲，歌搖萬年泫啼。

（1892年初寫本）

# THE SORROW OF LOVE II

The brawling of a sparrow in the eaves,
The brilliant moon and all the milky sky,
And all that famous harmony of leaves,
Had blotted out man's image and his cry.

A girl arose that had red mournful lips            5
And seemed the greatness of the world in tears,
Doomed like Odysseus and the labouring ships
And proud as Priam murdered with his peers;

Arose, and on the instant clamorous eaves,
A climbing moon upon an empty sky,              10
And all that lamentation of the leaves,
Could but compose man's image and his cry.

(Final Printed Version, 1925)

# 085. 情殤 之二·八六子❶

雀單飛，繞檐爭嘴，❷
星河皓月同輝，
願混跡和融草葉，
寄言衝突心圖，搵乾泫啼。

朱唇情劫傷悲，
普世淚泉泓邃，
英雄十載鄉思。奧德賽，風帆命中撕裂。❸
兩強矛舞，獨夫頭斷。❹

重聞屋角翻飛鳥語，
虛空流瀉蟾暉，
草離離，❺
殷勤撫平泫啼。

（1925年重寫本）

# AFTER LONG SILENCE

Speech after long silence; it is right,
All other lovers being estranged or dead,
Unfriendly lamplight hid under its shade,
The curtains drawn upon unfriendly night,
That we descant and yet again descant                    5
Upon the supreme theme of Art and Song :
Bodily decrepitude is wisdom; young
We loved each other and were ignorant.

## 086. 長久緘默過後❶

長久緘默過後，真想盡情傾訴，
昔日情侶皆疏遠，或作生死別，
殘燭搖影冷無情，❷
無情之夜，重重窗簾隔，
來吧，你我細細道來，
只祇把詩畫宏旨共評說：
皮囊衰老即智慧，但憶年輕時
彼此相愛，卻渾然不覺。

# Ernest Dowson (1867-1900)

## IN SPRING

See how the trees and the osiers lithe

Are green bedecked and the woods are blithe,

The meadows have donned their cape of flowers,

The air is soft with the sweet May showers,

And the birds make melody:                                          5

But the spring of the soul, the spring of the soul,

Cometh no more for you or for me.


The lazy hum of the busy bees

Murmureth through the almond trees;

The jonquil flaunteth a gay, blonde head,                           10

The primrose peeps from a mossy bed,

And the violets scent the lane.

But the flowers of the soul, the flowers of the soul,

For you and for me bloom never again.

# 艾內斯特·道森 (1867-1900)*

## o87. 春 玉蝴蝶慢 ❶

望處柳枝垂葉，

滿身染綠，萬樹歡顏，

草地茵茵，花色覆蓋披肩。

氣清列，甘霖五月，

百鳥鬧，旋律清甜。

惜春天，暮春魂斷

你我心田。

貪看，羣蜂採蜜，不知悲苦，

杏樹之間，細語嗡嗡，

壽星❷逗得少年癲。

翠苔地，一花❸領艷，

步小徑，賞紫羅蘭：

惜心間，枯花長謝

你我心田。

# William Henry Davies (1871-1940)

## THE EXAMPLE

Here's an example from
  A Butterfly;
That on a rough, hard rock
  Happy can lie;
Friendless and all alone                5
On this unsweetened stone.

Now let my bed be hard
  No care take I;
I'll make my joy like this
  Small Butterfly;                 10
Whose happy heart has power
To make a stone a flower.

# 威廉・亨利・戴維斯 (1871-1940)*

## o88. 風範 如夢令二首

彩蝶飄然飛落，
　　風範啟人思索；
棲息壁巖間，
　　不失向來歡樂；
孤覺，孤覺，
任爾石間污濁。

堅硬眠床如鐵，
　　我已無心關切；
孤苦化甘飴，
　　效此袖珍蝴蝶；
欣悅，欣悅，
頑石吐芳萌蘗。

# Ralph Hodgson (1871-1962)

## THE HAMMERS

Noise of hammers once I heard,

Many hammers, busy hammers,

Beating, shaping, night and day,

Shaping, beating dust and clay

To a palace; saw it reared;                                          5

Saw the hammers laid away.


And I listened, and I heard

Hammers beating, night and day

In the palace newly reared,

Beating it to dust and clay:                                        10

Other hammers, muffled hammers,

Silent hammers of decay.

# 拉爾夫・霍奇森 (1871-1962)*

## o89. 鐵錘❶

曾聞忙碌鐵錘聲，
鐵錘多多不勝數，
錘擊造型夜復日，
造型錘擊塵與土。
為建宮殿高高揚，
大廈落成撤閑處。

我曾聽，我曾聞，
鐵錘錘擊夜復日。
新造宮殿何輝煌，
錘擊催它歸塵土：
此錘別樣悄悄錘，
堪使宮墻化朽腐。

# Robert Frost (1874-1963)

## TREE AT MY WINDOW

Tree at my window, window tree,
My sash is lowered when night comes on;
But let there never be curtain drawn
Between you and me.

Vague dream-head lifted out of the ground,     5
And thing next most diffuse to cloud,
Not all your light tongues talking aloud
Could be profound.

But tree, I have seen you taken and tossed,
And if you have seen me when I slept,     10
You have seen me when I was taken and swept
And all but lost.

That day she put our heads together,
Fate had her imagination about her,
Your head so much concerned with outer,     15
Mine with inner, weather.

# 羅伯特・弗羅斯特 (1874-1963)*

## 090. 窗前一顆樹

窗前一顆樹,窗扉樹,
夜幕低垂時,我拉下窗扉。
可是呵,你我兩心相知,
千萬別以簾幕分隔。

夢的腦袋依稀從地上抬起,
不知何物紛紛飄向雲霄,
你高聲喧嘩的亮麗舌頭,
並不都能深邃到哪裏。

可是樹,我看見你忐忑搖曳。
假如我睡著時你見到我,
你就見到我忐忑飛掠,
而那一切都已失落。

那天她把你我的頭頂弄到一起,
命運的想像真是奇異,
樹梢牽掛外面的天氣,
人心牽掛內在的晴雨。

# Edward Thomas (1878-1917)

## JULY

Naught moves but clouds, and in the glassy lake

Their doubles and the shadow of my boat.

The boat itself stirs only when I break

This drowse of heat and solitude afloat

To prove if what I see be bird or mote,                    5

Or learn if yet the shore woods be awake.


Long hours since dawn grew, — spread, — and passed on high

And deep below, — I have watched the cool reeds hung

Over images more cool in imaged sky:

Nothing there was worth thinking of so long;              10

All that the ring-doves say, far leaves among,

Brims my mind with content thus still to lie.

# 愛德華・托瑪斯 (1878-1917)*

## 091. 七月 水調歌頭

萬籟靜無念，但見白雲飄，平湖如鏡，

舟影輕蕩共雲搖。

劃破沉沉炎暑，

驅散絲絲寂寞，極目入林梢：

歸鳥或纖芥，

睡意幾時消？

曉天白，明霞染，碧空高，

撒落湖畔，葦間涼氣聚難銷，

映入悠悠雲水，

忘卻紛紛物我，沙漏滴悄悄，

臥聽斑鳩語，

詩意滿青霄。

# Cock-Crow

Out of the wood of thoughts that grows by night

To be cut down by the sharp axe of light, —

Out of the night, two cocks together crow,

Cleaving the darkness with a silver blow:

And bright before my eyes twin trumpeters stand,         5

Heralds of splendour, one at either hand,

Each facing each as in a coat of arms: —

The milkers lace their boots up at the farms.

## 092. 雞鳴 七律

夜孵思想森林旺，
光若斧頭斷樹椿，
雙唱金雞報曉色，
一吹銀響驅幽惶：
晨曦放眼角笳引，
信使增榮手臂揚，
擠奶鄉夫相對看，
軍靴戎服出農莊。

# THAW

Over the land half freckled with snow half-thawed
The speculating rooks at their nests cawed,
And saw from elm-tops, delicate as a flower of grass,
What we below could not see, Winter pass.

# 093. **解凍** 七絕 ❶

雪原半凝半化時，
俯瞰寒鴉啼高枝，
樹下木然人不覺，
殘冬花謝鳥先知。

# In Memoriam

The flowers left thick at nightfall in the wood
This Eastertide call into mind the men,
Now far from home, who, with their sweethearts, should
Have gathered them and will do never again.

## 094. 憶舊 七絕[1]

花叢林晚影深深，
復活節牽戰士心，
回望家園情侶遠，
芳菲同擷再難尋。

# Wallace Stevens (1879-1955)

## VALLEY CANDLE

My candle burned alone in an immense valley.

Beams of the huge night converged upon it,

Until the wind blew.

The beams of the huge night

Converged upon its image,                                    5

Until the wind blew.

# 華萊士・史蒂文斯 (1879-1955)*

## 095. 山谷燃燭❶

我身如燃燭，獨立浩浩山谷。
恢恢黑夜光束束，四面相逢身上聚，
直到風拂拂。
恢恢黑夜光束束，
凝聚燭心意象裏，
直到風拂拂。

# William Carlos Williams (1883-1963)

## THE BIRDS

The world begins again!
Not wholly insufflated
the blackbirds in the rain
upon the dead topbranches
of the living tree,                                                5
stuck fast to the low clouds,
notate the dawn.
Their shrill cries sound
announcing appetite
and drop among the bending roses                                 10
and the dripping grass.

# 威廉·卡洛斯·威廉斯 (1883-1963)*
## 096. 鶇鳥

世界又開始了！

沒有完全緩過氣來

那株活樹

樹梢垂死的枝條上

雨中的幾只黑鶇

迅疾沖向低雲

給破曉打個記號

它們昭示欲望的

尖亮的啼聲

滴落在彎枝的薔薇間

滴落在流翠的草葉上

# Sarah Teasdale (1884-1933)

## Epitaph

Serene descent, as a red leaf's descending
When there is neither wind nor noise of rain,
But only autumn air and the unending
Drawing of all things to the earth again.

So be it, let the snow fall deep and cover                    5
All that was drunken once with light and air.
The earth will not regret her tireless lover,
Nor he awake to know she does not care.

# 薩拉‧悌絲黛爾 (1884-1933)*
## 097. 墓志銘❶

悄然墜地，如一片紅葉飄零，
不見送客風，不聞喧嘩雨，
唯有蕭瑟秋氣，一陣陣，
拖曳萬物重掃茫茫大地。

秋無情，且讓冬雪深深落地，
覆蓋普天下一度迷醉光艷之人。
他愛大地如情侶，她卻不解人意，
他亦不復醒，焉知她如此薄情！

# Ezra Pound (1885-1972)

## IONE, DEAD THE LONG YEAR

Empty are the way,

Empty are the ways of this land

And the flowers

Bend over with heavy heads.

They bend in vain.                                              5

Empty are the ways of this land

Where Ione

Walked once, and now does not walk

But seems like a person just gone.

# 伊茲拉·龐德 (1885-1972)*
## o98. 伊昂妮離世的漫長一年❶

條條小徑，

空空蕩蕩寂寂。

簇簇野花，

低眉垂首，

徒然掩泣。

但憶當年附素足，

而今足音何處覓？

恰似離人方才去，

無聲息。

# Autumnus
## To Dowson — Antistave

Lo that the wood standeth drearily!

But gaunt great banner-staves the trees

Have lost their sun-shot summer panoplies

And only the weeping pines are green,

The pines that weep for a whole world's teen.                    5

Yet the Spring of the Soul, the Spring of the Soul

Claimeth its own in thee and me.


Lo that the world waggeth wearily,

As gaunt grey shadows its people be,

Taking life's burden drearily,                                    10

Yet each hath some hidden joy I ween,

Should each one tell where his dream hath been

The Spring of the Soul, the Spring of the Soul

Might claim more vassals than me and thee.

## 099. 秋：給道松——反其意而用之 玉蝴蝶慢❶

望處樹林悲慘，

挺如旗杆，瘦勁高昂！

夏日濃妝，飄盡敗葉飛黃。

聽秋聲，青松落淚，

不幸事、世界淒涼。

問春光，寄魂何處？

你我心房。

　

遙望，寰球困乏，戰兢搖晃，

灰色茫茫，人影森森，

眾生肩上苦難扛。

幸心底，尚存喜念，

說夢景，知在何方：

願春光，寄魂天下，

萬眾之王。

# Epitaphs

## Fu I

Fu I loved the high cloud and the hill,
Alas, he died of alcohol.

## Li Po

And Li Po also died drunk.                                    5
He tried to embrance a moon
In the Yellow River.

# 100. 墓誌銘●

傅奕

慕雲之高飛兮戀山之翠微，
嗚呼哀哉兮因酒而醉死。

李白

有酒之同好兮醉死而後已。
黃河夜泊兮波心月影
棄舟攬月兮逐水飄零。

# Thomas Stearns Eliot (1888-1965)

## HYSTERIA


As she laughed I was aware of becoming involved

in her laughter and being part of it, until her

teeth were only accidental stars with a talent

for squad-drill. I was drawn in by short gasps,

inhaled at each momentary recovery, lost finally          5

in the dark caverns of her throat, bruised by

the ripple of unseen muscles. An elderly waiter

with trembling hands was hurriedly spreading

a pink and white checked cloth over the rusty

green iron table, saying: 'If the lady and           10

gentleman wish to take their tea in the garden,

if the lady and gentleman wish to take their

tea in the garden ...' I decided that if the

shaking of her breasts could be stopped, some of

the fragments of the afternoon might be collected,          15

and I concentrated my attention with careful

subtlety to this end.

# 托瑪斯·斯特恩斯·艾略特 (1888-1965)*

## 101. 歇斯底里❶

她張口大笑，我意識到我正在捲入

她的笑聲，成為笑的一部分，直到她的

牙齒成為無意識震顫的明星❷，露出

新兵教練的才華，我被短促的喘息拉入，

在每個瞬間的康復中被吸進去，最後失落

在她喉頭的黑洞裏，被看不見的筋肉的漣漪

撞傷。一位年長的侍者

顫抖的雙手匆匆忙忙

把一件粉紅色白格子花桌布

鋪在綠鏽斑駁的鐵桌上，說：「如果女士

和先生到花園裏喝茶，

如果女士和先生到花園裏

喝茶……」我打定主意

假如她胸部震顫的起伏可以止息，午後的

一些碎片也許可以收集起來，

我集中注意力小心翼翼

關注這個結局。

# THE WIND SPRANG UP AT FOUR O'CLOCK

The wind sprang up at four o'clock
The wind sprang up and broke the bells
Swinging between life and death
Here, in death's dream kingdom
The waking echo of confusing strife                    5
Is it a dream or something else
When the surface of the blackened river
Is a face that sweats with tears?
I saw across the blackened river
The camp fire shake with alien spears.                 10
Here, across death's other river
The Tartar horsemen shake their spears.

# 102. 午夜陡起狂風

午夜陡起狂風，

撞擊生死警鐘，

摧折鐘錘搖擺律動。

眼下死滅夢幻王國裏，

混戰廝殺激蕩醒世回音，

幽暗河面如人臉，

汗水帶淚奔湧，

此景是夢非夢？

目光穿越暗河水，

但見異邦軍營邊，

長矛正共營火搖。

越過冥河，

韃靼鐵騎依舊舞長矛。

# Wystan Hugh Auden (1907-1973)

## THE DECOYS

There are some birds in these valleys
Who flutter round the careless
With intimate appeal.
By seeming kindness turned to snaring,
They feel no falseness.                              5

Under the spell completely
They circle can serenely,
And in the tricky light
The masked hill has a purer greennesss.
Their flight looks fleeter.                          10

But fowlers, O, like foxes,
Lie ambushed in the rushes.
Along the harmless tracks
The madman keeper crawls through brushwood,
Axe under oxter.                                     15

# 維斯坦·休·奧登 (1907-1973)*

## 103. 誘鳥❶

山谷裏幾隻誘鳥

繞著輕信的鴿子鼓翼

親昵地呼喚

以仁慈的表情練習誘捕，

彷彿壓根兒沒有誆騙之意。

完全由魔咒操縱

它們悄悄盤旋

在光影的把戲裏

遮掩的青山顯出更純的翠綠

它們更敏捷地飛行。

獵手，呵，像狐狸

埋伏在藤蔓裏

沿著無害的小徑

那護林的狂人爬過樹叢

腋下夾著斧柄。

Alas, the signal given,
Fingers on trigger tighten.
The real unlucky dove
Must smarting fall away from brightness
Its love from living.                    20

看，信號發出來了，
手指緊扣扳機。
真正不幸的鴿子
一陣劇痛從亮麗中墜落
它的愛活生生墜落。

# WHEN ALL OUR APPARATUS OF REPORT

When all our apparatus of report
Confirms the triumph of our enemies,
Our frontier crossed, our forces in retreat,
Violence pandemic like a new disease,
And Wrong a charmer everywhere invited,          *5*
When Generosity gets nothing done,
Let us remember those who looked deserted:
To-night in China let me think of one

Who for ten years of drought and silence waited,
Until in Muzot all his being spoke,          *10*
And everything was given once for all.
Awed, grateful, tired, content to die, completed,
He went out in the winter night to stroke
That tower as one pets an animal.

## 104. 當所有的新聞媒介

當所有的新聞媒介

確證了敵人的勝利，

我方前線被突破，大軍撤退，

暴力的瘟邪流行如新興時疫，

行騙的魔法師到處有人邀請，

當寬容一籌莫展時，

讓我們銘記那些似乎被遺棄的人：

今宵中國，讓我想起一位：


他十年欠收默默等候，

終於在慕佐盡情傾訴，

把一切表現得淋漓盡致，❷

敬畏、感激、甘願去死，完璧之後

在一個冬夜外出，去觸摸

那座城堡，宛如撫愛寵物。❸

# Epitaph on a Tyrant

Perfection, of a kind, was what he was after,

And the poetry he invented was easy to understand;

He knew human folly like the back of his hand,

And was greatly interested in armies and fleets;

When he laughed, respectable senators burst with laughter,     5

And when he cried the little children died in the streets.

# 105. 一個暴君的墓志銘 ❶

完美純淨，乃其盛年所求，
霸氣賦詩，辭章通俗易讀；
深諳蚩氓，熟如自己手背，
兵燹軍艦，引為無窮樂趣；
龍顏一笑，羣臣應聲噗嗤，
狼嗥徒起，童子死於街衢。❷

# Dylan Thomas (1914-1953)

## THE FORCE THAT THROUGH THE GREEN FUSE DRIVES THE FLOWER

The force that through the green fuse drives the flower

Drives my green age; that blasts the roots of trees

Is my destroyer.

And I am dumb to tell the crooked rose

My youth is bent by the same wintry fever.                    5


The force that drives the water through the rocks

Drives my red blood; that dries the mouthing streams

Turns mine to wax.

And I am dumb to mouth unto my veins

How at the mountain spring the same mouth sucks.              10


The hand that whirls the water in the pool

Stirs the quicksand; that ropes the blowing wind

Hauls my shroud sail.

And I am dumb to tell the hanging man

# 狄蘭・托瑪斯 (1914-1953)*

## 106. 引爆花朵的綠色導火索的力❶

引爆花朵的綠色導火索的力

驅策我青蔥的衰年；炸開樹根的力

是我的毀滅者。

我失語，無法告訴佝僂的玫瑰

同樣嚴寒的狂熱怎樣壓彎我的青春。❷


驅策水流穿越巖石的力

驅策我鮮紅的血液；蒸乾聒噪的溪流的力

把我的熱流凝結為蠟塊。

我失語，無法告訴我的血管

同一張嘴怎樣吸吮山澗泉水。


弄皺一池清水的手

攪拌流沙；捆綁陣風的手

牽引我風帆撕裂的裹屍布。❸

我失語，無法告訴那被絞死的人

How of my clay is made the hangman's lime.                    *15*


The lips of time leech to the fountain head;
Love drips and gathers, but the fallen blood
Shall calm her sores.
And I am dumb to tell a weather's wind
How time has ticked a heaven round the stars.                 *20*


And I am dumb to tell the lover's tomb
How at my sheet goes the same crooked worm.

我的腐土怎樣由同一個絞刑吏的石灰炮製。❹

時間張開水蛭的嘴唇貼近清泉吸血；
愛滴落再凝聚，但滴落的血
將平復她的傷痛。
我失語，無法告訴一陣季風
時間怎樣環繞羣星滴答出一片晴空。

我失語，無法告訴情人的墳塋
同一條病蟲怎樣在我的被單上蠕動。

# Gwendolyn Brooks (1917-2000)

## Piano after War

On a snug evening I shall watch her fingers,

Cleverly ringed, declining to clever pink,

Beg glory from the willing keys. Old hungers

Will break their coffins, rise to eat and thank.

And music, warily, like the golden rose                     *5*

That sometimes after sunset warms the west,

Will warm that room, persuasively suffuse

That room and me, rejuvenate a past.

But suddenly, across my climbing fever

Of proud delight — a multiplying cry.                       *10*

A cry of bitter dead men who will never

Attend a gentle maker of musical joy.

Then my thawed eye will go again to ice.

And stone will shove the softness from my face.

# 格溫多林・布魯克斯 (1917-2000)*

## 107. 戰後鋼琴❶

一個溫暖的黃昏，我將觀賞她的手指，

靈巧的指環，極為靈巧地鞠躬下行，

從期望的琴鍵祈求神恩。美聲可餐，

昔日餓鬼將破棺而出，❷吞食並感恩。

樂音，細膩地，如金色玫瑰，

有時會在日落後給西天添暖，

給琴房添暖，朗朗瀰漫

琴房和我，會重憶一段往事。

可是，穿越我得意的歡欣

躋攀欲燃過後，突然一聲號哭——

那是痛苦的陣亡者的哭訴，他們

再也不能聆聽輕盈彈奏的琴師。

然後，我解凍的眼睛將再度結冰，

石頭將硬化我臉上的柔潤。

# MENTORS

For I am rightful fellow of their band.
My best allegiances are to the dead.
I swear to keep the dead upon my mind,
Disdain for all time to be overglad.
Among spring flowers, under summer trees,                    5
By chilling autumn waters, in the frosts
Of supercilious winter — all my days
I'll have as mentors those reproving ghosts.
And at that cry, at that remotest whisper,
I'll stop my casual business. Leave the banquet.            10
Or leave the ball — reluctant to unclasp her
Who may be fragrant as the flower she wears,
Make gallant bows and dim excuses, then quit
Light for the midnight that is mine and theirs.

# 108. 良師

因為我是他們的羣體中正義的一員，
我最佳的忠誠獻給那些死難者。
我立誓要讓死難者活在我心中，
任何時候都不能洋洋自得。
在春天的花卉中夏日的樹蔭下，
在寒秋的溪水邊嚴冬的森林裏
——在我生命中的日日夜夜，我將始終
以縈繞心頭的亡靈為良師。
聆聽那悲哀的哭號，遙遠的絮語，
我不再做瑣屑之事。遠離筵席，
甚至離開舞會——因為她難於駕馭，
她可能像她佩戴的花朵一樣馥郁，
獻上殷勤的鞠躬並製造模糊的藉口，
然後把我午夜守靈的長明燈掐熄。

# 譯 註
## Explanatory Notes

### 001. 特羅勒斯情歌

＊傑弗雷・喬叟（1343-1400），「英國文學之父」，以中古英語寫詩，代表作為1387年開始主要以詩體寫作的《坎特伯雷故事集》（*The Canterbury Tales*）。

❶ 節譯自喬叟的詩體傳奇《特羅勒斯與克麗西德》（*Troilus and Criseyde*, Book I, 400-420）。這部傳奇取材於古希臘特洛伊戰中特羅勒斯與克麗西德的愛情悲劇，但揉進了中世紀背景。喬叟原詩譯自中世紀義大利詩人彼特拉克（Petrarch）致勞拉（Laura）十四行詩第八十八首，頗多誤譯，卻成為英詩經典。原文排版參照英詩選本，＊ 號前面的中古英文詞在右方注明其相應的現代英語詞。

### 002. 當造化創造她的傑作

＊菲里普・錫德尼（1554-1586），英國詩人，代表作為十四行詩組詩《愛星者與星》（*Astrophel and Stella*, 1591）和〈為詩一辯〉（*The Defence of Poetry*）等。

❶ 譯自錫德尼的十四行詩組詩《愛星者與星》第七首。拉丁文的「Stella」一詞意義為星，一般認為史黛拉是一個真實的美女，即錫德尼愛戀的Penelope Devereux，有一雙黑眼睛和一頭黑髮。原詩為義大利或佩脫拉克式十四行詩（Italian or Petrarchan sonnet），尾韻韻式為 abba，abba，cdcd，ee，譯詩押韻有變通。

❷ 此處的「他」指「愛星者」，原文「mourning weed」在此處意為喪服，但這只是一個比喻，意思是說，造化創造的史黛拉的黑眼睛，本身就像一曲富於愛心的哀歌，彷彿在悼念那些別的為無望之愛而殉情的男人。

## 003. 我們在世界大舞臺演戲

＊艾德蒙・斯賓塞（1552 -1599），英國詩人，有史詩《仙后》（*The Faerie Queene*）等名作。

❶ 譯自斯賓塞十四行詩組詩《愛情小唱》（*Amoretti*, 1595）第五十四首。組詩描寫詩人與一位女郎的婚戀。源於拉丁文「世界大舞臺」（theatrum mundi）的比喻，流行於文藝復興時期。斯賓塞式十四行詩（Spenserian sonnet）尾韻韻式為 abab，bcbc，cdcd，ee，譯詩押韻有變通。

## 004. 人性自然的一觸，世人都來套近乎

＊威廉・莎士比亞（1564-1616），英國文藝復興時期的大劇作家、詩人，著名劇作有悲劇《哈姆雷特》（*Hamlet*）、《奧賽羅》（*Othello*）、《李爾王》（*King Lear*）、《馬克白》（*Macbeth*），喜劇《仲夏夜之夢》（*Midsummer Night's Dream*）和《威尼斯商人》（*The Merchant of Venice*）等，還寫過一百五十四首十四行詩和兩首長篇敘事詩。

❶ 選譯自莎劇《特洛伊羅斯和克瑞西達》（*Troilus and Cressida*, Act III, Scene

III）。本劇通過希臘聯軍遠征特洛伊的戰爭和克瑞西達背叛愛情的情節，反映出時代、人性和價值觀的變化。這段話是尤里西斯（Ulysses，即奧德修斯）勸說一度因故不參戰的英雄阿基里斯（Achiles）的一段臺詞。由於莎劇版本不同，這段話個別詞的拼寫，尤其是標點的採用各有不同，而不同的標點可以引導讀者作出不同的解讀。這裏採用的是道森（Anthony B. Dawson）編輯的該劇版本（劍橋大學，2003 年版）。原文「nature」一詞在文藝復興以來兼有人性和大自然的意義。這句話往往被英語讀者從上下文中抽離出來作為名言引用，誤讀為人與大自然的親密關係，或粗淺的人際交往導致人們親如手足的情形。朱生豪的譯本略去了這句話。依照道森的解釋，這句話的原意是：One natural trait creates a common bond among all people. The implication, spellet out in what follow, is that the 'touch' is a failing or weakness.（一次自然的碰觸在所有的人們中間製造了一根共同的紐帶或一種親戚關係。從下文來看，暗含的意思是：這種『碰觸』是一個缺陷或一個弱點。）換言之，此處甚至帶有冷嘲熱諷的意味。這一行的詩意似乎在英國畫家羅姆尼（George Romney）的畫作〈大自然和激情關照的嬰兒莎士比亞〉（*The infant shakespeare attended by Nature and the Passions*）中得到絕妙的闡釋：人性或大自然輕輕觸碰出來嬰兒莎士比亞，把世界上所有的人們和他們所有的情緒都攪到一起來了，他們像親戚一樣，可是，這些貌似的親戚實際上或親或疏，甚至心懷敵意。

❷ 這是一句古希臘諺語。

❸ 指大阿賈克斯（Greater Ajax），另一位著名的希臘英雄。

❹ 在《伊利亞特》描寫的特洛伊戰爭中，幫助戰爭雙方的天神像人一樣看風使舵，戰神一度站在特洛伊一方。

## 005. 人類有良種，菁英求繁衍

❶ 莎士比亞十四行詩自成一體，共一百五十四首，大致寫於1592至1598年，第一到第十七首通稱「婚戀十四行詩」，這一系列每首都在勸導一個貴族青年成婚。第一首有開宗明義之意。英國式或伊麗莎白式十四行詩（English or Elizabethan sonnet）雖然不是莎士比亞首創的，但往往稱為莎士比亞式十四行詩（Shakespearean sonnet），在形式上可以分為兩部分，第一部分為三節四行詩，第二部分為兩行對句，尾韻韻式為abab，cdcd，efef，gg。譯詩或大致仿照原詩押韻，或有變通。

❷ 詩句「But as the riper should by time decease」中，定冠詞加比較級形容詞「riper」（更成熟的），用來比喻年齡較大的人或老人，「bear his memory」一語雙關：蓋上前人記憶的印章留下印記；生一個孩子（bearing a child）能攜帶前輩的記憶。

❸ 原文的「contracted」一詞，意思是簽訂契約或婚約，因此受簽約的另一方所制約。

❹ 此處雖然沒有點明蠟燭，但在莎士比亞的時代，蠟是日常生活中照明的主要燃料之一，因此，莎士比亞專家大都解讀為隱喻自戀的蠟燭意象。

❺ 在莎士比亞的時代，荒年挨餓、豐年暴食的現象往往交替而來。

❻ 原文的「content」一詞，此處可指精液（semen），這裏也許隱含衍生的

「自慰」之意。

❼ 這裏的形容詞「tender」含有稚嫩的、溫柔的、敏感的等多種意義，在第四行出現時譯為「稚嫩的」，此處譯為「精細的」，以彰顯這一行的矛盾語（oxymoron），加上接著而來的似非而是的悖論（paradox），這一句隱含既褒又貶的意味：你這個精細的粗人，自淫捨得射精，卻捨不得射精生個孩子。

❽ 結尾兩行以嚴詞警告。貪食（饕餮）是天主教所說的七宗罪之一。原文「due」一詞，原義是應得物，此處指應當得到的後嗣，意思是，你不生育就虧欠了這個世界，等於吞噬了埋葬了它的子孫——你自己的晚輩。因此，最後以「by the grave and thee」把兩者（墳墓和你）並置等同起來。


## 006. 問君何所似，可否比春日？

❶ 英國夏季明媚，相當於中國的春季，前人已有譯「Summer's day（夏日）」為「春日」之先例。

❷ 原詞「untrimmed」，此處應解讀為「stripped of beauty」。

❸ 原詩「that fair thou owest」，應當解讀為「that beauty thou possessest」，即你所具有的美。

❹ 原詞「growest」，此處應解讀為「becomes a part of」。這兩行直譯是：當你在永恆的詩行中成為時代（或時間）的一部分時，死神也不會誇口說你走在他的陰影裏。

## 007. 造化大手筆，為君繪容顏

❶ 原詞「master-mistress」，猶言陰陽人。

❷ 原詞「rolling」意為「roving」，即「rove（眼睛環視）」的動名詞。

❸ 原詞「hue」在此處意為「form」，即形態。

❹ 原詞「defeated」意為「cheated」或「defrauded」，即哄騙，下行的「one thing」指陽具。

❺ 原詞「pricked」意為「selected」，即挑選出，或用一個小點標出（男性特徵），名詞「prick（刺）」在現代英語俚語中指陽具。

## 008. 萬事令人煩惱，不如一死了之

❶ 原詞「Desert」意為「a deserving person」，即配得上更好的命運的人，是美德的人格化。以下首字母大寫的詞，均可視為抽象概念的人格化。

❷ 原詞「jollity」在此處意為精美服裝，或解讀為「pleasure（歡樂）」。

❸ 原詞「strumpeted」的名詞「strumpet（妓女）」，詞形和讀音接近「trumpet（喇叭）」，此句含有公開大聲羞辱童貞女子的意思。

❹ 此處詩無達詁，原詞「Doctor-like」，莎士比亞注家解讀為「pendant-like」或「as an academic doctor（貌似的學究或博士）」，甚至暗指馬婁（Christopher Marlowe）筆下愚蠢極致卻自以為可以操控技藝（control 'skill'）的浮士德博士（Doctor Faustus）。其他中譯多解讀為貌似博士的人。由於莎士比亞常用「Skill」一詞來指醫藝，「Doctor」一詞也被更確切地解讀為「a doctor of medicine（醫學博士）」，中譯因此取醫生之

義。

❺ 此處原文的「my love」可以寬泛地解讀為戀人、朋友或詩人所愛的戲劇和詩歌藝術。


## 009. 往古之時黑色豈能作風流

❶ 這是莎士比亞十四行詩中著重描繪一位「黑女郎」（dark lady）的第一首詩。關於這位天生黑膚的女郎身分，學者有多種臆說，沒有定論。

❷ 著喪服的比喻，化用了錫德尼〈當造化創造她的傑作〉詩中的比喻。


## 010. 良晨

＊鄧約翰（1572-1631），英國文藝復興時期的詩人和牧師，「玄學派詩人」的卓越代表，有《神聖詩歌》（*Divine Poems,* 1607）等詩作和文集。

❶ 這首詩的詩題，梁實秋、曾建綱均譯為〈早安〉，楊牧譯為〈良辰〉。儘管「good morrow」義同問候語「good morning」，但詩題加了定冠詞，故直譯為「良晨」（該詞在中國詩詞中並不鮮見，如陸遊《園中作》：「良晨不把酒，新燕解相嘲。」）原詩可視為「破曉歌」（Aubade），第一節是詩的主人公晨醒後追問夜夢，即追問兩人相戀之前的過去，第二節則面對良晨，繼續靈與肉雙重意義上的做愛。

❷ 此處原文「countrey pleasures」一語，既與大自然相關，又與性事相關，甚至可以說是「野合之趣」。

❸ 此處關於七睡人（seven sleepers）的傳說是：西元三世紀時以弗所

（Ephesus）城的七個男女基督徒青年為了逃避羅馬皇帝德夕阿斯

（Decius）的宗教迫害，躲在城外一個山洞裏，睡了一兩百年後才醒

來。或認為這裏同時暗用了柏拉圖《理想國》（*The Republic*）中「洞

喻」的典故：一羣手腳被捆綁關在洞中的囚徒，背後有一堆火，只能借

助火光看到某些東西在洞壁上迷幻的投影，卻誤以為是真實的事物。他

們只有出洞之後才能看到真相並走向光明。

❹ 此處詩無達詁，原文「Maps」，梁譯為「地圖」，並不為錯，但此地

圖，一般認為特指當時流行的可以顯示多個世界的「心形投影地圖」

（cordiform map），或說此詞指的是「星圖」（charts of the heaven），

似乎證據不足。

❺ 此處採用了「聯軛法」（zeugma）的修辭手法，意指把同一個動詞或名

詞像牛軛一樣加諸於一個句子（複合句）的兩個或多個組成部分（子

句），以便聯接起來，達到省略而簡潔等藝術效果。此行原文的動詞

「appears」就是如此，應當理解為：My face（appears）in your eye, and

your face appears in my eye。這種手法有點像中文的互文見義，活譯的「我

在你眼裏，你在我心裏」應當理解為：我在你眼（和心）裏，你在我

（眼和）心裏。接下來的意思是：各人心裏的愛，也會形之於色，即坦

誠地浮現在各自的臉上。

❻ 在鄧約翰的時代流行「人是微觀世界」的觀點，把兩個人喻為兩個半球

是很自然的。這裏的意思是：完美的愛的微觀世界避免了宏觀世界的問

題，即極地寒冷太陽西落的問題，幼稚的肉欲之愛由此提昇到永恆靈性

的層次。英詩注家認為這裏還暗示了希臘一個創世神話：相傳人本來像

一個滾動的圓球一樣，有兩個腦袋和四手四腳，由於冒犯神祇，主神宙斯以電火將人劈成兩半，從此各人開始尋找自己失落的一半，這就是愛情的起源。

❼ 英詩注家認為此處暗用的典故是：依照亞里士多德關於天體與地上萬物的理論，天體永恆不變，地上萬物則處在不斷變易中，因為合成塵世萬物的火、空氣、水、土「四根」，不是「均等和合」。詩人同時採用了繪畫的比喻：總是在染色或塗色的東西，就始終在變色，而「染色」（dyes）一詞又與「死亡」（dies）一詞諧音，因此，染色就是變色，變色就是趨近死亡。

❽ 此處仍然兼及靈與肉雙重意義上的愛：精神之愛令人不朽，奠基於此的肉體之愛也「性趣」無窮。像英國宮廷艷情詩中常見的那樣，性亢奮是不會洩氣終結的。在十七世紀英語中，死（die）一詞往往隱含性高潮之意，因為達到高潮就洩氣終結了，這種感覺無異於死。但這並不意味著沒有性高潮，而是這樣一個悖論（paradox）：既沒有高潮又高潮迭起。


## 012. 回聲之歌

＊本・瓊生（1573-1637），英國文藝復興時期的詩人和劇作家，莎士比亞的朋友。除抒情詩外，名作有諷刺劇《伏爾蓬》（*Volpone*）和《煉金術士》（*The Alchemist*）等。

❶ 譯自瓊生的劇作《月神的狂歡》（*Cynthia's Revels*, 1600），這首歌取材於希臘神話中的美少年納西瑟斯（Narcissus）自戀的故事，是愛戀他的

「回聲」姑娘所唱的哀歌。

## 013. 高貴品格

❶ 節譯自瓊生的一首紀念友人的頌歌（*To the immortal memory and friendship of that noble pair, Sir Lucius Cary and Sir H. Morison*），詩題為《英詩金庫》（*The Golden Treasury*）編者所加。

## 014. 勸女及時采薔薇

\*羅伯特・赫里克（1591-1674），英國詩人，代表作有詩集《金蘋果園》（*Hesperides*, 1648）。

❶ 譯自赫里克的詩集《金蘋果園》。詩題直譯是「給少女們，多多掙得時光」。「掙得（捕捉）時光（carpe diem）」這句拉丁文成語所蘊涵的人生哲理源於古羅馬詩人賀拉斯（Horace）的一首頌歌。首行同樣源自拉丁文，化用了田園詩人維吉爾（Virgil）的一句詩。譯詩以首行為題更符合中文習慣。

## 015. 獄中致阿爾西亞

\*理查・拉夫羅斯（1618-1657），英國宮廷騎士派詩人，有死後出版的詩集《盧卡斯塔》（*Lucasta: Posthume Poems*, 1659）傳世。

❶ 這首詩寫於倫敦威斯敏特的一所監獄。拉夫羅斯在國王查理斯一世與國

會的衝突中因保皇主張羈獄。阿爾西亞身世無考，可能只是詩人想像中的產物。

❷ 此處原文指泰晤士河。

## 016. 燕子 虞美人

* 亞伯拉罕・考利（1618-1667），英國詩人、政治家和航海家，有詩集《情婦》（*The Mistress,* 1647）和《詩歌》（*Poems,* 1656）等。

❶ 譯自考利《詩歌》中的一首阿克那里翁詩體（Anacreontics）詩歌，這是一種源於古希臘抒情詩人阿克那里翁（Anacreon）的專寫酒色的詩體。

## 017. 光之殤

* 約翰・密爾頓（1608-1674），英國詩人和思想家，曾參與清教徒革命活動，出版反對書報審查制的《論出版自由》（*Areopagitica,* 1644），王朝復辟後一度羈獄，晚年雙目失明，口述完成《失樂園》（*Paradise Lost,* 1667）、《復樂園》（*Paradise Regained,* 1671）和《力士參孫》（*Samson Agonistes,* 1671）等著名長詩。

❶ 這首義大利式十四行詩可能寫於1652年到1655年之間，即詩人雙目失明之後。原詩無題，後來的密爾頓詩集的編纂者所加的這個詩題，有些英詩選集不予採用，因為密爾頓沒有直接採用「blind」或「blindness」一詞，而是兩度採用含義更豐富的「light」一詞，縱觀密爾頓的其他作品，該詞有視力、才華、生命之光（神光或人的內光）等多種含義，甚至可解讀為時間（如中文稱時間為光陰），中文詩題因此改為「光之

殤」，在詩行中將此詞先後活譯為「晴光」和「明慧」。原詩為義大利式十四行詩，韻腳為 abba, abba, cde, cde，譯詩大致仿照原詩押韻。

❷ 關於人的年日或壽數（days），《舊約》有兩說：第一是《以賽亞書》（65：20）中的預言：在耶和華所造的「新天新地」，「將沒有數日夭亡的嬰孩，也沒有年日不滿的老人；因為青年應當活到百歲才死，罪人活到百歲才死就要被咒詛。」第二說是《詩篇》（90：10）：「我們一生的年日是七十歲，若是強壯可到八十歲；但其中所矜誇的不過是勞苦愁煩，轉眼成空，我們便如飛而去。」依照前一理想的說法，密爾頓寫這首詩時年日未過半百。

❸ 特倫原本羅馬帝國的金銀等硬幣的計量單位，引申為天資，典出《新約‧馬太福音》（25：14-30）中的比喻：一個主人出遠門時叫了三個僕人來託付家業，按著各人的天資，給他們數目不同的銀子：分別給五特倫、兩特倫和一特倫。主人回來後要三個僕人來結賬，頭兩個都用銀子做買賣賺了一倍，因此得到擢昇。第三個卻把銀子埋起來，一點沒有增值，原銀歸還。主人責怪他懶惰，把那一特倫給了頭一個有天資的，把懶惰的趕出家門扔進黑暗中。

❹ 此處的「true account」含有雙關意義：僕人與主人結算的實賬，詩人要向上帝交代他對社會的真實記述。

❺ 日工，每天的工作，典出《新約‧約翰福音》（9：4）：「趁著白日，我們必須做那差我來的工，天一黑，就沒有人能做工了。」密爾頓以寫作為日工。

❻ 首字母大寫的「Patience」，是人格化的堅忍。

❼ 十字架之軛既沉重也柔和，參見《新約·馬太福音》（11：30），耶穌說：「我心裏柔和謙卑，你們當負我的軛，學我的樣式，這樣，你們心裏就必得享安息。因為我的軛是容易的，我的擔子是輕省的。」

❽ 《舊約·詩篇》（27：14）：「要等候耶和華，當壯膽，堅固你的心。我再說，要等候耶和華。」耐心等候有站得穩的意思。據西方學者的評注，這一行的含義是：上帝對於人的價值是根據人是否各盡其力來判斷的。例如，一個呆木匠一天只能做兩把椅子，一個巧木匠能做五把，只要各盡其力就有同等價值。假如巧木匠只做了三把，那麼，與盡力日工的呆木匠相比，他就不值得尊重。如果一個木匠像密爾頓一樣殘疾了，不能做椅子只能觀望等候了，上帝仍然看得起他。隱含的意思是，詩人不能再像先前那樣積極介入政治了，但他的社會觀察和著述仍然很有價值。

## 018. 利西達

❶ 這首輓歌哀悼作者的一位有詩才的劍橋大學同學愛德華·金（Edward King）之死，但密爾頓把他提昇為高潔的牧童詩人利西達來描寫。利西達（或譯為利西達斯）原本是古希臘詩人希奧克里特斯（Theocritus）的牧歌中常見的牧人名字。牧人（Pastor）一詞兼有牧師之意，牧師或祭司就是最古老的詩人。晚清學者和翻譯家辜鴻銘曾經把這首詩稱為「洋離騷」，兩者之風格確有相近之處，故以騷體迻譯。

❷ 密爾頓所說的教士指當時英國教會腐敗的神職人員。

❸ 原文的古文詞「ye」，意為「你們」或「汝等」，「thou」的複數形式，像「you」一樣，主格和賓格相同。月桂、桃金娘和常青藤分別是日神阿波羅、美神維納斯和酒神巴克斯（Bacchus）的象徵。

❹ 原文的「bear」一詞等於「bier」，即靈柩的臺架。

❺ 依照希臘羅馬的牧歌傳統，密爾頓祈請繆思九姊妹唱一曲輓歌。位於海力孔山（Mount Helicon）的繆思靈泉（Aganippe）之高位，僅低於主神宙斯之寶座。

❻ 盛死者骨灰的骨甕，往往鐫刻以贊詞或死者生前事跡。

❼ 這裏採用 1638 年版本的「burnisht」一詞，後來的 1645 年版本作者改動了個別措辭，此處改為「westering」一詞。

❽ 原文的「the oaten Flute」，指維吉爾牧歌中牧神潘吹奏的麥稈製作的笛子。

❾ 羊人（Satyrs）或音譯為薩提爾，是希臘神話中半人半羊的好色之徒。林間精靈（Fauns）或音譯為方恩。密爾頓可能借以指劍橋大學的同學。

❿ 原文提及的達莫塔（Damoetas）是維吉爾牧歌中常見的牧人名字，密爾頓可能借以指劍橋大學的一位導師。

⓫ 此處的詩人和高僧均指德魯伊（Druids），即古老的凱爾特民族（Celt）的神職人員，在後世詩文中常以橡樹精的形象出現。莫奈山（Mona），位於威爾士西北愛爾蘭海上安格爾西島（Anglesey），該島有德魯伊教徒留下的石板墓等遺物，據說這裏是德魯伊教徒躲避羅馬入侵者的最後一個避難所。

⓬ 原文的「Deva」，即狄河（The river Dee），斯賓塞（Spenser）《仙后》

（*Faerie Queene*）中的一條神聖河流，英格蘭與威爾士的界河。詩人仿佛看到只有狄河神女在那裏噴射巫水，意即在那裏也見不到水澤仙姝的影子。

❸ 奧菲斯是日神阿波羅與一位繆思女神的兒子，詩人和樂師的首領，同時是日神和酒神的祭司。在他的妻子不幸被蛇咬死後，奧菲斯前往冥土營救，冥王被奧菲斯的音樂打動，允許他帶妻子還陽。但冥王提出一個條件：在奧菲斯引領妻子出冥土抵達陽世之前不得回頭張望。還陽路上，奧菲斯無意中回頭一看，他的妻子立即消失在黑暗之中。救妻失敗後，奧菲斯不再喜歡女人了，變成了同性戀者。因此，在他彈琴歌唱時，崇拜酒神的狂女向他扔樹枝石塊，可是，由於音樂的魔力，連樹枝石塊也不願擊中他。那些狂女蜂擁而上，把奧菲斯撕碎吞吃了。他的頭顱被扔進希伯魯斯河（Hebrus），卻在水面歌唱不已，一直漂到雷斯勃島的海岸（Lesbian shore）。對於密爾頓等許多詩人，奧菲斯是詩歌的偉大力量的化身。

❹ 彼岸花（Amaryllis）或音譯為阿瑪麗麗絲，交際花（Neaera），或音譯為涅埃拉，均為維吉爾牧歌中水澤仙姝的名字，古希臘也有名妓取名為涅埃拉，故採用意譯，密爾頓可能借以暗指當時的宮廷艷情詩人。

❺ 此處的「with」一詞，據英詩箋注家的解釋，可能是動詞「withe」的一種形態，意為「to twist」，即搓扭。

❻ 密爾頓把命運稱為狂女（Fury），好比希臘戲劇中的復仇女神（Eumendies）之一。在希臘神話中往往把命運人格化為三姊妹，一位編織生命之線，一位測量其長度，一位以剪刀剪斷，此處的這一形象顯然

指操剪刀的一位。

⓱ 佛布斯，即日神阿波羅，同時是詩歌之神。維吉爾牧歌中寫到佛布斯擰他的耳朵，警告他不要野心勃勃。

⓲ 原文的「foil」一詞，指鑲嵌在寶石背後用以襯托寶石的薄金屬葉片，有綠葉扶紅花之功。

⓳ 主神（Jove），即朱庇特，密爾頓借以指基督教的上帝。

⓴ 古泉（Arethuse），或音譯為阿瑞瑟莎，西西里一個海島上的古泉。明秀河（Mincius）是維吉爾故鄉哺育牧歌的河流。兩者分別象徵史詩和牧歌，通常認為史詩比牧歌詩情更為崇高。

㉑ 海王之使者：指人身魚尾的海神（Triton），繪畫中通常攜帶一隻螺號，傳遞海王（Neptune）的信息。

㉒ 原文的西坡塔德斯（Hippotades）在荷馬史詩中是風神（Aeolus）的綽號，是根據他母親名字取的，意思是「西坡塔斯（Hippotas）養的」。

㉓ 此處「Panope」是一位性格好靜的水澤仙姝，羅馬海員常為風平浪靜而祈求之。

㉔ 劍河，穿越劍橋大學校園的河流，是這所名校的象徵，此處被人格化了。

㉕ 在希臘神話中，阿波羅愛上了美少年雅辛托斯（Hyacinthus）卻誤殺了他，為了紀念他的死難，阿波羅讓他的血泊中長出風信子，並且在花瓣上寫下哀辭。此處暗示劍河上漂浮的莎草像風信子一樣含悲帶愁。

㉖ 耶穌門徒之一的彼得原本是加利利湖上的漁父。《新約‧馬太福音》（16：19）：耶穌對彼得說：「我要把天國的鑰匙給你」，《舊約‧以

賽亞書》（22：22）：「我必將大衛家的鑰匙放在他肩頭上。他開，無人能關。他關，無人能開。」

❷⑦ 《新約·約翰福音》（10：1）：耶穌說：「我實實在在告訴你們，人進羊圈，不從門進去，倒從別處爬進去，那人就是賊，就是強盜。」

❷⑧ 此處寫到的一種重型武器，一般認為是一種重到兩手才能揮動的重劍，依照前人中譯譯為雙刃劍。

❷⑨ 白水（Alpheus），依希臘文原詞意譯，或音譯為阿爾弗，是福樂之地阿卡迪（Arcady）的一條河流和河神的名字，傳說他追逐水澤仙姝彼岸花，黛安娜幫助彼岸花變為一股泉水脫逃，好色的白水仍然追獵不捨。

❸⓪.原文的「freaked」一詞意為胡亂地弄出斑點（flecked），「jet」一詞意為黑斑（black spots），但此處並無貶意，故譯為美人斑。

❸① 此處中譯的首領，在實際意義上指死者的頭部和衣領，也可以從象徵意義上來理解。

❸② 仙葩（Amaranthus），密爾頓在《失樂園》中寫到的伊甸園裏永不凋謝的花。

❸③ 原文的赫布里底羣島（Hebrides）是靠近蘇格蘭西海灣的羣島，加上前面的形容詞，意譯為「風雨羣島」。

❸④ 此處的「地角之寓言」（the fable of Bellerus old）中的貝勒斯（Bellerus）是神話中的大力士或大惡人，英國的地角或陸地之角（Land's End），即康沃爾郡（Cornwall），在羅馬時代亦稱為「Bellerium」，得名於「Bellerus」。貝勒斯的寓言，當指他被希臘英雄貝勒羅風（Bellerophon）殺死的故事，貝勒羅風亦得名於貝勒斯。

㉟ 上兩句的「警戒之山巒」（guarded Mount）指康沃爾郡附近的聖米高山（St. Michael's Mount）。聖米高是總領天使，密爾頓可能是想像聖米高從山頭眺望西班牙的納曼科（Namancos）和巴約納（Bayona）要塞，因為歷史上英國曾處在西班牙海上霸權的威脅之下。或認為此處的天使指利西達，無論指誰，此處的含義是：天使山頭眺望的目光會從西班牙方向轉向金的故鄉，並且不再悲傷了。

㊱ 海豚（Dolphins）被海員視為海上照看船隻的吉祥的動物。

㊲ 指耶穌曾行於海面上，事見《新約・馬太福音》（14：25-26）。

㊳ 典出《新約・啟示錄》（7：17）：「上帝也必擦去他們一切的眼淚。」

㊴ 原文的「Genius」一詞，意為地方精靈或守護天使。

㊵ 原文的「quills」一詞，指牧人吹奏的的空心葦管。

㊶ 「鄉間之小曲」（Doric lay），直譯是多里斯小曲，多里斯語是希臘牧歌詩人喜歡採用的一種方言。


## 019. 太空何靈異，難攀此華榮

＊亞歷山大・蒲伯（1688-1744），英國啟蒙時期的詩人，主要作品有文論詩《論批評》（An Essay on Criticism）、《論人》（An Essay on Man）和諷刺性長詩《鬈髮遇劫》（The Rape of the Lock）。

❶ 譯自蒲伯的長篇諷刺詩《鬈髮遇劫》（Canto II: ll. 1-18），以選詩的第一行為題。《鬈髮遇劫》描寫一個少年偷剪了一個少女的一絡金髮後兩

個家庭的爭執，諷刺了當時社會的奢華。選詩可以略見詩人寓貶於褒的諷刺筆法。

❷ 原文「the ethereal plain」，即天空。

❸ 原文「the purpled main」指被霞光染成紫紅色的大海，紫色是皇室權貴的象徵。

❹ 詩中描寫的女主人公當時正乘船從倫敦到漢普頓宮。

❺ 親吻十字架是改宗基督的表示。


## 020. 鄉村墓園哀歌

＊托瑪斯・格雷（1716-1771），英國詩人和學者，「墓畔派」的代表人物，一生只寫過十幾首，卻是廣為流傳的經典。

❶ 這首詩係詩人於1750年在白金漢郡的斯多克・瀦吉斯（Stoke Poges）的教堂墓地參訪時觸發靈感而作，久經錘煉後成為名作。原詩採用四行詩節（quatrains）和揚抑格五音步詩行（iambic pentameter），每節第一行與第三行押韻，第二行與第四行押韻。譯詩（「碑銘」除外）大致仿照原詩隔行押韻。

❷ 據英詩箋注家，此處原文的「Beetle」可以指任何有翼的昆蟲，螢火蟲亦屬其列，不宜譯為甲殼蟲。

❸ 當時的牧人以一頭被閹割的公羊並在它的脖子上掛一個鈴鐺充當頭羊，原文中的「folds」一詞意為羊羣或羊圈。

❹ 原文把鴞鳥即貓頭鷹喻為黑暗世界的女皇，所以不喜歡月光。

❺ 原文「cell」指囚室般的靈柩或墳墓。

❻ 此處和此後原文首字母大寫的許多詞，都是抽象概念的人格化，譯文一般加引號表示。

❼ 西方歷史上的紋章（heraldry，或紋章學），是記錄貴族及知名家族的宗譜、名譽及功績的徽章及其相關的學問。

❽ 這三行原文是一個倒裝句，主語是「hour」，謂語動詞是「awaits」，前面兩行為前置賓語。

❾ 此處原文中的「storied urn」指骨灰甕，往往繪以相關的圖畫，仿佛在講述死者生前故事。

❿ 此處分別指下述三人：約翰・漢普登（1594-1643），英國議會領袖，曾帶頭反抗理查一世攤派的苛捐雜稅；英國詩人密爾頓，曾在離斯多克・潑吉斯不遠的鄉村居住過；克侖威爾（1599-1658），英國資產階級革命領袖，他是漢普登的表親，曾經常到漢普登的鄉居拜訪。詩人回應了歷史上對克倫威爾的批評，認為克倫威爾沒有罪咎，把導致英國陷入內戰血泊的責任歸咎於他是不公正的。

⓫ 原詩這一節與下一節開頭的「Their lot forbade」三個詞形成一個倒裝句，即這一節均為謂語動詞「forbade」的前置賓語，意思是說，村民的命運妨礙了他們去從政並建樹政績。接著寫到村民自有其鄉野的樂趣。

⓬ 此處的「unlettered Muse」，直譯是「不精於讀寫的繆思」，以下的原文以女性人稱代詞來指稱這類沒有受過正規教育的「土秀才」。

⓭ 此處的「聖言」（Holy text）可解讀為聖經經文，原文「teach」一詞，據《英詩金庫》（*The Golden Treasury*）編注，由於前面的「text」一詞是

第三人稱單數，以嚴格的語法來要求，此處應當用「teaches」一詞。

⓮ 一般認為此處的「君」（thee，即「你」的賓格），當指格雷自己。

⓯ 據英詩箋注家，詩人將森林人格化了。此處人與樹像知己一樣，甚至渾然不分。

## 021. 羊羔

＊威廉・布萊克（1757-1827），英國詩人和畫家，浪漫主義先驅，作品極富神秘色彩,代表作有《天真之歌》（*Songs of Innocence*）、《經驗之歌》（*Songs of Experience*）、長詩《四天神》（*The Four Zoas*）和《耶路撒冷：神人愛爾比奧的投射》（*Jerusalem, The Emanation of The Giant Albion*）等。

❶ 譯自布萊克的《天真之歌》。

❷ 指基督。

## 022. 老虎

❶ 譯自布萊克的《經驗之歌》。

❷ 在布萊克的《四天神》中，詩人明顯地把老虎與敗北的烏理森（Urizen，或意譯為智力神）聯繫起來，詩中的烏理森說：「在那黑暗之夜，我呼喚縈繞腳下的星辰，星辰投擲他們的長矛，然後赤身裸體撤退了。」

## 023. 一株毒樹

❶ 譯自布萊克的《經驗之歌》。

❷ 原文「the pole」在此處指北斗星。


## 024. 友誼偽裝之愛 憶江南四首

＊羅伯特·彭斯（1759–1796），蘇格蘭詩人，以英文和蘇格蘭方言寫作，主要
作品有《蘇格蘭方言詩集》（*Poems, Chiefly in the Scottish Dialect*, 1786）。


## 025. 美后菲莉絲之歌

❶ 菲莉絲，本名 Philadelphia Barbara McMurdo，是彭斯一位朋友的美麗女
兒，啟迪了詩人的靈感。菲莉絲一詞來自希臘文，相當於拉丁文的弗洛
拉（Flora），意為草木花卉，源於羅馬神話中的花神和春神的名字。彭
斯詩中的菲莉絲是他想像中的「純美皇后」的化身，因此譯為芳心，
以便襲用陸譯的「素心」（Simplicity）一詞，寄寓素樸乃芳美之母的詩
意。

❷ 尼斯河（River Nith）是蘇格蘭境內流經彭斯的故鄉鄧弗利斯和加洛維
（Dumfries and Galloway）的一條河流。

❸ 依照另一種版本，此後每一節最後一行重複歌唱「Awa' wi' your belles,
&c.」，即合唱的第一句「遠遜你那麗質」。

❹ 原文的「woodbine」是忍冬屬植物，金銀花（soneysuckle）屬於此類植

物，在中文中別稱為金花或銀花。

## 026. 睡美人

*塞繆爾・羅傑斯（1763-1855），英國銀行家兼詩人，代表作有詩集《記憶中的歡樂》（*Pleasures of Memory*, 1792）。

## 027. 她幽居於鄉野之間

*威廉・華茲華斯（1770-1850），英國浪漫派詩人，「湖畔派」詩人之一，代表作有與柯勒律治合作出版的《抒情歌謠集》（*Lyrical Ballads*），此外有長詩《漫遊》（*The Excursion*）等許多重要作品。

❶ 這首詩最初載於《抒情歌謠集》第二版，是華茲華斯的五首〈露西〉（*Lucy*）組詩中的一首。露西身世不詳，可能是詩人想像的產物。原詩韻腳為abab, cdcd, efef，譯詩三節均為abab韻，同時採用詞牌「巫山一段雲」的句法。

❷ 鴿泉是英格蘭中部鴿河（Dove River）的源頭。

❸ 原文把露西喻為天際唯一一顆星（only one），當指金星（Venus），在西方文化中它是愛的象徵。中文對聯中有「東啟明西長庚」之語，是金星在凌晨和黃昏的兩個不同名稱，這一行因此譯為「昏曉第一星」。

## 028. 致蝴蝶 天香

❶ 華茲華斯先後於1802年3月和4月寫了兩首同題各自獨立成篇的〈致蝴蝶〉。當時，詩人住在英國湖區中心的格拉斯米爾（Grasmere）的鎮頭（Town-end）鴿舍（Dove Cottage），常在果園裏和他的詩人妹妹多蘿茜（Dorothy）一起種樹栽花，多蘿茜喜歡追蝴蝶，但並不抓捕。

## 031. 忽必烈汗

＊S. T. 柯爾律治（1772-1834），英國浪漫派詩人和批評家，主要作品有與華茲華斯合作出版的《抒情歌謠集》，詩作〈古舟子詠〉（*The Rime of the Ancient Mariner*）、〈克麗斯特貝爾〉（*Christabel*）、〈忽必烈汗〉（*Kubla Khan*），以及批評著作《文學評傳》（*Biographia Literaria*）等。

❶ 譯自柯爾律治的《克麗斯特貝爾》（*Christabel*, 1816）。這裏省略了詩前柯爾律治關於此詩的說明。詩人自言他在讀忽必烈汗營建宮殿的記載時，因神經痛服了鴉片酊，朦朧入睡，靈感勃發，一氣呵成兩三百行詩，醒來後奮筆疾書，不料被人打斷，耽誤一個多小時，結果失憶，再也無法續寫，僅剩下現在的五十四行。

❷ 學者一般認為，柯爾律治采用「阿爾佛」（Alph）一詞，是參照希臘文第一個字母的名稱「Alpha」，依照神話，伊甸園位於阿比西尼亞（Abyssinia，今埃塞俄比亞和蘇丹一帶），人類語言起源之地，有一條名為「Alpheus」的地下河流。

❸ 原文「the mingled measure」，語出科林斯（Collins）的頌詩〈激情：音

樂頌〉（*The Passions: An Ode for Music*），科林斯的原意是說，在一條鬧鬼的河流中，有各種混雜的音韻。

❹ 原文為阿比西尼亞姑娘。

❺ 或音譯為德西梅琴，一種形似瘦長蝴蝶有三根琴弦用兩個小錘敲擊的樂器，類似中國揚琴。

❻ 「Mount Abora」，或英譯為阿伯拉山，一般把它與密爾頓在《失樂園》中寫到的位於阿比西尼亞的阿瑪拉山（Mount Amara）山聯繫起來。

❼ 指抽鴉片的人。

❽ 柯勒律治的手稿表明「人間蜜露」指的是鴉片；在《柏拉圖對話集》（*Dialogues of Plato*）的〈伊安〉（*Ion*）篇中，談到詩人的靈感時，柏拉圖提到崇拜酒神的婦女從繆思的天國河流中吸取蜂蜜和乳漿。


## 032. 詩律啟蒙：示兒

❶ 詩題（Metrical Feet）直譯為「詩的音步」，最初係詩人為其長子哈特利（Hartley）所寫，後為其次子德文特（Derwent）改定。英詩的詩句，按音節（syllable）和重音（stress）來計算韻律，度量韻律的單位稱為「音步」（foot），這首詩論及最常用的雙音步（dimeter）和三音步（trimeter）。

❷ 原詩指英國湖區的斯基多山（Mount Skiddaw），經常出現在華茲華斯、柯爾律治等「湖畔派詩人」作品中的名山。

## 033. 希臘的見證

* G. G. 拜倫（1788-1824），英國浪漫主義詩人，代表作有敘事詩《恰爾德·哈樂德遊記》（*Childe Harold's Pilgrimage*）和《唐璜》（*Don Juan*）等。

❶ 節譯自拜倫的長詩《異教徒——一個土耳其故事的殘片》（*The Giaour: A Fragment of a Turkish Tale,* 1813）。詩題係譯者取自原詩中的一行並活譯為中文。這首長詩是詩人的「東方敘事詩」的第一首，主要情節是一個土耳其女奴與異教徒相愛，依照當地風俗被扔進海裏，異教徒憤而為她復仇。

❷ 塞莫皮萊是希臘東部一山隘，斯巴達三百勇士曾憑藉這一險關頑強抵抗波斯入侵。

❸ 薩拉米是夾在希臘半島與波羅奔尼撒半島之間的島嶼，歷史上的薩拉米海灣戰，是希波戰爭中雅典贏得馬拉松戰役之後的又一次輝煌勝利。

❹ 古希臘人以雅典的「地球之臍」自居，把不屬「文明」希臘人的異邦人，一概視為野蠻人。

❺ 在奧斯曼帝國統治下的希臘，雅典地方官由土耳其蘇丹宮殿的大宦官（the Kislar Aga）委任，缺乏教養的大宦官，實際上只是宮中婦女監護人的奴隸。


## 034. 她步入美

❶ 這首詩最初見於拜倫配有曲譜的《希伯來旋律》（*Hebrew Melodies,* 1815），詩中的「她」可能指拜倫的一位堂（表）姊妹，這位孀居的美

人著喪服在舞會上出現，啟迪了詩人靈感。但是，「她」的形象也可以視為一種藝術美的象徵。

❷ 這一行因為韻律的需要而倒裝，正常語序為「heaven denies to gaudy day」。其中的「heaven」一詞，英詩箋注家的理解略有不同，或認為是用來指代上帝，意即上帝不把那種柔光（tender light）賜予浮艷的白日（gaudy day）；或認為用來比喻這位美女，意即她不喜歡浮艷的白日，不會在太亮麗的場景中出現。中譯為求古譯韻味取義於後者。

❸ 原文這一行的「which」一詞指上文的「難言神韻」（the nameless grace），儘管難以名狀，詩人仍然欲罷不能，嘗試用各種比喻「狀難寫之境如在目前」。


## 035. 星辰山岳，悄然寂滅？少年游

❶ 節譯自拜倫《島嶼》（*The Island*, 1823）。詞牌名「少年游」，各家句讀多出入，譯詩依周邦彥別格填入。


## 036. 一八一九年的英格蘭

＊P. B. 雪萊（1792-1822），英國浪漫主義抒情詩人，偉大的理想主義者，主要作品有長詩《麥布女王》（*Queen Mab*）、《阿多尼斯》（*Adonais*）等。

❶ 這首十四行詩寫於1819年，直到1839年才發表於雪萊夫人編輯的四卷本《雪萊詩集》（*The Poetical Works of Percy Bysshe Shelley*）。全詩是一個長句，開始是一連串並置的主語，直到第十三行才出現了表示比喻意義

的系動詞「are」。原詩韻腳為 ababab，cdcd，ccdd，不同於傳統的英國十四行詩。譯詩大致仿照原詩的語法結構和韻腳。

❷ 指已經失明並患有精神病的英王喬治三世，死於雪萊寫作這首詩之後的次年。

❸ 主要指缺德的不受歡迎的攝政王子。

❹ 原文「field」一詞可以視上下文譯為田野或廣場，此處一詞多譯。詩中提及的殺戮指 1819 年 8 月發生在英格蘭曼徹斯特的聖彼德廣場（St. Peter's Field）的彼得盧屠殺（Peterloo Massacre），當時一隊騎兵衝入數萬和平集會要求改革的人羣，十五人被殺，數百人受傷。這次事件被命名為彼得盧屠殺，與四年前發生的滑鐵盧戰役中英軍的勝利形成反諷的對比。

❺ 指排斥非國教徒（Dissenters）和羅馬天主教徒的法規。


037. 西風頌

❶「這首詩構思於佛羅倫薩附近阿諾河畔的樹林裏，主要部分亦草成於此。當日，熱風卷著雲靄，氣溫驟然上昇，一場秋雨正在醞釀之中。果然不出所料，日落時分，狂風乍起，大雨滂沱，伴以阿爾卑斯山南地區特有的氣勢磅礴的閃電雷鳴。」——雪萊原注。原詩詩節採用義大利式十四行詩三連環體（terza rima），韻式為 aba，bcb，cdc，ded，ee，譯詩大體仿照原詩押韻。

❷ 在信奉「神人同形同性論」（anthropomorphism）的希臘神話中，西風

的人格化或神格化（deification）的「Zephyrus」是佔星之神（Astroeus）和黎明女神（Aurora）的兒子。就氣象學而言，雪萊所遇的西風，是阿爾卑斯山南夏末秋初的西風，後文寫到的「你青翠的陽春妹妹」，是另一股透露義大利西海岸春訊的西風。

❸ 此句譯文參考郭沫若譯筆：「在山野之中彌漫著活色生香」。

❹ 此處原文把西風稱為「破壞者保護者」（Destroyer and preserver），暗指印度教的破壞之神濕婆（Siva）和保護之神毗濕奴（Vishnu），雪萊當時從 Edward Moor 的《印度萬神殿》（*Hindu Pantheon*）等著作中了解到一些印度神話。

❺ 酒神的狂女（Maenad）或音譯為邁那得，是希臘神話中的酒神的女祭司或信徒，常披頭散髮，狂歌亂舞。

❻ 巴延灣（Baiae）位於義大利那不勒斯附近，是古羅馬海濱勝地的遺址。浮石是一種火山岩，那不勒斯一帶屬火山區。詩人於 1818 年 12 月 18 日從那不勒斯西岸乘船到巴延灣，在給友人的一封信中寫到航程中觀賞到的澄澈透明的海水和古代繁華留下的廢墟。

❼ 第三節末尾所詠的現象，博物學家是十分熟悉的。江河湖泊和海洋底部的水生植物與陸地植物一樣，對四時更替有類似的反應，因此也受季風的影響。——雪萊原注。

❽ 「詩琴」（lyre），七弦琴或小豎琴，在希臘神話中是風神的豎琴（Aeolian or wind harp）。

❾ 「預言的號角」，據西方注釋家，詩人此處暗用了《聖經·啟示錄》第一章的典故。

## 038. 哀歌

❶ 這首詩原為雪萊劇作殘篇《查爾斯一世》（*Charles I*）中一個宮廷小丑所唱的歌，原本有三節，收入雪萊《身後詩集》（*Posthumous Poems, 1824*）時題為「A Song」，後來雪萊夫人瑪麗（Mary Wollstonecraft shelley）單獨發表現在流行的這兩節。蘇曼殊曾以五言譯此詩，題為〈冬日〉。

## 039. 音樂輕柔曲散時 七絕二首

❶ 原詩無題，雪萊夫人瑪麗曾題為〈回憶〉（*Memory*），後來的詩選集一般以首行為題。

❷ 原詩最後兩行因韻律而採用倒裝句，依正常語序是：Love itself shall slumber on thy thoughts.（愛本身將陪睡在你的思緒上）。詩人致辭的對象（thou）性別不明，中譯作「君」或「汝」均可。死者思想不死，思想在睡夢中也會有神思飛揚之時，中譯取此深層結構的含義。最後一句改為「情愛將隨別緒棲」，則與原詩表層結構較為接近。

## 040. 世界游子

❶ 譯自《雪萊抒情詩和短詩》（*The Lyrics and Shorter Poems of Percy Bysshe Shelley, 1907*）。

## 041. 美女薄情仙 添字畫堂春六首

＊約翰・濟慈（1795-1821），英國浪漫主義詩人，主要作品有長詩〈伊莎貝拉〉（*Isabella*）、〈聖愛尼節前夜〉（*The Eve of St. Agnes*）、〈安狄米恩〉（*Endymion*）等。

❶ 原詩詩題取自法文，意為「無情的美人」，原詩有兩種略有差異的版本。一般認為，詩人把斯賓塞的《仙后》中耍欺騙手腕的妓女 Duessa 與仙后本人這兩個截然不同的女性形象揉合起來了。

❷ 原文「honey wild, and manna dew」，可能指柯爾律治的《忽必烈汗》中寫到的蜜露，即鴉片，瑪那（manna）原本是《舊約》中以色列人經過曠野時獲得的神賜的食物。


## 042. 憂鬱頌

❶ 譯自濟慈詩集《女妖，伊莎貝拉，聖艾妮絲節前夕及其他詩歌》（*Lamia, Isabella, The Eve of St. Agnes, and Other Poems*, 1820）。這首詩是濟慈著名的六首頌詩之一，其他五首分別是：〈希臘古甕頌〉、〈懶惰頌〉、〈夜鶯頌〉、〈靈魂頌〉和〈秋頌〉。〈憂鬱頌〉最初有四節，發表時由詩人刪去第一節。

❷ 詩人直接向讀者致辭。莫去遺忘河，即勸人不要自殺，不要嘗試忘卻憂鬱或以死來了斷憂鬱。以下多行均含此意。

❸ 山金車，學名「Arnica Montana」，有附子草（可入中藥）、狼毒（Wolf's Bane）等多種別名，一種可以用來自殺的有毒植物，也曾用來

毒殺狼群。

❹ 冥后普柔瑟萍，在羅馬神話中，是冥王把她綁架到冥土，迫使她每年在冥土滯留半年為后。

❺ 可能暗指最後奪去濟慈生命的結核病。

❻ 水松球果亦有小毒。

❼ 甲蟲是棺木的象徵；致命飛蛾是一種身上帶有骷髏般花斑點的蛾蟲。希臘神話中靈魂化身的美女賽姬（Psyche）以蝴蝶為象徵，因此，靈魂化蝶是理想，化蟲則不祥。

❽ 這一行的意思是，活著比死去好，有靈魂的痛苦比沒有靈魂要好，因為有靈魂，至少會有一種能夠欣賞生活美的審美意識。

❾ 此處的「情人」仿佛是個瘋女人，或可解讀為死亡女神。面對死亡，也應當處變不驚，理喻死亡的深意。

❿ 此處的「她」，兼指上面寫到的「情人」和憂鬱女神。

⓫ 此處歡樂被人格化為男性，接著的矛盾語「疼痛的愉快」（aching pleasure）在字面上與中文的「痛快」相似，但後者一般只用其偏義，在特殊情況下，有苦中之樂的複義。

⓬ 駕臨憂鬱之上的最高神祇，指濟慈史詩《海波利昂的敗落》（*The Fall of Hyperion*）中寫到的繆思母親記憶女神，她在詩中向詩人提出詩歌的本性等種種問題，作為對詩人的測試。

⓭ 此處化用莎士比亞十四行詩第三十一首中的詩行：「你如墳塋，被葬之愛蘇醒／我平生所愛，如戰利品懸掛墳前」（Thou art the grave where buried love doth live／Hung with the trophies of my lovers gone）。在莎士比

亞的時代，貴族階層的墳前往往插上喪旗，喪旗上飾以能展示死者功績的生前隨身物件作為紀念。莎士比亞用「trophies」（紀念品或戰利品）一詞可能還隱含性愛之意：情場如戰場，征服對方，無異於得到戰利品。

## 043. 致秋君

❶ 這首頌詩的詩題與其他五首頌詩不同，沒有采用「Ode」一詞，詩中的秋季既是神格化又是人格化的表現，因為詩一開頭就說秋是太陽（日神）的朋友，第二節起直接向秋致辭，勾勒了一個收穫者和音樂家的形象。濟慈曾在一封書信中說，詩人查特頓（Thomas Chatterton, 1752-1770）總是令他想到秋天。在詩歌語言方面，濟慈深受查特頓的影響，加上為詞曲體表述的方便，詩題譯為「致秋君」。

❷ 一般認為這一行詩是濟慈對查特頓的回憶，這位早熟的詩人碩果累累，甚至少年老成，把自己的作品偽託為中世紀詩歌。

❸ 原文「treble soft」（尖亮柔和）可以視為一種矛盾語，把蟋蟀雌雄兩性的歌聲揉合起來了。實際上，蟋蟀雄蟲好鬥，以翅膀摩擦發聲或鳴叫求偶，雌蟲不會鳴叫，故以中文擬聲詞譯為「雄唧唧，雌默默」。

❹ 即歐亞鴝，俗稱知更鳥。

## 044. 離燕 河傳

＊威廉・豪易特（William Howitt, 1792-1879），英國詩人，長期與他的妻子

Mary Botham 共同從事文學創作，曾合作出版《森林游吟詩人及其他詩作》（*The Forest Minstrels and other Poems,* 1821）。

❶ 詩人把追求自由的靈魂喻為一隻燕子。唐詞〈河傳〉，唐宋人所作令詞，字數句逗韻腳，極不一致。但前後兩片皆前仄韻，後平韻，平仄互換，則大抵相同耳。譯詩依李珣詞填入，分行依照原詩。


## 045. 水娘 西江月

＊托馬斯・胡德（1799-1845），英國詩人和幽默作家，代表作有〈襯衫之歌〉（*The Song of the Shirt*）、〈嘆息橋〉（*The Bridge of Sighs*）等詩篇和死後出版的十卷本《胡德著作：亦莊亦諧插圖本詩文集》（*The Works of Thomas Hood: Comic and Serious in Prose and Verse with All the Original Illustrations,* 1873）。

❶ 譯自《托馬斯・胡德詩集》（*The Poetical Works Of Thomas Hood,* 1861）。這首詩是在濟慈的朋友、英國畫家塞弗恩（Joseph Severn, 1793-1879）的一幅水彩畫的啟迪下創作的。


## 046. 紫杜鵑

＊R.W. 愛默生（1803-1882），美國哲學家、散文家和詩人，十九世紀中期美國超驗主義（Transcendentalism）運動的領銜人物，主要著作有《詩集》（*Poems,* 1847）、《大自然》（*Nature: Addresses and Lectures,* 1849）、《代表人物》（*Representative Men,* 1850）、《英國人的特性》（*English Traits,* 1956）和《五月

及其他詩》（*May Day and Other Poems*, 1867）等。

❶ 譯自愛默生《詩集》。

❷ 紫杜鵑先開花後長葉，原詩「leafless blooms」一語，並不意味這種花根本不長葉子。

❸ 原詩「simple ignorance」一語，西方學者或注釋為：This is a wise, though simple question, such as a child might ask.（這雖然是一個兒童也許會提出的簡單的問題，卻是一個高明的問題。）

❹ 最後一行「the self-same Power」一語，暫譯為「同源自力」。張愛玲譯本〈紫陀羅花〉譯為「一種大能」，龍應臺譯本〈紫杜鵑〉譯為「緣起」。西方學者認為此處指上帝。愛默生一度擔任過牧師，但後來日漸偏離了當時的主流宗教信仰，領銜超驗主義運動，認為萬物都是宇宙的縮影。寫作此詩前後，愛默生經常提到「自恃」（Self-Reliance）的概念，並於1841年以此為題發表著名散文。這一概念強調每個個體均遵循自身的本能或觀念，既避免合羣（conformity），尤其是假意的一致性（false consistency），又不是反社會反社羣的。詩人與社羣的關系，可以說是疏而不隔。這首詩似乎表現了愛默生類似的哲學思考和人生態度。

## 047. 康科特讚歌

❶ 譯自《愛默生全集》（*The Complete Works of Ralph Waldo Emerson*, 1904）中的定稿。這首詩是作者為謳歌美國革命英雄而作。美國麻省康科特小鎮康科特河流經的老北橋（The Old North Bridge），是美國獨立戰爭第一

次戰役——美國民兵抗擊英軍的列星頓及康科特戰役（Battle of Lexington and Concord）所在地。愛默生的祖父曾參與這次戰役。這首詩寫於老北橋附近的愛默生故居（The Old Manse）。

## 048. 辯白

❶ 譯自愛默生《詩集》。

## 049. 希倫·包爾斯的希臘奴隸

＊E.B. 勃朗寧（1806-1861），又稱勃朗寧夫人（羅伯特·勃朗寧的夫人），英國女詩人，代表作有《葡萄牙十四行詩集》（*Sonnets from the Portuguese*, 1850），其最後的詩集是詩人去世後由她的丈夫羅伯特·勃朗寧整理出版的。

❶ 譯自勃朗寧夫人的《葡萄牙十四行詩集》。詩人曾與她丈夫羅伯特·勃朗寧一起到義大利拜訪當時寓居弗羅倫薩的美國雕塑家希倫·包爾斯（Hiram Powers），在他的工作室見到「希臘奴隸」雕像，雕像展現的是土耳其人正在中東奴隸市場販賣一位白人女奴的情形。

## 050. 靈魂的表現

❶ 譯自勃朗寧夫人的詩集（*The Poems Of Elizabeth Barrett Browning*, Volume 1, 1853）。

051. 人生禮贊——年輕人心靈對歌者所言

＊H. W. 朗費羅（1807-1882），美國詩人和教育家，是歐洲與美國文學的橋樑，
主要作品有抒情詩集《夜籟》（*Voice of the Night*, 1839）、《經過之鳥》（*Birds of Passage*, 1841），長篇敘事詩〈伊芳吉琳〉（*Evangeline*, 1847）、〈海華沙之歌〉（*The Song of Hiawatha*, 1855）等。

❶ 譯自朗費羅的詩集《夜籟》。該詩副標題的「歌者」，當指作為《舊約・詩篇》作者的大衛王。

❷ 耶和華對亞當說：「你原本是塵土，也將歸於塵土。」見《舊約・創世紀》第三章。

❸ 此句化用古希臘名醫希波克拉底（Hippocrates）的格言：「人生短，藝術長，機會飛」（英譯：Life is short, [the] art long, opportunity fleeting.）。希波克拉底所說的「藝術」主要指醫藝，後來用以兼指包括文學藝術在內的各種技藝和學問。

❹ 這一行在全詩中頗為重要，甚至可視為「詩眼」，因為朗費羅一度把這首詩改題為〈死亡禮贊〉（*A Psalm of Death*），後來為了強調積極的人生觀才放棄了這個詩題。


052. 橋巫山一斷雲

❶ 譯自朗費羅的《布魯茨的鐘樓及其他詩》（*The Belfry Of Bruges And Other Poems*, 1845），這首詩寫於詩人喪妻之後，構思於詩人常去的波士頓查

理斯河上的橋頭（The bridge of the Charles）。1907年為紀念這位詩人，該橋改名為郎費羅橋。橋雖已部分重建，但仍然可見當時木碼頭等景觀。譯詩以原詩每兩節為一曲「巫山一斷雲」，第二曲換韻，最後剩下單一的一片，故特意不依照原詩標明詩節。

❷ 當時在橋頭附近的布萊頓碼頭有一個熔爐，入夜有「紅星亂紫煙」的景象。

## 053. 〈伊芳吉琳〉序曲 玉蝴蝶慢

❶ 譯自郎費羅的長詩〈伊芳吉琳〉序曲，原詩或分節，或不分節，此處分節不依慣例，而是依照譯詩的「玉蝴蝶慢二首」每首各有上下片來分節，以便英漢對照。這部史詩性的長詩以十八世紀的法印戰爭（The French and Indian War）為背景，敘述北美阿卡狄亞一個和平村莊遭英國殖民者焚毀，少女伊凡吉林與其未婚夫悲歡離合的故事。

❷ 此處原文「Druids of eld」意為督伊德高僧，是古老的凱爾特族（Celt）的神職人員，在後世詩文中常以橡樹精的形象出現。

❸ 此處省略了原文中村莊的名字：格蘭德・普列（The village of Grand Pré），是十七世紀的法國人在北美阿卡狄亞移民區建立的一個村莊，見證過歷史烽煙，現在是加拿大的國家歷史遺跡之一。

❹ 這一行省略了原文中的地名「阿卡狄亞」一詞。

## 054. 神的正義

❶ 這首詩最初是古希臘一位不知名的詩人的作品，經多次翻譯和轉譯，在英語中以朗費羅的意譯流行。

## 055. 鐘鈴

＊愛倫‧坡（1809-1849），美國詩人、小說家、編輯和文學評論家，被尊為美國浪漫主義運動的推手之一，以懸疑、驚悚小說著稱，詩歌成名作為〈烏鴉〉（*The Raven*, 1845）。

❶ 譯自《愛倫‧坡詩作》（*The Poetical Works of Edgar Allan Poe*, 1888）。英文中的同一個詞「bell」，在中文中根據其大小而譯為鐘或鈴。俄羅斯大作曲家拉赫曼尼諾夫（Sergei Rachmaninoff）曾根據這首詩創作了交響樂《升C小調前奏曲》（*Prelude in C# Minor, p. 3, No. 2*）。

❷ 北歐古代呂那文字的（Runic）韻律，帶有神秘色彩。

❸ 斑鳩有類似中國鴛鴦的象徵意義，在基督教文化中是一種象徵愛的獻祭的鳥，愛倫‧坡時代的婚禮往往在月夜舉行。這裏暗示了這樣一種意境：斑鳩棲身在背後有月亮在樹枝上，仿佛棲身在月亮中。

## 056. 滴滴無端淚

＊阿爾弗雷德‧丁尼生（1809-1892），英國詩人和劇作家，代表作有悼念友人哈勒姆（A. Hallam）的哀歌〈悼亡〉（*In Memoriam*, 1850）和戲劇獨白詩〈莫

德〉（*Maud:a Monodrama*, 1855），詩集有《抒情詩及其他》（*Poems, Chiefly Lyrical*, 1830）等。

❶ 這首詩原為丁尼生的敘事長詩〈公主〉（*The Princess*, 1847）中的一首歌，原詩是無韻詩（blank verse）。從第二節起，原詩每節都是一個倒裝句，主語是後置的（似水）年華（the days），省略了表達比喻意義的系動詞「are」。

## 057. 雄鷹 攤破浣溪沙

❶ 詩中的雄鷹可以視為浪漫主義孤獨的局外人的寫照。

## 058. 海鷗

❶ 原詩最後一行是動賓倒裝句，「lands」是動詞的第三人稱單數，意為「To catch and pull in」。這一結果與前面宏大的渲染形成一種反諷（irony）。

## 059. 一個悲劇故事

＊威廉・梅克比斯・薩克萊（1811-1863），英國小說家，《浮華世界》（*Vanity Fair*）的作者。

❶ 譯自薩克萊的《歌謠集》（*Ballads*, 1855）。這首詩是德裔法籍詩人沙米索（Adelbert Chamisso, 1781-1838) 的〈悲劇故事〉（*Tragische Geschichte*）的意

譯，原詩頭三行的大意是：曾經有個人，一根辮子牽掛到他心裏，那根辮子是掛在後面的，他想換一個方式。

## 060. 海外鄉思

＊羅伯特・勃朗寧（1812-1889），維多利亞時期的英國詩人和劇作家，主要作品有《戲劇抒情詩選》（*Dramatic Lyrics*, 1842）、《戲劇傳奇和抒情詩集》（*Dramatic Romances and Lyrics*, 1845）、長詩〈指環與書〉（*The Ring and the Book*, 1868）。

❶ 寫於詩人和他的夫人1845年寓居義大利之時。

## 061. 麥田上 鵲橋仙

＊H.D. 梭羅（1817-1862），美國詩人、作家和思想家，代表作有散文集《瓦爾登湖》（*Walden*, 1854）和詩集《梭羅詩選》（*Collected Poems of Henry Thoreau*, 1965）。

## 062. 煙

❶ 譯自梭羅散文集《瓦爾登湖》。

❷ 希臘神話人物伊卡魯斯（Icarus），憑藉用蠟黏合的翅膀高飛，蠟被陽光熔化後墜海遇難。

## 063. 月亮

❶ 引自英國詩人和政治家羅利（Sir Walter Raleigh）的詩作〈讚美月神美好無害之光〉（*Praised be Diana's fair and harmless light*）。

## 064. 明朗的子夜

＊瓦爾特・惠特曼（1819-1892），美國詩人和散文家，以詩集《草葉集》（*Leaves of Grass*, 1855）著稱。

❶ 這首詩是惠特曼《草葉集》（Leaves of Grass）1881年版本中的詩組〈從中午到星夜〉（From Noon to Starry Night）中的最後一首。

## 065. 鐵窗吟

＊艾內斯特・鐘斯（1819-1869），英國詩人、政論家、小說家和文藝評論家，左翼工人運動憲章運動（the Chartist movement）的領袖人物，在1948年歐洲革命風暴中因政治宣傳繫獄兩年，獄中寫有史詩《印度起義》（*The Revolt of Hindostan*）等詩作，於出獄後出版。

❶ 這首詩最初載於鐘斯出獄後編輯的《人民通訊》（*Notes to The People*）1850年第一期，是詩人血書的獄中詩之一，即詩人以指頭鮮血寫於撕下來的聖經書頁上的詩作。詩中化用了《舊約・詩篇》中的詩語，例如詩篇第一百一十八篇中的詩行：「他們環繞我，圍困我，我靠耶和華的名，必剿滅他們。」

譯文二・鐵窗吟（七律）：

怒銷囹圄黑柵欄，化作頭盔面世間。百煉熔爐心欲火，千錘膽略志淩天。指頭如削鑄彈道，霜骨作砧堆鐵磚，鎧甲摩登護舊疾，鋼條向敵如揮鞭。

原文把監獄柵欄或鐵窗欄杆人格化，直接對其致辭。怒視的（scowling）柵欄與詩人應當是相互怒目相向的。譯詩已經把柵欄的憤怒轉換為詩人的憤怒。

## 066. 多佛海灘

*麥修・阿諾德（1822-1888），英國維多利亞時期的詩人和文論家，詩作主要收集於《詩集》（*Poems*, 1853）、《詩二集》（*Poems: Second Series*, 1855）和《新詩集》（*New Poems*, 1867），文論著作有《批評論集》（*Essay in Criticism*, 1865）和《文化與無政府》（*Culture and Anarchy*, 1869）等。

❶ 譯自阿諾德的《新詩集》。這首詩的寫作年代無法確定，可能早在1848年的歐洲革命之後就已有了部分詩行的草稿，一般認為寫於1851年，正當西方宗教信仰在工業革命和社會達爾文主義的衝擊下日益衰落之時，當時詩人攜新婚妻子到英國東南部肯特州的英吉利海峽多佛海灘度蜜月，下榻之處，面對彼岸法國港口城市加來。

❷ 上句中的「the light」當指燈塔之光。燈塔顯隱，像潮汐一樣，是詩人所信奉的基督教信仰盛衰的象徵。雖然燈塔始終亮著，不會熄滅，但能否見到燈塔之光及其明亮朦朧的程度，取決於航海者或觀察者與燈塔之間

的距離、角度、天氣等各方面的因素。

❸ 英格蘭的懸崖峭壁是容易被風雨海浪剝蝕的石灰巖。此處景觀都是與後文相呼應的信仰危機的象徵。

❹ 原文的「the grating roar Of pebbles」一語延後迻譯於此。此處動名詞「grating」的動詞原形「grate」，意思是發出刺耳摩擦聲，包含似非而是的悖論（paradox）、擬人和誇張等多種修辭手法，因為，即使卵石摩擦有聲，也不是吼叫聲（roar）。既被潮汐捉弄又相互摩擦的卵石，是既被命運捉弄又相互牴牾的人類個體或小羣體的象徵。

❺ 西方詩歌箋注家認為這一行詩獨出心裁卻難於解讀。多家中譯把「girdle」一詞譯為彩帶或腰帶，此處當指該詞的另一個意義，即一種類似於女性連衣裙的內衣，詩人也許把人類的信仰衰落喻為衣裝脫落，這樣才能與下文的「裸體砂石」的比喻相呼應。

❻ 古希臘悲劇詩人索福克勒斯在悲劇《安提戈涅》中說：諸神像狂風掀起的潮頭一樣，將不斷光顧一代代人留下的廢墟。

❼ 依照西方箋注家，此處暗用典故：希臘歷史學家修席底德（Thukydides）在《伯羅奔尼撒戰爭史》中記敘了一次海灣夜戰，入侵西西里敘拉古王國的雅典軍隊黑暗中不辨方向敵我，自相殘殺。這一史實也可以用來暗示歐洲革命的盲目性的一面，或英國維多利亞時期各種價值觀的混亂和混戰，乃至現代世界的普遍的盲目性。

## 067. 安魂曲

❶ 譯自《麥修・阿諾德詩集》（*Poems by Matthew Arnold: A New Edition, 1853*）。詩人哀悼的對象生平不詳，中國詩人吳宓曾把此詩譯為五言體，題為〈輓歌〉，認為阿諾德哀悼的是一位歌妓舞女。

❷ 「Yew」，水松或紫杉，樹質堅硬，常用為製造武器的木材。在凱爾特神話中，它是葬禮的象徵，但一般適合於勇士的葬禮，故譯為勁松。

## 068. 菲洛美拉

❶ 譯自《麥修・阿諾德詩集》。在希臘神話中，菲洛美拉是雅典公主和道里斯（Daulis）城邦國王鐵修斯（Tereus）的妻子普柔克尼（Procne）的妹妹。依照阿諾德的版本，鐵修斯迷上了菲洛美拉，喜新厭舊，割掉了妻子普柔克尼的舌尖並把她關押在山洞裏，佯稱她已經死了。普柔克尼織成一幅錦繡，委婉地痛說自己的故事，托人以此向妹妹陳情。菲洛美拉獲悉後救出姊姊。憤慨中為了報復，姊妹倆殺死了鐵修斯與普柔克尼生的嬰兒 Itys，剁成肉塊給鐵修斯吃。暴君發現吃的是自己的兒子之後，追殺兩姊妹。兩姊妹在神的幫助下逃亡，普柔克尼變為喑啞的燕子，菲洛美拉變為啼血的夜鶯。這個故事在流傳中有多種變異的版本，或說鐵修斯借機強暴了菲洛美拉並割掉她的舌尖，是她在被關押的山洞中織出錦繡向姊姊陳情，或說變為夜鶯的是普柔克尼。夜鶯啼血的意義也有兩說，一是「Itu」，「Itu」即值得紀念的作為無辜犧牲品的嬰兒的名字，二是「Tereu」，「Tereu」即暴君鐵修斯的名字（因為舌尖被割掉

而發音不全），表明她永遠不忘記這個暴君的罪行。鐵修斯也變成一隻鷂鷹或戴勝鳥，牠啼叫的意思是「在哪裏？在哪裏？」表明暴君追殺獵物的本性難移。依照奧維德《變形記》中的敘述，菲洛美拉一詞的語源是「歌的戀人」（一般認為這是一種誤讀），後來的神話原型學派把夜鶯視為詩人或藝術家的原型。

❷ 原文的「Thracian」一詞是色雷斯（Thrace）的形容詞，色雷斯是包括道里斯城邦在內的一個廣袤的東南歐歷史地理區域。

❸ 原文的「Cephissian」一詞是河神西菲塞斯（Cephissus）的形容詞，道里斯城邦是以河神的女兒的名字命名的。

## 069. 閃光

\* D.G. 羅塞蒂（1828-1882），英國詩人畫家、詩人和翻譯家，前拉斐爾派（the Pre- Raphaelite）的創始人之一，主要著作有《羅塞蒂詩集》（*Poems by D.G.Rossetti*, 1870）和《歌謠和十四行詩》（*Ballads and Sonnets*, 1881）。

❶ 譯自羅賽蒂第一本詩集《詩歌：獻給蘭開夏郡》（*Poems: An Offering to Lancashire*, 1863）。第三節有兩個版本，因為用韻的緣故，譯詩取第一個版本。

## 070. 維納斯・心靈的轉化者

❶ 這首十四行詩寫於1868年，同題繪畫約作於 1863 年到 1869 年之間，題目取自拉丁文，原意是維納斯可以把婦女的心轉化為美德，但羅塞蒂反

其意而用之，把希臘羅馬神話與聖經中禁果的典故揉合起來，描寫維納斯的誘惑力如何把男人的愛情專一之心轉化為貳心。

❷ 指拐走海倫導致戰亂的特洛伊王子甘尼梅德（Ganymede）。

## 071. 寒意吟 八六子

＊C.G.羅塞蒂（1830-1894），英國維多利亞時期的女詩人，D. G.羅塞蒂的妹妹，主要詩集有《妖怪集市及其他詩》（*Goblin Market and Other Poems*，1862）和《王子的歷程及其他詩》（*The Prince's Progress and Other Poems*，1866）。

❶ 譯自羅塞蒂的《王子的歷程及其他詩》。詞牌「八六子」（又名「感黃鸝」），原詩的第二、三節合為譯詩的下片。依照格律，該詞牌平仄葉韻之外，前片第四句以一去聲字領六言兩對句，後片第四句以三仄聲字領六言一句，四言兩對句，第七句以兩平聲字領六言兩對句。譯詩依照英文原詩分行排列，以便對照。

譯文二·寒意吟：

寒夜風刀刺骨，羊羔何處安宿？依偎母羊厚絨褥，慈心通宵呵護

／永夜寒露侵骨，雛雀何處安宿？母鳥豐羽蓋被褥，直到天明日出。

／身羈荒原野樹，我心亦盼安宿，何處可得一暖巢？見者請君告訴。

## 072. 希望 漁歌子三首

＊艾密莉·狄金森（1830-1886），美國詩人，生前只發表過十首詩，遺作陸續出版後被公認為傑出女詩人。詹森（Thomas H. Johnson）編輯的《狄金森詩全

集》（*The Complete Poems of Emily Dickinson*, 1951），收錄了詩人一千七百七十五首詩以及一些殘篇，原詩無題，依照時間順序編號。其他一些選集大都以首行爲題。以下選詩或以首行爲標題，或依照別的版本靈活處理。

## 074. 細品味，此酒無人釀

❶ 毛地黃（foxglove），有酒壺花、山煙根等多種別名。
❷ 雪帽，比喻白雲。

## 075. 快哉長夜濃睡

❶ 此處「lid」一詞指棺蓋或被蓋。

## 076. 伉儷

＊A.C. 斯溫伯恩（1837-1909），英國維多利亞時代的詩人、劇作家、小說家和批評家，代表作有《卡里頓的阿塔蘭達》（*Atalanta in Calydon*, 1865）等。
❶ 譯自斯溫伯恩的詩集《詩與歌謠》（*Poems and Ballads*, 1866）。

## 077. 自由女神塑像

＊埃瑪・拉扎勒斯（1849-1887），生於紐約的美籍猶太裔女詩人和作家，主要著作有兩卷本《埃瑪・拉扎勒斯詩集》（*The Poems of Emma Lazarus: Narrative, Lyric, and Dramatic*, 1888）。

❶ 譯自《埃瑪・拉扎勒斯詩集》。這首十四行詩原本為一個基金會集資建造自由女神塑像底座的基金會而作，後來被鐫刻在銅板上置於自由女神塑像內部，1945 年從內部移出來安置於塑像底座正面。詩人把當時即將豎立的自由女神塑像視為希臘羅德島巨像（The Colossus of Rhodes）的革新。羅德島巨像塑造的是希臘神話中泰坦神族的赫利歐斯（Titan Helios）的形象，是古代世界七大奇跡之一，毀於西元前 226 年的地震。詩中所寫到的風雨顛簸而來的大批流亡的貧民主要是經由紐約艾利斯島（Ellis Island）抵達美國的。傅譯第一稿原載 1999 年 8 月 17 日紐約美東版《自由時報》，後被收入美國民主基本文獻（Basic Readings in U.S. Democracy）網頁（未注明譯者）。這裏發表的是修改稿。

❷ 原文的形容詞「brazen」兼有「無恥的、無禮的」和「黃銅制的」等多種意義。據說這尊塑像叉開雙腿橫跨於港口之上，來往的船只要從他胯下經過。

❸ 此處的海港指紐約港，雙城指原本分開的紐約和昆斯（Queens，即現在的紐約皇后區），直到 1883 年才連為一體。


## 078. 柏枝壓霜雪

＊A.E.豪斯曼（1859-1936），英國古典學者和詩人，代表作為詩集《什羅普郡一少年》（*Shropshire Lad*, 1896）。

❶ 譯自豪斯曼的詩集《什羅普郡一少年》。

❷ 柏枝在西方被視為死亡的象徵。

❸ 水松或稱杉樹，根葉均有微毒。

❹ 迷迭香在西方常用於葬禮中。

❺ 英國古民歌中以柳枝象徵愁和怨恨，見莎士比亞《奧瑟羅》第四幕第三景之歌。


## 079. 給 W.P.

＊喬治‧桑塔耶納（1863-1952），生於西班牙的美國哲學家、美學家、詩人和作家，詩集有《十四行詩和其他詩作》（*Sonnets and Other Verses*, 1896）等。

❶ 這首詩最初發表於1896年。W.P. 指詩人的摯友 Warwick Potter，1893年死於船難。

❷ 指詩人所在的美國麻省的海域。


## 080. 白人的負擔

＊魯德亞德‧吉卜林（1865-1936），生於印度孟買的英國詩人和小說家，1907年諾貝爾文學獎得主，主要作品有詩集《營房謠》（*Barrack-Room Ballads*, 1892）、《曼德勒》（*Mandalay*, 1890）和動物故事《叢林之書》（*The Jungle Book*, 1894）等。

❶ 這首詩寫於美西戰爭之後，即美國在菲律賓擊敗西班牙接管菲律賓之時，是一首備受爭議的名詩，仿作甚多。

❷ 此處涉及西方殖民者的種族歧視。由於殖民者要推行關於禮儀和正派行為的西方觀念，被殖民者的舉止行為可能被視為近乎魔鬼的道德墮落現

象。

❸ 清道夫在印度種姓制度中是近乎奴隸的下等人。

❹ 此處涉及1898年美國與西班牙簽訂的《巴黎和約》的一個條款，根據這一條款，美國在美西戰爭中吞并的菲律賓和波多黎各，以及實際上控制在手的古巴，應當在十年後交還給本國人。到時候，美國人就可能進不去了。

❺ 此處用《舊約·出埃及記》中的典故：以色列人在曠野挨餓時，抱怨引領他們出埃及的摩西。


## 081. 藍玫瑰

❶ 譯自吉卜林《消失的光線》（*Light That Failed Memoirs*），同時見於他的詩集《書中歌》（*Songs from Books*, 1914）。大自然中原本不存在的藍玫瑰，在文學中是愛、非分之想或神秘性的象徵，因此有把白玫瑰染藍製作「藍色妖姬」的傳統。


## 082. 牧神的祭司

＊威廉·巴特勒·葉慈（1865-1939），愛爾蘭詩人和劇作家，1923 年諾貝爾文學獎得主，主要詩集有《葦間風》（*The Wind Among the Reeds*, 1899）和《塔》（*The Tower*, 1928）等。

❶ 這是葉慈早期未發表的詩作之一，後收入葉慈詩集《月下》（*Under The Moon: The Unpublished Early Poetry*）。

❷ 原詩「oriads」係希臘神話中的山林仙女，譯詩化用《楚辭‧山鬼》首句：「若有人兮山之阿」。

## 083. 他講述完美

❶ 譯自葉慈詩集《葦間風》。

## 084. 情殤 八六子

❶ 這首詩最初發表 1892 年，即詩人認識女演員、愛爾蘭民族主義者毛德‧崗（Maud Gonne）兩年之後的熱戀中。

❷ 指引發特洛伊戰爭的海倫。

## 085. 情殤 八六子

❶ 1925 年詩人重寫這首詩，借懷古抒寫他對毛德‧崗的無望之戀以及對愛爾蘭民族獨立運動的思考。

❷ 葉慈把舊版的「The quarrel of the sparrows」（幾隻麻雀的口角）改為「The brawling of a sparrow」（一隻麻雀的爭嘴），曾引起一位批評家的質疑：「一隻麻雀能爭嘴嗎？」實際上葉芝在散文〈人之魂〉（Anima Hominis）中已回答了這個問題：「借重與別人爭嘴，我們造出雄辯術，借重與自己爭嘴，我們造出詩歌。」（We make out of the quarrel with others, rhetoric, but of the quarrel with ourselves, poetry.）可見這首詩修改後

的起句，有類似於禪宗公案的意義。

❸ 「奧德賽」的意思即奧德修斯的故事，原文點明希臘英雄奧德修斯的名字。

❹ 原文點明特洛伊國王普萊姆（Priam）的名字。這個傲慢的國王在特洛伊陷落後被希臘英雄阿基里斯（Achiles）的兒子殺死。

❺ 「離離」一詞，含義豐富，除了可以狀濃密貌、隱約貌之外，還可以狀悲痛貌，如《楚辭》中錄劉向〈九歎‧思古〉：「曾哀悽欷，心離離兮。」因此可以涵蓋原文含有的悲慟之意。


## o86. 長久緘默過後

❶ 這首詩是葉慈的二十五首抒情短詩《也許可配曲的歌詞》（*Words for Music Perhaps*, 1932）中的一首。第一行的「it」是強調句型的先行代詞（It is right,...that），中間是插入語。多家中譯把「that」後面的一般現在時態「we descant...」誤解為已經完成的行為。葉慈專家 David Clark 在整理葉慈手稿時，對這首詩作了直白的解釋，其中一句是：「來吧，讓我們談論愛。」（Come, let us talk of love.）。

❷ 原文「lamplight」一詞可以依上下文語境指電燈、油燈、蠟燭等各種燈照光亮；「shade」一詞可以指暗影，並不特指多家中譯所譯的燈罩。葉芝曾多次修改這首詩，在另一份手稿中，此兩行為燭光（The heavy curtains drawn-the candle light／Waging a doubtful battle with the shade）。

## o87. 春　玉蝴蝶慢

* 艾內斯特・道森（1867-1900），英國詩人和作家，有死後出版的《道森詩集》（*The Poems of Ernest Dowson*, 1962）等著作。

❶ 這首詩以春天的樂景寫詩人心中的悲涼，龐德曾針對詩人的頹廢傾向，寫了〈秋：給道松——反其意而用之〉，參看後文同樣以詞牌「玉蝴蝶慢」譯出的龐德詩。

❷ 指長壽花，亦稱壽星花。

❸ 指報春花。

譯文二・春：

看那林中柳枝垂葉，滿身綠衣萬樹歡顏，草地披上了百花編織的披肩。清氣和煦夾帶甜美的五月陣雨，爭鳴的百鳥旋律清甜。可那靈魂之春，靈魂之春，再也不會重臨你我心田。／／看那忙碌的蜜蜂悠悠飛舞，細語嗡嗡穿行在杏樹之間，壽星花逗弄金髮少女頑皮少年。苔蘚苗床上報春花領先綻放，小徑旁綴滿芳香的紫羅蘭：可那靈魂之花，靈魂之花，再也不會綻放在你我心田。


## o88. 風範　如夢令二首

* W.H.戴維斯（1871-1940），威爾士出生的英國詩人和作家，有詩集《靈魂的毀滅者及其他詩作》（*The Soul's Destroyer and Other Poems*, 1905）和死後出版的詩全集（*Complete Poems*, 1963）等著作。

## 089. 鐵錘

＊拉爾夫・霍奇森（1871-1962），英國詩人，其詩集《公牛》（*The Bull, 1913*）曾流行一時，二〇年代到三〇年代曾在日本仙臺東北帝國大學教授英文，並從事日本古典詩歌《萬葉集》的英譯工作。

❶ 譯自霍奇森的詩集《最後的黑鶇及其他詩作》（*The Last Blackbird and Other Lines*, 1907）。

## 090. 窗前一顆樹

＊羅伯特・弗羅斯特（1874-1963），美國詩人，以描寫新英格蘭的田園詩見稱，有詩集《波士頓之北》（*North of Boston*, 1914）和《山間》（*Mountain Interval*, 1916）等。

## 091. 七月 水調歌頭

＊愛德華・托瑪斯（1878-1917），英國詩人和作家，第一次世界大戰爆發後應徵入伍，在法國東北戰場犧牲，主要作品有以筆名出版的《六首詩》（*Six Poems*, under pseudonym Edward Eastaway, Pear Tree Press, 1916），死後出版的《詩歌》（*Poems*, Holt, 1917），《最後的詩歌》（*Last Poems*, Selwyn & Blount, 1918）和《詩選》（*Collected Poems*, Selwyn & Blount, 1920）。

❶ 這首詩和下一首詩均寫於托瑪斯在英國應徵入伍尚未去法國之時。

## 093. 解凍 七絕

❶ 譯文二‧解凍：

大地上斑斑駁駁，薄冰殘雪／半是點綴半融化／榆樹上嘰嘰呱呱，幾只烏鴉／半是思索半猜測／高枝暖巢朝下看／冬亦過客，脆弱如敗葉殘花／人卻不能見察／只緣身在樹下。

## 094. 憶舊 七絕

❶ 這首詩是詩人奔赴法國前線後，對前一年（即 1915 年）復活節的回憶，堪稱絕命詩。

## 095. 山谷燃燭

\* 華萊士‧史蒂文斯（1879-1955），美國現代派詩人，主要詩集有《關於秩序的思想》（*Ideas of Order*, 1936）、《帶藍色吉他的人及其他》（*The Man with the Blue Guitar*, 1937）等。

❶ 譯自史蒂文斯的第一本詩集《小風琴》（*Harmonium*, New York: Knopf, 1923），這首詩是意象派的代表作。

## 096. 鶇鳥

\* W.C. 威廉斯（1883-1963），美國現代派詩人，代表作是長詩《裴特森》（*Paterson*, 1963）。

## 097. 墓志銘

＊薩拉・梯斯苔爾（1884-1933），美國女詩人，有《特洛伊的海倫及其他》（*Helen of Troy and Other Poems*, 1911）《奔流入海的河流》（*Rivers to the Sea*, 1915）、《戀歌》（*Love Songs*, 1917）和《月黑》（*Dark of the Moon*, 1926）等詩集。

❶ 選自悌絲黛爾的詩集《月黑》。


## 098. 伊昂妮離世的漫長一年

＊伊茲拉・龐德（1885-1972），美國詩人，意象派的開創者，曾根據一位東方學者的遺稿譯成中國古詩英譯本《華夏集》（*Cathay*, 1915），主要詩集有《比薩詩章》（*The Pisan Cantos*, 1948）。

❶ 譯自龐德早期詩集《大祓集》（*Lustra*, 1916），可能寫於1913年，一般認為詩人悼念的是他的情人，一位藝名伊昂妮（Ione de Forest）自殺身亡的法國芭蕾舞女。


## 099. 秋：給道松──反其意而用之 玉蝴蝶慢

❶ 譯自《龐德早期詩選》（*Collected early poems of Ezra Pound*, 1926, New Directions Publishing, 1982）。詩人道森在〈春〉（參看本書同樣以詞牌「玉蝴蝶慢」翻譯的道森詩）中寫到春天萬物復蘇的景象，用以反襯詩人的心境：「只有靈魂的春天，靈魂的春天／再也不會為你我到來」。龐德因此寫了這首詩給予回應。詩題中的「antistave」一詞或拼寫為

「anti-stave」,「stave」是古英文詞,意同「chapter」(章、篇),活譯為反其意而用之。

譯文二.秋:給道松——反其意而用之:

看那樹林森然挺立,樹幹如瘦勁的旗桿,褪盡了陽光下盛夏的濃妝。唯有低垂的松柏一片青蔥,枝枝葉葉哭訴著世界的悲涼。靈魂的春天,靈魂的春天,在你我身上寄寓它的芬芳。//看那寰球困乏地搖晃,世人憔悴的身影一片灰暗,把生存的重負扛在肩上,可我覺得他們各有內在的愉悅,講得出哪裏是他的夢想:靈魂的春天,靈魂的春天,君臨萬眾,比你我更配稱王。

## 100. 墓誌銘

❶ 譯自《面具:龐德短詩集》(*Personae: The Shorter Poems of Ezra Pound*, 1926)。傅奕,初唐文人,《舊唐書・傅奕傳》:「又嘗醉臥,蹶然起曰:『吾其死矣!』因自為墓誌曰:『傅奕,青山白雲人也。因酒醉死,嗚呼哀哉!』」。兩節詩係龐德依據 H. A. Giles 的《中國文學史》(*A History of Chinese Literature*, 1901)中關於傅奕和李白的故事改譯。

## 101. 歇斯底里

＊T.S.艾略特(1888-1965),英國詩人、劇作家和文藝評論家,1948 年諾貝爾文學獎得主,長詩〈荒原〉(*The Waste Land*, 1922),詩集《普魯弗洛克及其它觀察到的事物》(*Prufrock and Other Observations*, 1917)是二十世紀現代派

詩歌傑作，此外有《詩選》（*Poems*, 1920）和《四個四重奏》（*Four Quartets*, 1945）等詩集。

❶ 這首詩最初發表於 1915 年 11 月的《天主教文集》（*Catholic Anthology*），後收入艾略特的詩集《普魯弗洛克及其他觀察到的事物》（*Prufrock and Other Observations*, 1917）。2005 年，英國「巡沙劇團」（Inspector Sands）和「衝擊劇團」（Stamping Ground Theatre），在這首詩的靈感的啟迪下合作創作了一出長達一小時的先鋒話劇，在國際劇壇轟動一時。

❷ 此處用來比喻一排牙齒的「accidental stars」是奇特而費解的，有英詩注家解讀為「marching artificial stars」。中譯依照「accidental」一詞的近義詞「unintentional」及這首詩濃烈的精神分析意味，暫譯為「無意識震顫的明星」。

## 102. 午夜陡起狂風

❶ 這首短詩最初作為三首〈多里斯夢歌〉（*Doris's Dream Songs*）之一，於 1924 年發表於期刊《詩歌小冊子》（*Chapbook*）。詩中夢景表明一個幽靈一直在詩人心頭徘徊，同時反應了西方「文明人」對東方「野蠻人」，尤其是對成吉思汗橫掃千軍的鐵騎心有餘悸。

## 103. 誘鳥

*W. H. 奧登（1907-1973），英國出生的美國詩人，作品大多收錄於《短詩結集》（*Collected Shorter Poems*, 1927-1957）和《長詩結集》（*Collected Longer*

*Poems*, 1969）。

❶ 譯自奧登的詩集《演說者》（*The Orators*, London, 1932），誘鳥是獵人馴養用來誘捕同類的鳥，也有獵人以紙鳥為誘鳥。

## 104. 當所有的新聞媒介

❶ 譯自奧登的《來自中國的十四行詩》（*Sonnets from China*, XIX, 1938）第 19首，以首行為題。奧登與同性戀情人伊修伍德（Isherwood）於1938 年同赴抗日烽火中的中國，合著詩文集《戰地行》（*Journey to a War*, 1939），其中奧登的組詩《戰時》（*In Time of War: A Sonnet Sequence with a Verse Commentary*）後來重新題為《來自中國的十四行詩》。

❷ 奧登沒有提及名字的一位指奧地利詩人里爾克（Rainer Maria Rilke, 1875-1926）。里爾克從1912年起開始在義大利杜伊諾城堡寫作《杜伊諾哀歌》（*Duino Elegies*），大約沉寂十年之後，1922年在瑞士慕佐城堡（the Chateau de Muzot）寓居的別墅中完成這一名篇以及組詩《致奧菲斯十四行詩集》（*Sonnets to Orpheus*）。

❸ 這裏的寵物既是城堡也是里爾克的作品的象徵。最後兩行引用了里爾克在完成《致奧菲斯十四行詩集》後寫給友人的一封書信（1922 年 2 月 11 日）：「我外出觸摸了小慕佐，這座城堡為我保護了它（我的作品），最後把它賜給我，像一個碩大的老動物」。

## 105. 一個暴君的墓志銘

❶ 譯自奧登的《另一個時代》(*Another Time*, Random House, 1940)。一般認為這首詩是二戰爆發之前奧登針對希特勒而作的。希特勒追求的那種完美,是絕對權力的完美,也可以說是金髮碧眼的純種雅利安人種統治世界的妄想,依照這種偏見,猶太人、吉普賽人乃至奧登這樣的同性戀者,均屬於應當清除之例。

❷ 十九世紀美國歷史學家莫斯利(J. L Mosley)在《荷蘭共和國的崛起》(*Rise of the Dutch Republic*)一書中把荷蘭獨立運動領袖奧蘭治親王威廉(William of Orange,1533-1584,通稱「沉默的威廉」:William the Silent.)贊揚為照耀荷蘭民族的北斗星:「當他去世兒童在街頭哭泣」(When he died, the little children cried in the streets.)。奧登基於歷史事實把這句話反過來寫。「cried」一詞原本兼有(鳥獸)叫喊和哭泣等多種意義,在後一種意義上,此處可意譯為「鱷魚流淚」。如果直接借用莫斯利的話來描寫暴君,則具有莫大的反諷意味,而這同樣是歷史事實。

## 106. 引爆花朵的綠色導火索的力

＊狄蘭・托馬斯(1914-1953),生於威爾士的英國詩人和作家,出版的詩集有《詩18首》(*18 Poems*, 1934)、《詩 25 首》(*Twenty-Five Poems*, 1936)、《愛情的地圖》(*The Map of Love*, 1939)、《死亡與出路》(*Deaths and Entrances*, 1946)和《詩選》(*Collected Poems*, 1934-1952)等。

❶ 譯自托馬斯的第一本詩集《詩 18 首》。

❷ 原文每一詩節重復的「I am dumb to tell」一語包含一個重要的悖論或語言學和詩學的觀點：無法用語言描繪的真實，或不可言詮的真理，卻有可能甚至只能用詩的語言來表達，含有奧妙道理「只可意味，不可言傳」之意。

❸ 這裏可能暗示了揚帆出海的維京人死後帆布裹屍的喪葬傳統。

❹ 此處涉及西方執行死刑之後的一種習俗：撒上石灰防止屍體散發臭味，卻說成是為了保護屍體防止其腐爛，因此，屍體好像是用石灰來加工製作。


## 107. 戰後鋼琴

＊格溫多林・布魯克斯（1917-2000），美國非裔女詩人，代表作有詩集《布龍斯維爾的一條街》（*A Street in Bronzeville*, 1945）和《安妮・艾倫》（*Annie Allen*, 1949）。

❶ 譯自布魯克斯的詩集《布龍斯維爾的一條街》（*A Street in Bronzeville*, Harper & Brothers Publishers, 1945）。這首詩與下一首〈良師〉構成姊妹篇。詩的主人公是二戰中盟軍的一位戰士，他想像自己倖存後聆聽一位女鋼琴師彈奏小夜曲的情形，懷念陣亡戰友。

❷ 耶穌基督曾使得歷盡苦難的麻風病患者拉薩路在死後破棺而出，復活昇天，事見《路加福音》和《約翰福音》，此處化用這一典故。

# 參 考 文 獻
## Bibliography

Abrams, M.H. (gen. ed.),et al. *The Norton Anthology of English Literature* ( W. W. Norton & Company, 1962).

Baym, Nina, (ed.), *The Norton Anthology of American Literature* (W. W. Norton & Company, 1979).

Bryant, William Gullen, (ed.), *Library of World Poetry More than 1,400 poems* (Avenel Books,1970).

Driver,Paul,(ed.), *Eighteenth-Century Poetry* (Penguin, 1996a).

Driver,Paul,(ed.), *Early Twentieth-Century Poetry* (Penguin, 1996b).

Driver,Paul,(ed.), *Romantic Poetry* (Penguin, 1996c).

Driver,Paul,(ed.), *Sixteent-Century Poetry* (Penguin, 1996d).

Driver,Paul,(ed.), *Seventeent-Century Poetry* (Penguin, 1996eb).

Driver,Paul,(ed.), *Victorian Poetry* (Penguin, 1996f).s

Ellmann, Richard, and O'Clair, Robert, (ed.), *The Norton Anthology of Modern Poetry* (New York and London: W.W. Nordon and co, 1973).

Ferguson, Margaret, Salter, Mary Jo, Stallworthy, Jon, (ed.), *The Norton Anthology of Poetry* (W W Norton,2005).

Freer, Allen, and Andrew, John,(ed.), *Cambridge Book of English Verse 1900-1939*(Cambridge University Press, 1970).

Gardner, Helen,(ed.), *The New Oxford Book of English Verse*( Oxford University

Press, 1972).

Gardner, Helen, (ed.), *The Metaphysical Poets* (Middlesex: Penguin Books, 1868).

Graham,Stephen, (ed.), *100 Best Poems in the English language* (London: Ernest Benn,1952).

Hayward, John,(ed.),*The Penguin Book of English Verse* (London : Allen Lane, 1978).

Kermode, Frank, and Hollander, John, (ed.), *The Oxford Anthology of English Literature* (Two-volume edition, Oxford University, 1973).

Monson, Andrew, and Larkin, Philip, ( ed. ) , *The Oxford Book of Twentieth Century English Verse*(OUP Oxford; repr edition, 1972).

Palgrave, Francis Turner, (ed.), *The Golden Treasury of English Songs and Lyrical Poems in the English Language* (Oxford University Press, 1929).

Quiller-Couch, Arthur, (ed.), *Oxford Book of English Verse 1250-1900* (Oxford University Press, 1900).

Stedman, Edmund Clarence, (ed.), *An American Anthology, 1787–1900* ( Houghton Mifflin, 1901).

Untermeyer, Louis, (ed.), *A Treasury of Great Poems: English and American* (New York: Simon and Schuster, 1942).

Wain, John,(ed.), *Oxford Anthology of English Poetry* (Oxford ; New York : Oxford University Press, 1990).

Williams, Oscar,(ed.), *Master Poems of the English Language* (New York: Washington Square Press, 1967).

英美抒情詩新譯／傅正明著 · -- 初版 ·
-- 臺北市：臺灣商務，2012.06
面 ； 公分. --

ISBN 978-957-05-2696-7(平裝)

873.51                          101002305

# 英美抒情詩新譯

譯註者◆傅正明

發行人◆施嘉明

總編輯◆方鵬程

主編◆葉幗英

責任編輯◆王窈姿

美術設計◆吳郁婷

出版發行：臺灣商務印書館股份有限公司

台北市重慶南路一段三十七號

電話：(02)2371-3712

讀者服務專線：0800056196

郵撥：0000165-1

網路書店：www.cptw.com.tw

E-mail：ecptw@cptw.com.tw

網址：www.cptw.com.tw

局版北市業字第 993 號

初版一刷：2012 年 6 月

定價：新台幣 390 元